KINGS OF MAFIA

# HUNTED BY A SHADOW

USA TODAY BESTSELLING AUTHOR
## MICHELLE HEARD

**Cover Designer:** Okay Creations

**Editor: Sheena Taylor**

# TABLE OF CONTENTS

Dedication

Songlist

Synopsis

Hunted By A Shadow

Chapter 1

Chapter 2

Chapter 3

Chapter 4

Chapter 5

Chapter 6

Chapter 7

Chapter 8

Chapter 9

Chapter 10

Chapter 11

Chapter 12

Chapter 13

Chapter 14

Chapter 15

Chapter 16

Chapter 17

Chapter 18

Chapter 19

Chapter 20

Chapter 21

Chapter 22

Chapter 23

Chapter 24

Chapter 25

Chapter 26

Chapter 27

Chapter 28

Chapter 29

Chapter 30

Chapter 31

Chapter 32

Chapter 33

Chapter 34

Chapter 35

Chapter 36

Chapter 37

Chapter 38

Chapter 39

Chapter 40

Chapter 41

Chapter 42

Epilogue

Published Books

Connect with me

Acknowledgments

# Dedication

In every book I write, you'll find the words *'a kaleidoscope of butterflies.'*
It's a thing between my editor and me.

Sheena, thank you for all your patience with me over the years. This one is for you.

---

# Songlist

Thousand Eyes – Of Monsters and Men

Oats In The Water – Ben Howard

In The Shadows – Amy Stroup

Raise The Dead – Rachel Rabin

Do You Really Want To Hurt Me – Denmark + Winter

Warm Shado – Fink

It Had To Be You – Tommee Profitt, Tiffany Ashton

When It's All Over – RAIGN

Silhouettes – Of Monster and Men

Crystals – Of Monsters and Men

Get On The Road – Tired Pony

# Synopsis

When I finally get a life-saving kidney transplant, I think the worst
is behind me.

*Boy, am I wrong.*

I start feeling eyes on me wherever I go.
I'm being watched. Stalked. Hunted.
It's downright scary.

Then the hunter steps out of the shadows, and my life implodes.
I'm taken by Renzo Torrisi, a dangerous and unforgiving man.

Turns out the kidney I received belonged to one of his men and I
have to repay the debt. Only the terms are unclear, and the rules
change on a whim.

Held prisoner in his penthouse, I have to serve the ruthless mafia
boss like the god he is.
Whether I'll survive being Renzo's captive is up for debate, though.

# Hunted By A Shadow

*Mafia / Organized Crime / Suspense Romance*
**STANDALONE in the KINGS OF MAFIA**
**Book 3**

### Authors Note:
This book contains subject matter that may be sensitive for
some readers.
There is triggering content related to:

Brutal and Graphic Violence
Kidnapping
Organ Transplant
Loss of a family member

18+ only.
Please read responsibly.

*"Sometimes even to live is an act of courage."*

—— **Lucius Annaeus Seneca**

# Chapter 1

## Skylar

*Renzo; 35. Skylar; 30.*

Life used to be amazing.

*Dame*, the restaurant where I worked as a sous chef, had just gotten their first Michelin Star because of me.

I had an interview lined up at one of the top restaurants in New York.

If I got the position as head chef, I would've been able to create my own signature dishes.

I was on fire and was ticking off one goal after the other.

But the higher you fly, the harder you fall.

*And boy, did I fall.*

Lying in the hospital bed with a dialysis machine humming next to me, I try to process what Dr. Bentall said.

End-stage renal disease. I'm out of time. If I don't get a transplant soon, I'll die.

At thirty.

My fabulous life came to a crashing halt three years ago when I was in a car accident with Mom. Mom was in a coma for eight months before we made the heartbreaking decision to take her off life support.

I thought that was the darkest moment of my life, but things just kept getting worse. Dad has flown in the best doctors from around the world and paid so much money, but nothing has worked.

After the car accident, my shattered pelvis healed. My reconstructed bladder is functioning. But the damage done to my kidneys is irreversible. If it weren't for dialysis, I would've died months ago, but now, not even that's enough.

I need a kidney in the next couple of weeks, or I'll die.

Slowly, my gaze shifts to the tubes filled with my blood.

Twenty minutes ago, Dad left with Dr. Bentall, and I haven't seen them since.

The past three years have been torturous for me, but it's been a hell of a lot worse for Dad. He lost Mom, and now he's going to lose me as well.

Every time I look at him, I see the feverish panic in his eyes. The desperation to find a kidney for me is etched in deep lines on his face.

I hate seeing what my deteriorating health is doing to Dad.

I hate that he has to watch me slowly die.

I hate that I'm stuck in this hospital bed, and a machine is fighting to keep me alive.

*Is it even worth it?*

There are dark moments where I feel it would be better for me to die right now. It would stop the torture, and Dad would be able to mourn my death before going on with his life.

I'm tired of the sword hanging over my head.

I'm tired of just existing until my next dialysis.

What is life if it's not filled with hopes and dreams? What's left when all possibilities have been stripped from it?

It's morbid and soul-destroyingly tiring.

*I can't do this anymore.*

Movement by the door pulls me out of my dark thoughts, and I lift my eyes to where Dad's staring at me with excruciating grief already carved into his face.

Unable to wallow in the death blow that I've been dealt, I have to be strong for my father.

Somehow a smile curves my lips. "It's going to be okay, Daddy."

He shakes his head, his red-rimmed eyes welling with tears.

Coming closer, Dad sits down on the side of the bed and takes my hand in both of his. With his head bowed it looks like the weight of the world rests on his shoulders.

"It's okay," I whisper.

He shakes his head again and clears his throat before his eyes meet mine. For the longest moment, Dad just stares at me as if he's memorizing every inch of my face.

He clears his throat again, then says, "We're not giving up. Be strong for a little while longer. Okay?"

*I don't have any strength left, Daddy.*

Knowing I can't speak the words out loud, I lie, "Okay, I will."

From his hopeless expression, I can see he doesn't believe me.

That's all we've done for the past few months. Lie.

Not a single word of truth has passed between us.

I stare at the man who's raised me as his own. When he met Mom, I was six years old, and not a day has passed where he's treated me like a stepdaughter.

He's the best person I know, and I hate seeing him like this.

Unable to keep up the act, tears flood my eyes, and I whisper, "I love you, Daddy."

He lowers his head and presses a kiss to the back of my hand. His fingers tremble as he tightens his grip on mine.

I let my tears flow, and scared I'll run out of time and won't get a chance to say everything that's in my heart, the truth falls over my lips. "Thank you for being the best father a girl could ask for. Thank you for being everything I needed and taking care of me. Thank you for loving me."

A wounded sound comes from Dad, and it makes my tears fall faster.

"When I'm gone, I want you to live a beautiful, long life. Fall in love again. You're not too old to have another child. Live and be happy."

Dad's eyes snap to mine with so much anger, then he cries, "Stop talking like that. I'm not letting you die, and I sure as fuck don't want other kids. I want you, Skylar. You're my daughter, and no one can take your place."

Tilting my head, I give him a pleading look. "Daddy."

He lets go of my hand, and climbing to his feet, he angrily wipes the tears from his cheeks. "You're not dying."

Before I can say anything else, he storms out of the hospital room.

*God, this is too hard.*

How do I say goodbye to my father, knowing he'll be all alone in this world? How do I ask him to carry on after I'm gone?

I would do anything to save him from the grief and loneliness.

# Chapter 2

## Renzo

While I'm checking the status of all the shipments with Elio, I hear Giulio's infectious laughter as he spars with Fabrizio and Vincenzo.

"Giulio, it's no use sparring," I mutter. "I'll never make you a guard."

He stops mid-punch and pulls a disgruntled face. "Come on, Renzo. I'm almost as good as Fabrizio and Vincenzo."

I let out a snort while Vincenzo says, "You wish." Just to prove his point, he swipes Giulio's feet from under him, making him fall on his ass.

Elio's booming laughter fills the air as he shakes his head, his tone filled with sarcasm as he drawls, "Yeah, you've gotten real good."

With a scowl, Giulio climbs to his feet. "I was caught off guard."

Getting up from the chair, I say, "Elio, make sure the shipment to China isn't late. The contract with the Triads is important."

"Will do, boss."

When I walk to the door, Giulio catches up to me. "Where are we going?"

"The restaurant," I reply as I leave the warehouse.

"For lunch?" he asks. "I'm starving. Sparring with the guys has worked up an appetite."

I shoot him a glare. "No. To check that everything is running smoothly. Do you ever not think of food?"

"Of course. When I'm training to become your guard, I don't think about food at all."

Letting out a sigh, I say, "You're my driver, and that's the end of the discussion."

Giulio's only twenty years old. His father, Santino, was my father's driver until he passed away from a heart attack a couple of years ago. Since then, Giulio's practically been my shadow, and to keep him busy, I made him my driver.

Growing up, I saw more of Santino than my own father, and I always considered Giulio family.

By being around me, he's slowly learning everything about the business, and when he's ready, I'll make him Elio's underboss.

I'm close with many people, but Giulio's like a little brother to me, which means I'm protective of him.

Sure, I care about all my men, but there's a handful I love like they're my own blood. Elio, Francisco, Vincenzo, and Giulio are right at the top, along with the other heads of the Cosa Nostra.

Giulio opens the door of the black Bentley, and after I climb inside, he shuts it and hurries around the front of the car to get in behind the steering wheel.

As he drives us away from the warehouse, he's quiet.

Five minutes away from La Torrisi, the restaurant I opened when I was twenty-one, Giulio asks, "Why?"

Keeping my gaze on the view outside the window, I say, "Why won't I let you be my guard?"

"Yes."

"Because it's my job to protect you. Not vice versa."

"But –"

"Enough, Giulio," I snap. "Christ."

When he parks the car in front of the restaurant, his tone is remorseful when he says, "I didn't mean to upset you." Glancing over his shoulder, his eyes meet mine. "I just want to be able to keep you safe."

Letting out a sigh, I look at him and reply, "And I want to keep you safe. As the oldest between us, it's my duty."

Leaning forward, I place my hand on his shoulder and give him a squeeze. "I promised your dad I'd look out for you. Let me keep my promise."

The corner of his mouth lifts, then he nods. "Okay."

Shoving the car door open, I say, "Come. Let's get you some food."

He chuckles as he climbs out, and the moment we walk into the restaurant, I hear Giulio's stomach growl loudly.

"Place your order, then meet me in the office," I mutter before leaving Giulio in the main section of the restaurant.

Just as I step into my office, my phone starts to vibrate, and when I pull it out, I see Franco's name on the screen.

Franco's one of the heads of the Cosa Nostra. I'm close with Dario, Angelo, and Damiano, but Franco's my best friend.

Answering with a smile, I say, "Hey. What's up?"

I hear him yawn before he mutters, "Fuck, I'm going to die of sleep deprivation."

I chuckle as I take a seat behind my desk, and while I switch on the laptop, I say, "That's what happens when you have triplets."

Franco got married a few years ago and has just become a proud father of three beautiful babies. I haven't seen much of him, because his family takes up all of his time.

Come to think of it, I haven't seen much of Angelo as well. He's just as busy with his wife and child.

I'm not the only single one in the group. It doesn't look like Dario and Damiano will settle down anytime soon, so I still get to hang out with them every other week.

"Yeah-yeah." Franco yawns again before clearing his throat. "Your shipment reached Peru without any problems."

"Thanks for the update." Leaning back in the chair, I ask, "When are we getting together?"

"You can always come over and help with the kids."

Laughter explodes from me. "I'm going to pass. I don't do well with crying babies."

Giulio comes into the office and takes a seat across from me.

Just then, I hear a baby cry on the other end of the phone, and Franco lets out a tired sigh. "Gotta go."

"Good luck," I chuckle before ending the call.

"Franco?" Giulio asks.

"Yeah. He's tired as fuck. The triplets are keeping him up."

Guilio stares at me momentarily, then asks, "Are you ever going to get married and have kids?"

21

Shaking my head, I turn my attention to the laptop screen. "No."

"But you need an heir to take over when you retire."

My eyes flick to his face before returning to the screen. "I have Elio."

Giulio takes a pen from the holder on my desk, and grabbing a sticky note, he starts drawing cartoons. "Yeah, but Elio's older than you. What if he retires?"

"Christ, you're just full of questions today," I mutter.

I open the document listing the restaurant's stock and check that Alain, the head chef, didn't order too many ingredients. The fucker once ordered enough trout to feed an army, and three-quarters of it had to be thrown in the trash.

Giulio leans forward and sticks the little square of paper to the screen before grinning at me.

He drew a cartoon man holding a screaming baby.

Chuckling, he says, "That could be your future."

I rip the sticky note off the screen, and when I attempt to toss it at him, it floats to the desk.

"Stop playing around and learn something."

I wait for Giulio to scoot his chair to my side of the desk and start explaining the ins and outs of a restaurant's kitchen.

22

Not even five minutes later, the fucker yawns before grumbling, "Where's my food?"

Leveling him with a serious look, I say, "Do you want to be a driver forever?"

He quickly shakes his head. "Of course not."

"The quicker you learn everything, the faster you'll get promoted."

His eyebrow lifts. "Promoted?"

I wanted to put off the conversation about Giulio training to take over, but thinking he needs the incentive, I say, "I want to train you to be Elio's underboss. Think you can handle that?"

Shock tightens his features, and he stares at me for a solid minute as he processes what I just said.

There's a knock at the door, and I call out, "Come in."

Sophia, one of the waitresses, enters the office with a tray and comes to set it down on the corner of the desk. Usually, Giulio would flirt with the woman, but he's still staring at me with a gobsmacked expression.

"Will that be all?" Sophia asks, her eyes glued to Giulio. It's clear she has the hots for my little brother.

"Yes. You can leave," I murmur.

When the door shuts behind her, the corner of my mouth lifts as I place my hand on his shoulder. "Now, do you understand why I won't let you train as a guard?"

Eagerly, he nods, and then his features tighten with emotion.

"It's going to be a lot of hard work," I warn him.

He nods again, still struck speechless.

I gesture at the tray. "Eat before your food gets cold."

Giulio's eyes remain locked on me, and his voice is filled with disbelief as he asks, "You want to make me an underboss?"

"You're my little brother, Giulio. There's no one else more suited to take over when Elio and I retire." I don't say it often, but it's common knowledge.

A smile splits across his face, and looking happy as fuck he shoots forward to hug me.

"I won't disappoint you, Renzo," he promises, his tone tense.

Patting his back, I reply, "I know."

# Chapter 3

## Skylar

With every passing day, I become weaker, and Dad grows more frantic.

When Dr. Bentall told us I was out of time, I struggled to process the fact that I'd die soon. A million things went through my mind.

How unfair life is.

I'm too young.

I've barely had a chance to live.

What happens when you die?

Is there a heaven, or is it like before you were born, where everything is just black?

I'll never get to run my own kitchen.

I'll never make food for Dad again.

I'll never get married, and Dad won't walk me down the aisle.

I won't have children.

*It's unfair.*

But the thoughts slowly faded, and in their place, a weird acceptance that 'it is what it is' settled in me.

There's no fighting the inevitable.

Whenever I think something is too hard or impossible to handle, I somehow manage to overcome it. It's the same with dying. In the end, I've made peace with what's coming, so I don't lose my mind.

Dad comes into the hospital room, and a tired but happy smile tugs at my mouth. After I accepted my fate, I decided to enjoy every second I have left with my father.

When I'm gone, I want him to remember my smiles and not my tears.

"Hey, Daddy," I murmur, my tone filled with all the love I have for him.

"Hi, sweetheart." He sits down on the armchair next to my bed and takes my hand in both of his. Like always, he presses a kiss to the back of my fingers before his eyes drift over every inch of my face.

My smile grows wider, then I say, "Remember when you were dating Mom? Whenever you came over, I would hide in the same stupid spot." A chuckle escapes me.

The corner of Dad's mouth lifts. "Behind the curtains in the living room. Your feet would stick out."

Again, I chuckle. "You'd make a big show of looking everywhere for me." My fingers tighten around Dad's. "I have so many special memories thanks to you."

Dad's chin quivers, and he clears his throat before he says, "And we'll make many more."

His cell phone starts to ring, and letting go of my hand, he digs the device out of his pocket, and walking out of the room, I hear him say, "Please give me good news... I don't care how much it costs...Yes...Yes..."

I can't hear more as his voice fades away, but minutes later, he returns with intense relief on his face. Leaning over me, he frames my face, and his eyes lock with mine.

"You're getting a kidney tomorrow, sweetheart."

Shock hits me hard, and I can only whisper, "What?"

"I've found someone who can help us. The surgery will be tomorrow." Dad leans closer and presses a kiss to my forehead. "You're going to be okay."

The desperate hope I've been suppressing explodes in my chest, and instantly, a sob bursts over my lips. For a moment, it feels like I'm having an out-of-body experience, my skin tingling and my heart racing a mile a minute.

Tears sneak from Dad's eyes, and his voice is hoarse as he says, "You're going to be okay, sweetheart."

I can only sob as I nod.

Where my life was over a second ago and I was waiting to die, I'm now filled with dizzying relief and hope.

I'm getting a kidney.

I won't die.

———————

# Renzo

Checking the time, I frown when I see it's six am.

Giulio went to a club last night and didn't return. I figured he hooked up with some girl, but he's always home by six, so he can shower and grab breakfast before we have to head out.

Picking up my phone from the kitchen counter, I dial his number while I take a sip of my coffee.

Instead of ringing, the call goes straight to voicemail, and I wait for the beep before I say, "You better be here in the next five minutes."

I end the call and tuck the device into the breast pocket of my jacket. Dressed in a dark blue three-piece suit tailor-made for me, I'm ready to get to work. There's a shitload that needs to be done.

I hate waiting, and Giulio knows this.

*He never ignores my calls.*

*This isn't like him.*

My phone begins to vibrate, and thinking it's Giulio, I feel relieved as I pull the device out. Instead of seeing Giulio's name, it's Elio's.

Answering, I mutter, "Yes?"

"You have to come right now. I'm in an alley near the NewYork-Presbyterian hospital. I'll send you the coordinates."

A frown forms on my forehead as I ask, "Why? What happened?"

"Just come, Renzo!"

The worry I felt a second ago returns with the force of a nuclear weapon detonating in my chest. "Is it Giulio?"

"Yes."

"I'm on my way!"

Dropping the cup of coffee in the sink, I run out of the kitchen and head for the elevator of my penthouse. During the ride down to the garage, I worry about every single possible thing that could've happened to Giulio.

*Was he in a fight?*

When the elevator doors slide open, I rush out, and Vincenzo and Fabrizio instantly stand on guard.

"What's wrong?" Vincenzo asks.

"We need to get to Giulio," I answer as I climb into the back of the Bentley.

Fabrizio slides in behind the steering wheel and asks, "Where is he?"

I forward the coordinates to Fabrizio's phone. "It's near the NewYork-Presbyterian hospital. Elio's already there. Hurry."

During the drive, I dial Elio's number, and the moment he answers, I ask, "What happened? Is he okay?"

"I'll tell you everything when you get here," Elio says, and from the tension in his voice, I know it's bad.

*Giulio.*

"Tell me now," I order, my tone not leaving space for any argument.

"Antonio got a call from his cousin, who's a nurse at the hospital. She recognized Giulio when she was roped into doing a shady job."

When Elio pauses, I snap, "Is he alive?"

"Renzo," he groans.

*No.*

An icy sensation rushes through me, and it's followed by a ruthless pain tearing through my heart.

Elio clears his throat, then says, "You have to get here now."

"We're a couple of minutes out," I say, my tone coated with the ice filling my chest.

*He's not dead.*

*He's only twenty.*

*I've done everything to protect him.*

*Giulio's not dead.*

*There's no way.*

My mind keeps reeling, and when we pull up to the entrance of the alley, I shove the Bentley's door open, and the moment my feet touch the ground, I break out into a run.

"Where are you?" I growl into the phone.

"I see you," he answers as he comes into view.

When I reach him, we rush past dumpsters lining the side of the alley until it opens up to an empty lot. An unmarked truck is surrounded by my men.

"It's fucked up, Renzo," Elio says. "Brace yourself."

My eyes flick to my right-hand man. "For what?"

He shakes his head, his complexion gray, and it looks like he's about to puke.

As we approach the open door at the side of the truck, he says, "Organ trafficking."

Living in a world of crime, I know exactly what that means.

Destructive rage fills every inch of my being until it feels like my body is vibrating.

There's no bracing myself, and when I climb the four steps and enter the truck, the air is knocked from my lungs.

The inside of the truck has been rigged into a mobile surgical unit.

Antonio, one of my men, is standing next to a woman who I assume is his cousin.

Two bodies of unknown men lie on the floor. Cooler boxes are set out on a table, and then my eyes lock on Guilio's body.

*Christ.*

I've seen a lot of shit, but the sight makes my stomach churn, and I struggle not to puke.

There's a cut running from the top of his chest all the way down to his abdomen.

"I tried to stitch him up," the nurse says with a trembling voice.

My eyes snap to her, and she recoils, trying to hide behind her cousin.

"Tell me what happened," I order, my tone low and deadly.

"I was approached by one of the doctors who asked if I wanted to make extra money. When he told me what the job would entail, I agreed because I knew the Cosa Nostra is against organ trafficking and would need all the information I could get. I also thought I'd be able to help the patient. I called Antonio, and he rushed over, but by the time I arrived, they already had Giulio on a bypass machine." The words leave her in a rush, each one filled with fear. "They already removed his organs and were getting ready to transport them." She covers her mouth with a trembling hand. "I'm so sorry, Mr. Torrisi. There was nothing I could do."

"Everyone get out," I growl as my eyes lock on Guilio again. "Now!"

Only when the door shuts behind the last person to leave do I move to the side of the operating table and look down at Giulio's bruised face. His nose is broken, and his left eye's swollen. There's dried blood on the side of his head and purple marks around his neck.

I continue to inspect him, noticing the broken skin over his knuckles. There are no gunshots or stab wounds.

My eyes flick back to his face, and seeing the deathly paleness of his skin, the heartbreak slams so fucking hard into me, it forces me to take a step back.

Lifting a hand, I grip the back of my neck as I start to shake my head.

"No." The single word is nothing more than a groan.

I move closer to the operating table he's lying on, and leaning over my little brother, I frame his beaten-up face with trembling hands.

Feeling how cold he is, a breath explodes over my lips before a broken cry is ripped from my very soul.

Pressing my forehead to his, the unbearable pain of losing my brother makes it feel like my soul is hemorrhaging.

In my line of work, I've experienced loss before, but nothing like this.

The grim sorrow mixes with uncontrollable rage, driving me to the brink of insanity.

Straightening up, I'm barely able to control my breathing as I glance around the room again. Seeing the cooler boxes, I dart around the operating table to get to them and open one after the other, only to find organs.

They're marked, indicating which organ is which and where they're heading.

Seeing his heart, a hard tremor wracks through my body. It's so fucking intense it feels like the fucking ground quakes beneath my feet.

I can't think rationally, and picking up the container with Guilio's heart, I sink to my ass and grip it to my chest.

Closing my eyes, I hear my breaths saw over my lips.

And then I hear Giulio's laughter.

I see his infectious smile.

Every memory I have of him bombards me. I have no idea how much time passes before I come to my senses.

My sorrow blends with rage until it becomes a murderous need for revenge.

*I'll hunt every single person involved until rivers of blood fill the streets of New York.*

# Chapter 4

## Renzo

Opening the door, my eyes land on the nurse, and I order, "Open him up and put his organs back in his body."

Pale as fuck, she nods as she cautiously steps into the truck.

Elio follows her inside, his face torn with worry and grief as he says, "This is fucked up."

"Was Antonio the first man here?" I ask, my eyes already locking on my soldier.

Antonio comes closer as he nods and gestures at the dead bodies on the floor. "I just reacted without thinking to keep one of them alive for information. I'm sorry, boss."

"Tell me everything," I order. "Leave nothing out."

He points at the bodies again. "I found the fuckers removing Giulios organs and killed them before calling Elio."

My eyes flick to where Bianca's opening the cut on Giulio's chest before returning to Antonio.

"One of his kidneys has already been taken for a transplant," Bianca says, drawing my attention back to her. "I couldn't stop it without giving myself away. I had to sign the documents with the doctor, so it looks legit."

My rage multiplies until it's a violent storm, and I can only utter two words. "Which doctor?"

Her eyes are still wide with fear as she answers, "Dr. Bentall."

"Who got the kidney?" I ask, my tone growing grimmer by the second.

"A woman," Antonio answers on behalf of his cousin. "As soon as Bianca is done here, she can get all the information for us." He glances at his cousin before looking at me again. "I'll need protection for Bianca. Just until the problem's taken care of."

The shock of losing my brother hits again, and crossing my arms over my chest, my gaze returns to Giulio's body.

Bianca handles each organ with care while tears roll over her cheeks.

When she closes the wound and takes a moment to clean Giulio's chest, I say, "Elio, assign guards to keep Bianca safe. Have them take her to the house in the Hamptons and make sure she's comfortable."

Bianca's eyes dart to my face. "Thank you, Mr. Torrisi. I'm sorry I couldn't do more."

Nodding, I mutter, "Keeping you safe is the least I can do to repay your loyalty to the family."

Gesturing to the door with a jerk of my head, I order, "Antonio, take two men and go with Bianca while she gets the information regarding the transplant. I want someone watching the doctor around the clock."

When the group leaves, I look at Vincenzo. "Call our contact at the morgue and have Giulio moved so he can be readied for..." Unable to say funeral, I can only shake my head.

"On it, boss," Vincenzo replies, his voice hoarse.

Everyone who knew Giulio will feel the loss. His death will leave a gaping hole in our lives.

"Should we take the mobile surgical unit to the warehouse?" Elio asks. "Maybe we can find something that will help us track down the group trafficking in New York."

As I nod, there's a commotion outside, and a second later, a man is dragged inside by Carlo and Emilio, two of my soldiers.

"We found this fucker sniffing around, boss," Carlo explains.

With every ounce of rage I feel, I order, "Take him to the warehouse. I'll deal with him when I'm done here."

"Yes, boss," Carlo replies before they drag the man away.

"We should notify Franco and the others," Elio mentions.

There's so much to do, my mind reels, and I struggle to focus as I pull my phone out of my pocket.

Going into the group chat I have with the other heads of the Cosa Nostra, I press the video call icon.

One after the other, they connect, and their faces fill the screen.

Dario's the first to ask, "What's up?"

My eyes flick to Giulio's body, and I have to swallow hard before I say, "Giulio's been killed."

Every face on the screen turns to stone.

"Christ, Renzo. I'm coming over," Dario says, already on the move through his penthouse. "Where are you?"

"No. Stay near your computers. As soon as I know more, I need you to start digging for me."

Only then does Franco recover enough from the initial shock to say, "I'm so fucking sorry."

Angelo and Damiano also give their condolences, then Damiano asks, "Do you know who killed him?"

I shake my head. "It was for organ trafficking."

"Fuck," Angelo mutters. "That's not something we deal with often."

"If ever," Dario adds.

Damiano, who's the *capo dei capi* – the boss of bosses – has a dark expression tightening his features. "Find out who's trafficking in our area and eliminate them."

Nodding, I glance at Giulio again. "I'll call when I have more information."

Before any of them can say anything else, I end the call and walk closer to the operating table. The grief that's taken a backseat to my rage returns with a soul-crushing blow as I stare at my little brother.

Leaning down, I press a kiss to his forehead, then whisper, "*Addio, fratello. Ti vendicherò.*"

Straightening up, I turn away from Giulio and meet Elio's eyes. "Stay here until everything's taken care of."

"Where are you going," he asks.

"To the warehouse." Walking to the door, I add, "Let me know the second you find out anything new."

"Okay."

With Fabrizio and Vincenzo flanking me, we head down the alley.

*He didn't deserve to die like that.*

*In some fucking mobile surgical unit at the back of an alley.*

*Cut open like he's nothing more than cattle.*

The rage in my chest turns deadly and merciless, and when we reach the sidewalk where the Bentley is parked, pedestrians scatter out of my way, fearful expressions on their faces as they shoot glances at me.

I'm going to hunt every last person responsible for Giulio's death.

No one will escape my wrath.

———————————

Walking into the warehouse, I'm met with the sorrowful faces of my men. Here and there, one of them gives me a chin lift or pays their respects, but most are quiet.

I head to the back and up the steps to the room where Carlo has the fucker they found sniffing around in the alley kneeling on the concrete floor. Emilio's already laid out all the torture instruments and stands ready behind the man.

I unbutton my jacket, and shrugging it off, I lay it across a table before I undo the buttons of my cuffs and roll up my sleeves.

Not bothering to look at the fucker, I ask, "Do you know who I am?"

"Renzo Torrisi," he answers without hesitation.

I walk to the spread of tools we use to pry information from unwilling people and pick up a pair of pliers.

To inflict the most pain possible, I always start off with something small and work my way up. That way, it increases the pain and breaks down the man's resistance.

Just as the fucker gets used to the pain, I hit harder.

Killing the man is not a priority. I want every ounce of information he can give.

When I walk to where he's on his knees, I ask, "What's your name?"

"Joe."

My voice is calm as I ask, "Who do you work for, Joe?"

He shrugs. "Whoever pays the most."

"Who hired you for this job?"

"I never see the people who hire me." He tips his head down, gesturing to his pocket. "We only communicate via a chat room."

My eyes flick to Emilio, and he moves forward to dig the phone from Joe's pocket before handing it to me.

"Password," I order.

"One. V."

I swipe over the screen, then lift an eyebrow at Joe.

"Second icon at the top of the screen," he gives the information I need.

Tapping on the app, I'm taken to a black screen with numerous topics.

"Bottom right is chats," Joe offers.

I enter the chats and tap on the top one. I read the short texts, and it confirms Joe's just a man for hire. He was instructed to collect the pancreas and deliver it to a hospital on the other side of the city.

Letting out a sigh, I mutter, "Untie him."

After Emilio carries out the order, Joe stands up and meets my eyes.

"Can you find out who hired you?" I ask.

When he nods, I continue, "Betray me, and I'll kill you so fucking slow, you'll go insane from the pain."

I hold his phone out to him, and when he takes it, he says, "I wasn't aware the organ belonged to one of your men. I never would've taken the job if I'd known that."

"You'll communicate with Carlo," I inform him with ice in my voice. "You have seventy-two hours to find out who hired you."

He nods before turning his attention to Carlo. As the men leave the room, I drop the pliers back on the table and grab my jacket. When I shrug it on, I feel my phone vibrating and pull it from my pocket.

Answering Elio's call, I say, "What did you find out?"

"I'm on my way to the warehouse. Wait there for me."

When I head down the steps to the lower level, I see Joe talking with Carlo.

I don't believe in killing the messenger, especially if he can lead me to the person or group responsible. But the second I get all the information from Joe, he's dead for the part he played in Giulio's death.

As I wait for Elio, the entire morning replays in my mind, and I'm hit with blow after blow of debilitating grief.

*He's gone.*

*Giulio's gone.*

"Fuck," I hiss from the sharp pain tearing through me.

I hear the roar of an engine, and my eyes flick to where the mobile surgical unit is brought into the far side of the warehouse.

A moment later, Elio comes rushing toward me, and I forcefully shove the grief back. When he nods in the direction of the office, I follow him, and after shutting the door, he pulls his phone out of his pocket.

"Give me a second. I can't remember half the shit Bianca found out."

As I cross my arms over my chest, he comes to stand next to me so I can see the screen of his phone, and I see a medical chart.

"So the kidney went to a woman named Skylar Davies," Elio says. "Her father, Harlan Davies, has been paying the hospital bills, which are staggering. The man must be loaded. Dr. Bentall performed the surgery. I have men keeping an eye on all of them."

Elio opens Google, and typing in Harlan Davies, article after article pops up. He's big in the financial sector and on the list of wealthiest people in New York.

"Davies lost his wife in a car accident, and the daughter suffered damage to her kidneys in the same accident. She was out of time, hence Harlan buying a kidney on the black market."

My eyes flick to Elio's. "Why Giulio?"

"Giulio and Skylar Davies are both O-negative." He gives me a questioning look. "Did Giulio ever donate blood? Bianca thinks they could've gotten his information from a blood bank and matched him with Skylar Davies."

"Yeah. He used to date a girl who worked at the local blood bank. He did it to impress her."

I almost chuckle, but then the realization that Giulio's dead washes over me again.

"I suggest we grab Harlan and the doctor and find out who they bought the kidney from because looking into the blood bank to see who's selling information is like looking for a needle in a haystack," Elio mentions.

My little brother was fucking killed and his organs harvested because of his blood type.

*Giulio was meant for greater things than that.*

Walking to the couch, I slump down on it and rub my palms over my face.

The grief is downright unbearable and so fucking raw it's oozing pain.

"What do you want to do?" Elio asks.

Knowing I can be honest with my right-hand man, I mutter, "I don't know. I can't think right now." I rub a hand over my chest as if it will soothe my heart. Lowering my head, I close my eyes. "Giulio's gone." My voice becomes hoarse from all the pain. "He's dead."

Elio takes a seat next to me and places his hand on my shoulder. "We all feel the loss. I'm going to miss the sound of his laughter."

Nodding, I struggle to cling to my composure.

Giulio is dead, and I don't have time to mourn him. I have to follow every lead while it's hot.

I have to get up and be the fucking head of the Torrisi family people fear.

Once everyone involved is dead, I can be Giulio's brother and grieve my loss.

Taking a deep breath, I lift my head and say, "Organize the funeral and get men to sniff around the hospitals and blood banks for information. Don't spook Davies or the doctor, and let the men continue watching them until I decide what to do. I don't want word getting out that I'm looking for the fuckers who are trafficking organs in my city."

When I stand up, Elio asks, "What are you going to do?"

"I'm going to the hospital."

# Chapter 5

## Renzo

For the past couple of hours, I've been watching Harlan Davies.

The man is in his mid-fifties and looks like any other wealthy man in New York.

*But he isn't just any other man. He's the fucker who paid for Giulio's kidney.*

My phone rings for the hundredth time, but again, I ignore it.

After Harlan buys something to eat in the cafeteria, he takes a seat at one of the open tables.

Figuring he'll be here for at least fifteen minutes, I turn around and head to the hospital room Davies' daughter is in.

Unlike Angelo, Franco, and Dario, I don't have a problem with killing a woman. But I'm not as bad as Damiano, who won't hesitate to wipe out an entire family.

For the past ten hours, I've tried to process Giulio's death while trying to figure out how I'm going to approach this shit show.

If I wipe out the Davies family, I won't get to the fuckers who are peddling organs in New York. That's my priority right now.

Nearing the room, my fingers curl into fists, and no matter what I do, I can't brace myself enough when I walk inside. The lights are dimmed, and the moment my eyes land on the redhead lying on the bed, the pain is excruciating.

*A part of Giulio is still alive.*

Slowly, I move closer until I stare down at the woman's sleeping face. For a split second, I realize she's beautiful even though she's thin as fuck.

Her hair is on the lighter side and more ginger than red.

The moment passes, and my eyes narrow on her.

*You're the reason my brother was killed.*

Her breathing changes and her eyelids flutter open. The most striking blue irises are revealed, but it's clear she's out of it as she tries to focus on me.

My voice is soft but filled with a world of rage as I say, "The kidney belongs to me."

A frown forms on her forehead as she mumbles, "Huh?" Already passing out again, a soft smile tips her lips up as she whispers, "Thank you."

I watch as she falls back to sleep, and pulling my phone out of my pocket, I open the camera and take a photo.

"Don't get too attached to the kidney," I growl before I turn around and walk away.

Heading down the hallway, my eyes land on Harlan Davies as he comes from the opposite direction. He glances at me, and a second later, his eyes widen with recognition.

I'm not surprised.

Most of the rich fuckers in New York know about the Cosa Nostra because we have our fingers in every fucking slice of pie.

He tips his head, but I don't bother acknowledging the greeting. Right now, it's taking all my strength not to kill the fucker in this hallway.

I can't lose my shit. I have to focus on finding every single person involved with Giulio's death.

Leaving the hospital, I climb into the Bentley and steer the vehicle toward Dario's place.

Usually, I'd go to Franco, but I really can't handle crying babies right now.

My phone vibrates again, and pulling it out of my pocket, I answer, "What!?"

"Where are you?" Vincenzo asks, his tone tense as fuck.

"On my way to Dario's place."

"We'll meet you there."

The call ends, and I toss the device on the passenger seat. Driving through the busy streets, the horror of seeing Guilio on the operation table rips my soul to shreds.

*Giulio's dead.*

My eyes start to burn with unshed tears, and after I park the Bentley, I grab my phone and take the elevator up to Dario's penthouse.

When the doors slide open, Dario's head snaps to me from where he's sitting on a couch in his living room. He shoves the laptop off his lap and darts to his feet.

"Jesus, Renzo."

My feet move, my burning eyes locked on my friend.

Without having to say a word, Dario grabs me in a crushing hug. "I'm so fucking sorry. We'll find who did this and kill them."

Bringing a hand up, I grip his shirt as I struggle to breathe through the excruciating pain.

Somehow, I remain standing.

51

Somehow, the tears don't fall.

I pull away from Dario and walk to the table where a bottle of Macallan stands next to five tumblers. I open the whiskey and pour a couple of fingers before bringing the tumbler to my lips, and dowing the amber liquid.

I hear the elevator doors open, then Elio's voice snaps, "I was worried out of my fucking mind! Why didn't you answer your phone?"

I pour myself another glass of whiskey before I turn around.

Vincenzo and Fabrizio stand next to Elio while Dario's walking toward me to pour himself a drink.

"Anyone else want a drink?" Dario asks.

"No, thanks," Elio answers, his worried eyes locked on me. Letting out a sigh, he walks toward me and places his hand on my shoulder. "You okay?"

*Not by a long shot.*

I take a sip of the whiskey, then nod.

*'Thank you.'*

The memory of Skylar Davies slams into my gut, and I quickly drink the rest of the amber liquid.

*She won't be thanking me when I cut Giulio's kidney out of her body.*

Setting the tumbler down on the side table, I walk to the floor-to-ceiling windows and look at all the lights of New York City spread out before me.

Pushing my hands into the pockets of my pants, I say, "I want to know every single detail about Harlan and Skylar Davies."

"On it," Dario replies, and I hear him move as he takes a seat on one of the couches.

The fact that he's not asking who they are tells me he's already started digging for answers regarding Giulio's murder.

Elio comes to stand next to me, crossing his arms over his chest. "All the arrangements have been made. The funeral is the day after tomorrow."

Keeping my eyes on the city lights, I can only nod.

"Someone has to break the news to your mother," he murmurs solemnly.

My voice is hoarse when I whisper, "I'll tell her tomorrow."

When the elevator doors open again, and I glance over my shoulder, I'm not surprised to see Franco. His eyes land on me, and within seconds, he closes the distance and yanks me into a tight embrace.

Unlike when Dario hugged me, I can't keep the tears from sneaking from my eyes, and I grip my best friend in a crushing hold.

I've been friends with Franco since school, and besides Giulio, he's the person I'm closest to.

"I've got you," he whispers, and that's all it fucking takes for the pain to explode from me.

My grief is so fucking intense it shudders through my body.

"Come," Franco says.

Keeping an arm wrapped around my shoulders, he steers me up the stairs and into one of the guest bedrooms.

As capos, we can't break down in front of our men. No matter what, we always have to remain strong.

But the second I'm alone with Franco, my legs give way, and my knees slam into the floor. Bracing my hands on my thighs, I can't even breathe through the intense pain.

I feel Franco's arm wrap around my shoulders again. He's a solid force beside me while I break into a million pieces.

My voice is hoarse and filled with sorrow and rage as I whisper, "They fucking gutted him open like a fish."

My stomach burns with bile.

"His heart was in a fucking box."

"Christ, Renzo," Franco murmurs. "I'm so fucking sorry."

Turning my head, I lock eyes with my friend. "They fucking gutted my little brother."

Franco's face is strained, and I can see he feels my pain. "We'll kill every last fucker."

Nodding, I suck in a desperate breath of air.

I'll leave Skylar Davies for last.

Only when I bury Giulio's kidney with his body will I find some semblance of peace.

# Chapter 6

## Skylar

Waking up the day after the surgery, I feel groggy as hell.

An image of an attractive man standing next to my bed flits through my mind, and a frown forms on my forehead.

Was it real or a dream?

I can remember him vividly. He had black hair cut in a sharp faux style, the sides trimmed short. His eyes were a unique color, light brown irises with a dark green ring around them. Almost cat-like.

He even growled like a tiger.

*"The kidney belongs to me."*

My eyes widen as the thought that I might have seen a freaking ghost hits me.

"Don't be absurd," I mutter to myself as I gingerly try to sit up.

My midsection and abdomen are tender from the surgery, but the pain is a lot less than I expected.

Leaning back against the pillows, I let out a sigh.

Just then, Dad comes into the room, and when he sees I'm awake, a smile spreads over his face.

"How do you feel?"

The corner of my mouth lifts into a grin as I answer, "Stronger."

Leaning over me, Dad presses a kiss to my forehead before taking a seat on the armchair next to the bed.

Taking my hand, he asks, "No pain?"

I shake my head. "There's just a little discomfort."

"Let me know if you're in pain. Okay?"

I nod, then stare at Dad, who looks younger with all the worry gone.

"You need a vacation after all the torture I've put you through. I'm sorry for all the worry."

He lets out a relieved breath. "There's nothing to apologize for, sweetheart. You have a healthy kidney, and hopefully, I can take you home next week."

Scrunching my nose, I chuckle. "Yeah, I'm tired of the hospital."

Suddenly, I'm hit with an intense wave of emotion, and the realization that I'm not going to die overwhelms me.

Dad moves forward, and wrapping his arms around me, he says, "It's over, sweetheart. Thank you for fighting to stay with me."

The memory of the visitor from the night before flits through my mind, and I pull back so I can ask, "Do you know who the donor is?"

Dad shakes his head. "It was an anonymous donation."

*Shoot.*

My eyebrows draw together then I ask, "Do you think I can write a thank you letter? Would they give it to the person?"

Again, Dad shakes his head. "There's no way to contact the person."

Before I can continue the conversation, Dad brushes some strands away from my forehead and says, "Focus on getting better so your body accepts the kidney."

Taking a deep breath, I relax back against the pillows.

There's no way the man I saw last night donated a kidney. He'd still be out of it from the surgery like I was.

Yeah, it was probably just a dream.

*Hey, at least my mind conjured up a hot man.*

---

# Renzo

Sitting in the back of the Bentley as Vincenzo brings it to a stop at the cemetery, my grief darkens until it suffocates the last of my humanity.

I throw the door open, and even though it's raining lightly, I don't wait for one of my men to bring an umbrella and walk to where the hearse has stopped.

*Even the heavens weep for you, Giulio. That's how fucking special you were.*

I don't wait for the funeral director and open the doors at the back of the hearse.

Looking at the black casket, the pain is so fucking intense, I struggle to cope with the grim reality of the day.

A memory of Giulio learning to shoot a gun flits through my mind. He turned around, and everyone ducked to the damn floor, cursing him. He laughed so hard tears ran down his face.

When Elio, Vincenzo, and Fabrizio join me, I wait for Vincenzo and Fabrizio to pull the casket out until Elio and I can take hold of the front.

As we start to carry Giulio to his final resting place, Franco falls in behind me while Dario takes up position behind Elio, and the weight of the casket lessens.

Angelo and Damiano also join us, and walking to the hole in the ground, I glance at the chairs, forming a half-circle around the grave.

My soul feels numb by the time we place the casket on the green straps that will keep it suspended over the hole.

As the other men go to take a seat, Franco stays next to me while I look down into the hole.

*This isn't right.*

*Giulio was supposed to bury me. Not the other way around.*

Minutes later, Franco whispers, "Everyone's here."

I nod, but my feet refuse to move.

More minutes pass, then I growl, "You can start, Father."

The priest's voice begins to drone, but I don't hear a word.

I keep staring at the fucking hole I'm supposed to leave my little brother in.

I feel a hand on my lower back, and turning my head, it's to see my mother. Her face is streaked with tears.

Lifting my arm, I wrap it around her shoulders and pull her tightly to my side.

She was a mother to Giulio, and today, she's burying a son.

My eyes burn as if they're on fire when she sobs.

The rage swirls like a tornado in my chest, creating chaos and destruction.

"Mr. Torrisi?" Father Parisi says to get my attention.

I have to say something.

Sucking in a deep breath of air, I turn around and lead my mother back to her chair. Once she's seated, I place my hand on her shoulder and look at everyone who's come to pay their respects.

It's not just my men. An army of soldiers crowd the space around the grave.

I'm supposed to say something about Giulio. Maybe share a funny or sentimental moment.

When I open my mouth, there's only fire and brimstone as the words rumble from me. "They killed my brother. We will hunt every last person who was involved. We'll fucking burn New York to the ground."

A chorus of agreement sounds up.

Turning to the casket, I move closer again and crouch down to grab a fist of dirt. When I straighten up, I bring up the last memory I have of Giulio.

*'Don't stay out late. We have a lot to do tomorrow," I mutter to Giulio.*

*He comes closer and steals a fry from my plate. After popping it into his mouth, he chews before saying, 'You'd make a good father. You've had me to practice on.'*

*'Because of you, I'm never having kids. You're a fucking handful,' I say with a playful tone lacing the words.*

*The infectious smile that's synonymous with Giulio tips his mouth up. "I won't be late. Don't go to bed too early, old man."*

*"Fuck you," I growl.*

*His laughter fills the open-plan kitchen and living room as he walks to the elevator.*

Slowly, the dirt slips through my fingers, falling on the casket.

My voice is hoarse as I say, "I'll miss you so fucking much, Giulio."

# Chapter 7

## Skylar

Waking up in the middle of the night, I'm still clutching a pen. I fell asleep while making a list of things I have to do when I get released from the hospital.

I'm so excited about the second chance I've been given, I can't wait to get out of here.

While I set the pen down on the bedside table, I pat the covers in search of the notepad. When I don't find it, I reach for the remote so I can turn the lights on.

Movement catches my eyes, and as they flick to the door, I don't see anyone.

*I could've sworn I saw something move.*

Switching on the light, I glance at the covers, but not seeing the notepad, I frown and search the floor around the bed.

"Where did it go?"

Just then, my eyes land on the bedside table, and I see the notepad.

*I must've put it there before falling asleep.*

Getting comfortable on the bed again, I pick up the notepad and pen and flip to the page I was writing on.

I read over the list I've made, then my eyes widen, and a gasp escapes me.

**A life for a life.**

The words are practically carved into the page.

*What the hell?*

Staring at the harshly written words, I'm filled with confusion.

I have no idea how the words got onto my notepad. Surely I didn't write that before I fell asleep?

Why would I?

Still, the pen was in my hand when I woke up.

Unable to make sense of it, I close the notepad and set it down on the bedside table.

Lying back against the pillows, I stare up at the ceiling.

Weird things have been happening since the surgery. Besides the man I saw the night of the surgery, I've been seeing shadows move. As if someone's watching me.

If I believed in ghosts, I'd think whoever donated the kidney died, and now they're haunting me.

But there is no such thing as ghosts.

*Right?*

Zipping the bag closed, I grin at Dad. "Let's get out of here."

Dad takes the bag, and smiling from ear-to-ear, he wraps his other arm around my shoulders. "Finally, I get to take you home."

As we walk out of the room and toward the exit of the hospital, emotion builds between us.

Neither of us thought this day would come.

After the car accident, our lives came to a standstill, and I've practically lived in the hospital ever since.

It feels like I'm being freed from prison after having been handed a life sentence.

When we walk out of the hospital, and I'm met with the sun shining brightly, tears sting my eyes.

I'll never take life for granted again. Every day will be special.

A happy smile curves my lips when we reach Dad's Mercedes, and when I open the passenger door and climb inside, I exhale a breath of relief straight from my soul.

Dad climbs in behind the steering wheel, and as he starts the engine, excitement bursts in my chest.

"I'm going home," I shriek, and leaning over the center console, I hug the everloving crap out of Dad.

He pats my back and chuckles. "I can't wait for you to make me something to eat."

Pulling back, I say, "We have to stop at the store so I can get fresh ingredients. I'm going to make so much food that all you'll do for the next week is eat."

Dad steers the Mercedes away from the hospital, and my eyes drink in every car and person on the road. I stare at the buildings and trees.

Everything looks brand new as if I'm seeing it for the first time.

The leaves on the trees are greener, and every other color looks brighter than I remember.

When we reach our neighborhood, I'm hit with another wave of relief.

I get to live.

I'll get a job at a five-star restaurant.

I'll create my own dishes.

I'll get married, and Dad will walk me down the aisle.

My cheeks hurt from all the smiling, and when Dad parks the car by the store, my body vibrates with strength and energy.

Grabbing a cart at the entrance, I head down aisle after aisle to stock up on everything I'll need.

"Can we stop to get some meat and fish?" I ask while I search through the vegetables for the freshest ones.

"Sweetheart, consider me your chauffeur. We can go wherever you want," Dad says.

I grin at him as I put a bunch of carrots in the cart. "You're the best."

"Don't you ever forget that," he teases me.

"Not a chance."

When I have everything I can think of, we head to the checkout. Before I can start scanning the shopping, Dad says, "I don't want you to overdo things. Let me take care of this."

Watching Dad scan product after product, I feel like the luckiest woman in the world.

The worst is finally behind me, and I can breathe again.

I can hope and dream.

I can live.

"What do you feel like eating?" I ask.

"Anything, sweetheart."

"How about lamb rib eye with garlic and sage roasted potatoes?" I ask, watching Dad's face closely.

His smile wavers for a moment before brightening again. "You're mother's favorite. I think it's fitting for today."

Leaving the store, we stop by the butcher shop I love before heading home.

When I walk into my family home, it feels like the love of a million memories wraps around me. It feels like Mom will come down the grand staircase at any moment and scold us for going to the store without her.

Or her laughter will sound up somewhere in the house.

"Oh my God," Louisa, our housekeeper, shrieks from my left. "You're home!"

She's worked for us since I was in elementary school, so she's practically family.

She comes to give me a gentle hug, then says, "I'm so happy."

"That makes two of us," Dad murmurs. "Louisa, will you get the bags from the car, please?"

"Of course, Mr. Davies." She pats my arm. "Get settled in bed. I'll bring you a cup of tea."

I let out a groan. "I'm not going to bed."

"You need to rest, sweetheart," Dad says.

"I'll rest in the living room," I negotiate. "I've spent months in a bed."

"Okay. As long as you're not on your feet for long periods of time."

I give Dad a playful scowl. "Dr. Bentall said moving around is good. It promotes healing."

"Yes, but I know you. If I give you half a chance, you'll stand in the kitchen and cook for the next three days."

I scrunch my nose and pretend to pout as I walk in the direction of the living room. "I'll rest for two hours, but then I'm making food."

"Listen to your father, Skylar. We don't want you to go back to the hospital," Louisa chastises me.

"I promise to get a lot of rest, but I also want to get back to cooking. I need a lot of practice before I can return to work."

"You're going back to work?" Dad asks as he follows me.

"Eventually. Dr. Bentall said I should be able to return to work after three months."

I sit down on the couch I've adopted as mine and grab the remote for the TV. Lying down, I tuck one of the throw pillows beneath my head.

Giving Dad a sweet smile, I say, "I won't overdo it. I promise."

"Okay."

"Can you bring my pillow from my bedroom?" I ask as I switch on the TV.

"Sure. Should I bring your blanket as well?"

I point at the throw draped over the back of the couch. "I'll use this one if I get cold."

Dad looks at me for a moment before he leaves to get my pillow.

I hear Louisa carry the shopping to the kitchen and then become aware of the familiar sounds of the house.

*I missed this.*

Using the remote, I scroll to my selection of cooking videos and press play.

Dad comes back into the living room with my pillow, and after he places it under my head, I snuggle into it.

"Can I bring you anything else?" Dad asks.

"No, thanks." My eyes leave the TV screen to rest on him. "Are you going into the office today?"

He shakes his head. "I'm working from home this week." When he heads to the doorway, he adds, "I'll check in on you later."

"Okay."

I turn my attention back to the show and watch as the chef rubs spices into a filet.

Before the meat even gets to the pan, my eyes drift shut.

# Chapter 8

## Renzo

Unresolved anger is like cancer. It fucking spreads and destroys everything in its path.

I swing the bat at the fucker's hip for the fourth time, and he howls with pain.

After posing as a buyer, Dario set up a meeting with this guy. He's the one who sold Giulio's information at the blood bank.

"Who the fuck did you give the information to?" I shout, unable to control my rage, as I slam the bat into his lower back.

"Please," he begs through snot and tears. "Don't kill me."

We have him stripped down to his underwear, his body covered in bruises and blood.

Caught in a haze of white-hot wrath, I beat the fuck out of him until I'm breathless, and he's a whimpering mess at my feet.

My body vibrates from the destructive emotions, and my voice is ice fucking cold as I ask, "Who did you sell the information to?"

"I only have…an email," he whimpers. "I never…saw the person."

"Give us the email," I demand.

He lifts his head and tries to crawl a couple of feet away from me. "It's on my phone."

My eyes flick to Emilio, who quickly digs through the man's clothes. Finding the cell phone, he brings it to me.

There's no password, and when I go into the emails, I bark, "Which email?"

"The one from zero-three-six-snap," he answers quickly, terror trembling in his voice.

Finding it, I forward the email to Dario with a request that he trace it.

I toss the device back to Emilio, then glare at the fucker on the floor. With hatred raging in my chest, I repeatedly bring the bat down on the fucker until I'm sure he's dead.

*That's another one down, Giulio. I'll find them all.*

Dropping the bat to the floor, I mutter, "Clean up the mess."

Leaving the room, I take the steps down and head to the restroom, where I wash my hands and splash water on my face. When my eyes lock on my reflection in the mirror, all I see is the rage carved into my features. My breaths fall heavy over my lips, and I focus on slowing them down.

After I'm done drying my hands, I go to the office where Elio's working. He's been taking care of everything while I've been hunting leads.

When I enter the office, Elio's on a call. I take a seat on the couch, and pulling my phone from my pocket, I dial Dario's number.

"I just saw the email," he answers.

I exhale a tired sigh. "It should lead us to whoever set up the deal with Davies."

"I'll let you know when I find out anything."

"Thanks, brother."

"How are you holding up?" he asks.

I'm not, and I'm getting fucking tired of everyone constantly asking me how I'm doing.

Every lead I chase delivers nothing of substance we can use to find whoever's behind the trafficking of organs.

Joe, the fucker we caught in the alley, couldn't get any information, and after his seventy-two hours were up, I had Carlo kill him.

"I'm fine," I mutter, my tone laced with impatience.

"I got the cameras you asked for. Want to swing by and get them?"

"I'll be there in an hour."

We end the call, and I listen as Elio negotiates terms for a shipment of Uzis with the Yakuza.

When he finally puts his phone down, he mutters, "Fucking bastards. I'm tired of them always trying to negotiate a discount."

He looks exhausted.

"Are you okay handling the workload? I can get Carlo to help out."

He shakes his head. "I'll manage."

"Thank you." My words have his eyes flicking to mine. "I wouldn't be able to do this without you."

Letting out a deep breath, he nods before asking, "Did you get anything from the fucker?"

"An email address. I've sent it to Dario."

The corner of Elio's mouth lifts. "Good." His gaze narrows on my face. "What are you doing about the doctor and the Davies family?"

"I'll deal with them soon." Climbing to my feet, I leave the office and give Vincenzo and Fabrizio a chin lift so they know we're heading out.

They're busy cleaning their guns and quickly assemble the weapons before jogging to catch up with me.

"Where to, boss?" Vincenzo asks.

"Dario's place."

I climb into the back of the Bentley and pull my phone from my pocket again. Bringing up the photo I took of Skylar Davies, I stare at the woman.

I haven't seen her since I left the message in the notepad for her.

As soon as I know which group is behind the trafficking of organs, I'll kill the doctor. I'm leaving Harlan and his daughter for last.

*Especially the daughter.*

Honestly, I'm torn between cutting the fucking kidney out of her while she's conscious or making her suffer for the rest of her life.

I've memorized every stand of ginger hair on her head, but I still stare at the photo.

She looks vulnerable and weak. It would be the easiest thing to snap her neck like a twig.

I imagine my fingers wrapping around her throat and squeezing until tears spill down her cheeks.

She'd whimper and beg for mercy.

She'd fucking gasp for air, and I'd show no mercy.

"Boss?" Vincenzo says to get my attention.

I'm so deep in thought I didn't realize we're at Dario's place already.

Shoving the door open, I climb out of the vehicle and stalk to the elevators. I let out a sigh as I step inside, scanning the access card for the penthouse.

I have a key for Dario and Franco's homes. It's in case shit goes sideways, and we need to get inside.

The doors slide open, and not seeing Dario in the living room, I head to the kitchen.

"Where are you?" I call out.

"Taking a leak."

I open the fridge and help myself to a bottle of water. As I take a sip, Dario calls, "Where the fuck did you go?"

I swallow the water, then answer, "Kitchen."

A few seconds later, he comes in with a small box and sets it down on the island in the middle of the kitchen.

"I got four cameras. Make sure nothing obstructs their view, or we won't see shit." He tilts his head. "Maybe I should plant them."

"No. I'll do it."

I take a look at the cameras lying on a bed of bubble wrap. They're no bigger than a button. There are also double-sided adhesive pads.

When I pick up the sheet, I ask, "Will this work?"

"It's either that or you take a glue gun. Those will work just fine, though."

"They better," I mutter.

"Ungrateful ass."

The corner of my mouth lifts, and it has Dario smiling as if a miracle just happened.

"Need anything else?" he asks.

"Not that I can think of. I'll be in touch." Taking the box, I head toward the elevator.

"My ballet company is performing this weekend. Want to come to a show?"

Chuckling, I shake my head. "Opera and tutus are your thing, brother." Stepping into the elevator, I shake my head. "You're the only one who likes that shit."

"I'm the only one with taste," he shouts before the doors shut.

There's an actual smile on my face for the first time in two weeks, but it quickly fades when I think about breaking into Harlan Davies' house so I can plant the cameras.

I want to see every move Skylar makes.

After using a wireless alarm jammer that cost way too fucking much, I enter the mansion through one of the windows.

When my feet touch the tiles, I glance around and find myself in the dining room.

With my eyes already used to the dark, I move to the doorway and search the wide open space of the foyer for movement before I creep toward the left, where I find the kitchen.

Glancing around, I decide to stick the tiny camera near the vent, figuring it's not something they'll look at often.

Not making a fucking sound, I use one of the stools by the island to climb onto so I can reach the vent, and when I'm done, I quickly move the stool back into place before sneaking out of the kitchen.

*One down. Three to go.*

I find the living room and hide a camera by the TV stand, and heading upstairs, I'm on high alert.

Not sure which bedroom belongs to Skylar, I carefully check through the rooms until I find hers.

I only spare the sleeping woman a glance before I quickly find a spot by her dressing table to plant the camera. When I turn around, my eyes land on the bed where Skylar's kicked off her covers. Slowly, I move closer and stare at her right side, where the T-shirt has ridden up.

Seeing the bandage, a growl almost escapes me, and I have to fight the urge to rip the fucking bandage off and dig Giulio's kidney from her body with my bare hands.

"Your time will come, and I'll show you the same mercy Giulio received when they fucking butchered him," I whisper, a world of vengeance coating my voice.

The woman stirs and mumbles sleepily, "Huh?"

Creeping out of her bedroom, I head back to the staircase, where I hide the last of the cameras before getting my ass out of the mansion.

When I make it back to the Bentley without being caught, I find Vincenzo chewing on his thumb nail.

When he sees me, he complains, "My heart can't handle this shit. Next time, I'll go in."

"Let's get out of here," I order while climbing into the vehicle.

As we drive away from the mansion, the corner of my mouth lifts.

Now I can watch every little movement my prey makes.

# Chapter 9

## Skylar

The stitches were removed a few days ago, and Dr. Bentall says my body is adjusting to the transplant at a satisfactory rate.

Honestly, I feel as good as new, and with every passing day, I'm becoming stronger. I'm even gaining weight again.

While I fill little pockets of dough with shredded beef so I can make steamed dumplings, Louisa places a cup of tea on the counter.

"You're spending too much time in the kitchen," she chastises me. "You promised to take it slow."

"If I take it any slower, I'll be in bed twenty-four-seven," I mumble. I shoot her a grin. "It feels like I've been released from a prison sentence. Let me enjoy life."

"I just don't want anything going wrong."

Giving her a reassuring smile, I say, "Nothing will go wrong. I feel healthy, and as soon as I get tired, I'll take a nap."

She lets out a sigh before walking out of the kitchen, and I take a quick sip of the tea then continue making another dumpling.

Suddenly, the tiny hairs on the back of my neck prickle with a weird sensation as if I'm being watched. Even though I know I'm alone in the kitchen, I still glance around me.

I've been getting the feeling more and more.

*It's your imagination.*

*But...*

My hands still as I think about the dream I had last week. I didn't see the man, but I could feel him in my bedroom, watching me. He said something I can't remember.

It feels like it was the same man I dreamed about the day I got the transplant.

I mentioned the dreams to Dr. Bentall, who said some patients might have disturbing dreams and poor sleep. It isn't unusual.

Taking a deep breath, I continue to prepare the dumplings, and while they're steaming, I make sesame noodles.

I find Asian cuisine fascinating and would love to specialize in it. With a bit of luck, I'll become a head chef at a Michelin Star restaurant where I can create my own signature Asian-inspired dishes.

I let out a frustrated sigh, wishing I could return to work already. I want to get my life back to how things were before the car accident.

My thoughts turn to Mom, and there's a pang of sadness in my chest.

*I miss her.*

I hardly had time to mourn her death when I was forced to face my own impending demise. Three years have passed, and I've only been to her grave twice.

I should get some flowers and visit her grave.

Dad comes into the kitchen and grabs a bottle of water from the fridge. "When are we eating?"

"In ten minutes." I glance at him, then say, "I'd like to visit Mom's grave tomorrow. Can you squeeze it into your busy schedule?"

"What time?"

"Whenever suits you."

Dad thinks for a moment, then suggests, "How about four pm?"

"Works for me."

When he leaves the kitchen, I check the dumplings before making the noodles, which don't take long to cook.

When the food is ready, I prepare three plates. Placing two plates with chopsticks and soy sauce on a tray, I carry it to Dad's office so I can eat with him.

Passing Louisa, where she's wiping down the handrail by the stairs, I say, "Your food is in the kitchen."

"Thank you."

Walking into Dad's office, I set the tray down on the coffee table, and take a seat on the couch.

"Come eat, Daddy."

He gets up from behind his desk and sits down beside me. Picking up his chopsticks, he murmurs, "It looks delicious, sweetheart."

I've put off discussing my plans with my father, and after swallowing a bite of a dumpling, I say, "I want to start looking at apartments."

Dad's eyes snap to my face. "So soon?"

"I'll probably look around for a month or so before finding a place."

"Which areas?"

"Manhattan. I want to be close to the restaurant where I hope to get a position."

"Let's see where you end up working, then I'll help you buy an apartment."

The corner of my mouth lifts into a smile. "You don't have to do that. My savings account is pretty healthy."

"I know, but let me do this for you. Consider it a gift for fighting so hard."

I nudge my shoulder against Dad's. "You spoil me rotten."

"Of course. You're my daughter."

I feel a little emotional as we continue to eat, and only when we're done do I say, "I wouldn't have survived without you, Daddy. Thank you for practically dragging me through the past three years."

He pats my knee before getting up and walking to his desk. With his back to me, he clears his throat before murmuring, "There's nothing in this world I wouldn't do for you."

I know. I'm the luckiest person alive to have him as my father.

---

Climbing out of the Mercedes, my eyes touch on the bouquet of lilies before I glance over the cemetery.

While I wait for Dad to walk around the car, a Bentley with blacked-out windows drives slowly past us.

Smiling at Dad, I hook my arm through his, and as we walk toward Mom's grave, I look at the neatly trimmed grass and well-maintained graves. There are flower beds and old trees, the nature blending with the headstones.

"It's actually pretty and peaceful here."

"I wouldn't associate the word pretty with a cemetery," Dad replies.

I glance to my right and see a man crouching in front of a headstone, his head slightly bowed. Before I can look away, he glances in my direction.

With the distance between us, I can't get a good look at his face, and quickly look away so he doesn't think I'm staring at him.

When we reach Mom's grave, I take the dead flowers from the holder attached to the headstone and put the fresh bouquet in it.

"We brought you lilies, Mom," I say as I read the words engraved on the granite.

"Hi, Sadie," Dad whispers while he wraps his arm around my shoulders. "I brought Skylar so you could see how good she's doing." His voice tenses with sorrow as he adds, "But she's just as stubborn as you and wants to do too much too soon."

I let out a chuckle. "No, Dad's being overprotective like always."

Silence falls around us as we stand by Mom's grave, and a moment later, I feel the eerie prickling sensation at the back of my neck.

Glancing to my right, I see the man still standing by the grave he came to visit, but his head's turned toward us.

He's just looking in our direction, but still, my body tenses and I feel a sense of danger.

"Let's go home, Daddy," I say, already turning away from Mom's grave.

As we walk back to the car, Dad asks, "Is there anywhere else you want to stop, or are we heading home?"

"Home. I want to get started with dinner."

We climb into the Mercedes, and I pull on the safety belt. When Dad steers us toward the gates of the cemetery, I say, "Since the transplant, I keep getting this weird sensation that I'm being watched."

Dad's eyes flick to my face. "But you've hardly left the house."

"I know. It's weird. Whether I'm cooking or watching TV, the feeling just pops up at the most random times."

"You're not one to be paranoid, sweetheart. Maybe we should make an appointment with a therapist. You've been through a lot the past three years, and talking about it could be good for you."

I let out a chuckle. "No, thanks. I'm not spilling my guts to some stranger. Talking to you is all the therapy I need."

"Maybe you should invite Oakley and Hallie over. You haven't seen them in a while," Dad mentions.

There's a reason I haven't seen them. They stopped coming to the hospital when things got too hard for them to handle.

Not ready to think about how my friends abandoned me in my darkest hour, I mutter, "I don't think so."

Dad's eyes flick to me again. "Did something happen between you and them?"

I shake my head and glance out of the window. "Our lives just went in different directions. It happens."

He's quiet for a moment before saying, "I'm sorry, sweetheart."

"It happens." Leaning forward, I turn on the radio and adjust the volume so the music isn't too loud.

Just as Dad pulls away from a traffic light, I relax against the seat again and glance out the window.

There's a black car to our right, and with the windows rolled down, I get a glimpse of the man in the back seat.

Recognition slams hard into my gut, but a second later, the car turns up a side street, and I can't see the man anymore.

I'm dead sure that's the man I dreamed about the night after I got the transplant.

I'd recognize those hazel eyes anywhere.

As the car drives away, I realize it's a Bentley.

*Is it the same one I saw at the cemetery?*

Not even a minute later, I'm second-guessing myself.

*Maybe it was just déjà vu?*

# Chapter 10

## Renzo

Sitting in my living room, I watch the livestream from the cameras I planted in Davies' mansion.

I bring the tumbler of whiskey to my lips and take a sip, my eyes glued to Skylar, where she's blow-drying her hair.

She's physically changed over the past three weeks. Her face isn't gaunt anymore, and her skin has a healthy glow. With the weight she's gained, she's gone from pretty to strikingly beautiful.

She's sitting at her dressing table, facing the camera, and when I look into her clear blue eyes, it feels as if she can see me.

Her movements slow down, and with a frown forming on her forehead, she switches off the hairdryer.

She glances around her, then tugs her bottom lip between her teeth before murmuring, "This is getting insane. There's no one there."

The corner of my mouth lifts in a predatory smirk. "Oh, I'm here."

Brushing her shoulder-length ginger hair with hard strokes, she says, "I better stop seeing ghosts everywhere, or Dad's going to drag my ass to the nearest therapist."

When she places the brush on the table, she stares into the mirror and lets out a sigh.

I get up and walk closer to the TV screen until I'm eye-to-eye with her.

*She's really fucking beautiful.*

Skylar gets up and walks to her bed. She's only wearing an oversized T-shirt, and when she crawls onto the mattress, and sits down with her legs folded in front of her, I have a direct view of her black panties and smooth inner thighs.

For a moment, my body betrays me, and I begin to harden.

She pulls her laptop in front of her, and knowing she'll be busy on it for at least the next hour, I finish the whiskey before setting the tumbler down on the coffee table.

Heading upstairs to my bedroom, I grab a pair of sweatpants from the walk-in closet before going to the bathroom.

I switch on the faucets in the shower, and while the water warms up, I strip out of my suit.

I place my gun on the counter, my thoughts circling Skylar like a vulture getting ready to swoop in for the kill.

Fuck, I'm growing impatient and have to decide what I'm going to do.

Watching Skylar Davies live her perfect life with Giulio's kidney in her body is torture.

Stepping beneath the warm spray, I begin to wash my body while one thought after another rushes through my mind.

I could go to the mansion and give them a quick death after getting all the information from Harlan.

Or I could have them taken to the warehouse, where I can slowly torture them.

*Or...*

I can take Skylar's precious freedom. Holding her captive would be the worst kind of torture for both of them. Harlan clearly loves his daughter more than life itself, and being separated from her would drive him insane.

Switching off the faucets, I step out of the shower and grab a towel. As the soft fabric wipes the drops from my body, the corner of my mouth lifts.

I like the idea of Harlan losing his fucking mind. I'll have his precious daughter, and there would be nothing he can do to save her.

Slipping on the sweatpants, I grab my gun from the counter and walk out of the bathroom. When I head down the stairs, the smell of microwaved popcorn hits me, and then I see Dario sitting on my couch while watching the camera feed like it's some goddamn movie.

When he sees me, he pops a kernel of popcorn into his mouth and says, "I got hungry from watching the woman cook. It looks like she has some serious skills."

Grabbing the remote from the couch, I glance at the TV screen and see Skylar busy making a dish that could easily be served in the best restaurants.

I press the button on the remote, and the screen goes black.

"The whole place smells of fucking popcorn," I mutter.

"Want some?" Dario asks with a smirk.

"No." I walk to the kitchen, and opening the bag of takeout I ordered earlier, I pull the burger and fries out and put it on a plate before warming it for a minute in the microwave.

"You need to eat healthier," Dario complains as he opens the fridge to help himself to a can of soda. His eyes sweep over the contents of the fridge. "You're going to die of a heart attack."

"Considering all the ways I could die, I'll take it," I mutter to aggravate him.

He shoots me a scowl. "I can send Esmerelda over twice a week to cook for you."

"Hell no. Keep your housekeeper to yourself."

I remove the plate from the microwave and take a huge bite of the burger.

Dario looks at the junk food with disgust.

The man is my opposite in every way. It's a fucking miracle we're friends because the only thing we have in common is the Cosa Nostra.

Opening the can, he leans back against the island before taking a sip. He clears his throat, then asks, "Have you found out anything new?"

I shake my head. "We keep chasing a bunch of emails and phone numbers. It's pissing me off."

"Maybe it's time to grab the doctor. He'll definitely know something we can use."

I nod while taking another bite, and only after I've swallowed do I say, "Yeah, I'm thinking the same thing."

"And Davies and his daughter?"

"Same thing." I take the can of soda from his hands and help myself to a couple of sips before passing it back to him. "I'll have Carlos and Emilio bring them to the warehouse after I've cleared out the shipment of AKs for the Mexicans."

"When is that happening?" he asks as he starts crunching on popcorn again.

"In three days."

His eyes meet mine. "Are you really going to kill the woman?"

I stare at him for a solid minute. "Eventually."

His eyebrows lift. "What does that mean?"

"I'm first going to torture them," I answer as I put the empty plate in the sink before walking to the living room.

Dario plops down on one of the couches. "Torture? The woman as well?"

The corner of my mouth lifts. "Careful. It sounds like you have a hardon for Skylar Davies, brother."

"Not by a long shot. I'm just thinking she might be innocent in this fucking mess."

My eyes flick to his. "Innocent? You're kidding, right? Giulio's kidney is buried in her fucking body."

Dario holds my stare as he says, "That's her father's doing, Renzo. She might not know where the kidney came from. Did you even think about that?"

I give him a look of warning. "I'm done talking about this."

He lets out a heavy breath, then nods. "I just don't want you doing something you'll regret."

"I fucking regret not protecting Giulio better, but I sure as fuck will not regret killing anyone involved in his death."

Considering the conversation over, I walk to the stairs. "You can let yourself out."

Dario darts up from the couch and grabs hold of my arm.

When I turn to face him, he says, "I'm sorry. The last thing I wanted was to upset you. I'm just looking out for you."

I lock eyes with him, and seeing the worry on his face, I say, "It's fine."

"We're good?"

I pat his shoulder. "We're good. I'm heading to bed. Switch off the lights on your way out."

"You're not going to give the junk you just ate time to digest?"

I shake my head. "No. Goodnight, Dario."

Walking to my bedroom, I sit down on the side of the bed and cover my face with my hands. I exhale a heavy breath as the grief and anger swirl in my chest.

# Chapter 11

## Skylar

A miracle happened today.

Dad finally let me go to the store on my own. It felt weird driving a car, but as I walk up and down the aisles, I feel empowered.

That's until the eerie sensation I've been experiencing since I left the hospital ripples down my spine.

Shaking my head hard, I do my best to ignore it as I grab flour and baking powder from the shelf.

Unable to help myself, I glance over my shoulder, and for a split second, I catch sight of a man in a light brown suit.

Like an idiot, I stand frozen while staring at the end of the aisle.

*I'm not insane, and there is no such thing as ghosts.*

Fear tightens my stomach, and tearing my eyes away from the spot where I saw the man, I push the cart to the next aisle.

I keep glancing around me, and by the time I reach the fruit and vegetables, I'm second-guessing myself once again.

I'm digging through zucchinis, looking for the biggest ones, when someone comes to stand slightly behind me. When I see the light brown suit from the corner of my eye, I freeze, and my heart explodes in my chest.

Abandoning the zucchinis, I take a few steps away, and as I glance over my shoulder, it's to see the back of the man as he walks away from me.

It's definitely not my imagination. That man is watching me.

Feeling a need to escape so I can get back to the safety of my house, I rush to the checkout point and quickly scan the groceries.

When I have everything packed and paid for, I exit the store, but as my eyes land on the Mercedes, it's to see the man leaning back against the car with his arms crossed over his chest.

*Shit.*

He's staring in my direction, watching as I stop walking, then he tilts his head in a sinister way.

My heart pounds against my ribs, and my lips part, my breaths rushing over them.

It's the same man I saw the day we went to the cemetery, and I'm one hundred percent sure it's the man I saw at the hospital.

*I'm being stalked.*

My chest rises and falls with heavy breaths as fear ripples over my body.

I'm just about to abandon my cart and dart back into the store when the man pushes away from the Mercedes and walks to where a black Bentley is parked.

*What does he want?*

*Why is he watching me?*

Only when the Bentley leaves the parking area do I rush to Dad's car and quickly load the groceries into the trunk. My heart is still racing a mile a minute, and feeling like I'm being hunted, I hurry to climb behind the steering wheel.

All the way home, I keep checking the rearview mirror, and I'm only able to suck in a relieved breath when I park the car in the garage.

When the door slides shut behind me, I switch off the engine and slump back against the seat. Sweat beads on my forehead, and with parted lips, I just stare at the steering wheel.

After what's just happened, I'm sure this man is watching my every move.

My eyes widen when I think of all the times it felt like I was being watched while cooking, watching TV, or sitting in my bedroom.

But that's insane. The mansion has an alarm system that's switched on at night, and half the time, the sensation of being watched happens in broad daylight when we're all awake.

*God.*

*Do I tell Dad?*

*What if he wants me to see a therapist or takes away the little freedom I've gained?*

*What if I'm overreacting and I make Dad worry for nothing?*

There's no reason for some strange, hot man to stalk me.

This is so freaking weird.

Opening the car door, I climb out and grab a couple of bags from the trunk. I carry the groceries to the kitchen while wondering how to handle the situation.

Honestly, I should feel flattered. The man might be interested in me and is looking for the right moment to approach me.

*Don't be freaking stupid!*

Chastising myself, I stand by the island and frown.

There's nothing flattering about being watched, and it feels sinister as hell.

I begin to unpack the bags while thoughts of the strange man keep flitting through my mind.

When I'm done putting everything away, I leave the kitchen and head to my bedroom. I change out of the dress I wore to the store, and put on a pair of shorts and a T-shirt.

Gathering my hair, I tie it in a ponytail before I sit down on the side of my bed.

I think about what to do for a few minutes, then decide to hold off on telling Dad. I don't want to cause him unnecessary worry.

If it happens again, I'll tell him.

Needing to relax, I grab my pillow as I get up and leave the room. When I come down the stairs, Dad walks across the foyer, heading to the kitchen.

When he sees me, he asks, "Did you get everything you wanted?"

I nod.

"You look tired," he murmurs. "Are you going to get some rest?"

"Yes. I'll watch some TV and take a nap on the couch," I say to set him at ease.

Dad's eyes scan over my face, then he asks, "Would you like to go out for dinner tomorrow night? You can pick the restaurant."

A smile curves my lips. "I'd love that."

As he continues to walk toward the kitchen, he says, "It's a date."

Heading into the living room, I grab the remote from the coffee table and lie down on the couch. Switching on the TV, I put on episodes of Chef's Table and snuggle into my pillow.

I struggle to pay attention to the show and think about my stalker. The suits he wears look expensive, and he's always well put together.

I didn't see his eyes, but I can still vividly remember they're light brown with a dark green circle.

He's so attractive that he'd stand out among a thousand people, but still, it feels like he's always cloaked in shadows.

Wracking my mind, I try to think of why he would want to watch me.

Unable to relax, apprehension spins in my stomach.

# Chapter 12

## Renzo

After concluding the deal with the Mexicans, I find myself watching Skylar Davies twenty-four-seven.

The other day, when I got close to her at the store, I could feel the fear vibrating from her.

She's aware I'm watching her, and even at home, she's constantly on guard and glancing around as if she expects me to creep out of the shadows.

I'm not going to lie. I'm enjoying this little game of cat and mouse way too fucking much.

Sitting on the other side of the restaurant, where Skylar and her father are enjoying dinner, the corner of my mouth lifts as I stare at her.

*Topolina.*

Calling her 'little mouse' seems fitting. Just like a cat, I'll play with her before biting off her fucking head.

I watch as she smiles at her father and says something before she gets up and walks to the back of the restaurant, where the restroom is.

I wait a few seconds before I climb to my feet and follow her. I glance around to make sure no one's paying attention to me before I slip into the restroom.

Finding the switch for the lights, I flick it off, plunging the room into darkness.

"Crap," I hear her mutter. It takes another few seconds before the stall door creeks open. "I can't see a freaking thing."

Standing right by the exit, she'll have to pass me to get out of the restroom, and I don't have to wait long.

I hear her cautiously moving closer, and suddenly, her hand brushes my chest. She must have her arms stretched out in front of her so she doesn't walk face-first into a wall.

A peep escapes her, making her sound just like the mouse she is.

Before she can pull away, I step forward, and as I wrap my arm around her neck, I move in behind her until her back is pressed to my chest.

"Oh my God," she whisper-shrieks.

My mouth finds her ear, then I growl, "Are you scared yet, *topolina*?"

She nods frantically. "Y-Y-Yes."

"Good." The word is nothing more than a threatening growl from deep in my chest.

I smell the soft vanilla scent drifting from her and feel how she trembles.

"Don't hurt me." Her voice is soft, quivering with fear. When I keep quiet, she asks, "Why are you doing this?"

My lips brush against the sensitive skin beneath her ear, and a hard shiver wracks through her body.

"You have something that belongs to me."

Not wanting to be caught in the restroom and figuring I've sufficiently scared the shit out of her, I let go. Stealthily moving around her, I open the door and leave her rattled in the dark.

Stopping by my table, I toss a few bills on the white cloth to settle the bill before I get my ass out of the restaurant. As I walk through the door, I glance back, but there's no sign of Skylar, who must still be shitting herself in the restroom.

"I'll see you soon, *topolina*."

It's time to implement the next stage of my plan.

---

# Skylar

I fumble against the wall, and finding the light switch, I turn it on. My eyes dart around the restroom, and seeing I'm alone, I suck in desperate breaths of air.

*My God.*

My hand darts to the side of my neck, where I can still feel the ghost of his lips on my skin. My mind reels, and my body is a trembling mess.

I almost had a freaking heart attack when my hand slammed into him, and when he grabbed me, I stopped breathing.

*That was freaking terrifying.*

Pressing my other hand against my stomach, I try to focus on slowing my breathing.

I'm going to have to tell Dad. This whole situation is getting out of hand.

Regaining some control over my frazzled mind, I dart forward and yank the door open. Rushing out of the restroom, I head straight for the table where Dad's cutting into his sirloin steak.

I quickly sit down, and only then do I glance around the restaurant, but there's no sign of my stalker.

"What's wrong?" Dad asks.

I turn my attention to him. "There was a man in the restroom."

His eyes widen, and he drops the cutlery on the table. "What?!"

"Can we take the food to-go? I just want to go home."

"Tell me what happened," Dad orders in a stern tone.

"I'll tell you once we get out of here." With a trembling hand, I tuck some of my hair behind my ear. "I just want to go."

Dad quickly gets a server and settles the bill. With our food in a takeout bag, we hurry out of the restaurant, and once we're in the Mercedes, he says, "Tell me what happened."

I pull the safety belt on while the words spill over my lips. "I've been seeing the same man everywhere. At first, I thought it was my imagination, but yesterday at the store, he got really close to me, and when I was done shopping, he was leaning against the car." My eyes meet Dad's worried ones. "Tonight, he came into the restroom and grabbed me from behind, asking me if I'm scared."

Dad starts the engine, and with screeching tires, he pulls away from the curb.

"What does he look like?" he asks.

"He has black hair that's cut in a sharp faux style and hazel eyes. He's easily two heads taller than me and wears expensive suits." When Dad drives in the direction of our house, I ask, "Aren't we going to the police?"

He shakes his head. "I'll hire a private security team."

"Why aren't we going to the police?" I ask, thinking that's the first thing we should do.

Dad hesitates for a moment before he says, "We don't have enough details for them to find the man."

Frowning at him, I argue, "But they can get information once they know I'm being stalked."

Dad's eyes flick to mine, and his tone is harsh as he snaps, "Let me handle this, Skylar." There's a flash of regret on his face, and he reaches across the console to give my hand a squeeze. "Sorry, sweetheart. I'm just worried. I'll get a private company to find the man, and then we'll go to the police. Okay?"

"Okay," I whisper before glancing out of the window.

A bad feeling sinks deep into my gut, and my teeth tug at my bottom lip.

# Chapter 13

## Skylar

Yesterday, Dad contacted the private security firm, and he said they're putting a skilled team together to protect me.

It doesn't make me feel any better, because I think we should go to the police, but Dad won't hear about it.

Sitting in Dr. Bentall's office at the hospital, we wait for him to arrive so he can give me a checkup. He's already twenty-five minutes late, and Dad's getting agitated.

"What's taking him so long?" Dad mutters as he pulls his phone out of his pocket.

I watch as he dials Dr. Bentall's personal number, but a moment later, he shakes his head. "It goes straight to voicemail."

Patting Dad's arm, I get up and say, "I'll check with Julia." Walking to the reception counter, I smile as I ask, "Do you know where Dr. Bentall is?"

She gives me an apologetic look. "I'm sorry you're waiting so long, Skylar. I've tried to call but can't get a hold of him. Do you want to wait a little longer, or should we reschedule? I can squeeze you in tomorrow afternoon."

Glancing over my shoulder, I look at Dad's worried expression, then nod. "Let's reschedule. Call me once you've confirmed the appointment with Dr. Bentall."

"I'll do that. I'm so sorry. I don't know what's keeping him."

"It's okay." Turning away from the reception counter, I walk back to where Dad's sitting. "Julia says she'll reschedule for tomorrow. Let's go home."

"What a waste of time," Dad mutters as he stands up. He wraps an arm around my shoulders and holds me close as we leave the office.

We're quiet as we head down the hallway toward the exit, and I feel tension coming off Dad in waves.

Walking through the double doors of the hospital, Dad steers me in the direction of the Mercedes.

Suddenly there's a screeching of tires as two white vans speed toward us. Dad turns us around, and grabbing my hand, he starts to run back to the entrance of the hospital.

I'm so freaking shocked I barely get to take in what's happening as the vans stop behind us. When I'm roughly grabbed from behind, a terrified scream tears from my throat.

Dad's fingers tighten around mine, but I'm yanked from his hold, and in absolute horror, I watch as two men forcefully restrain Dad.

I'm not strong enough to fight the man as he drags me into one of the vans, and before the doors slide shut, I hear Dad shout, "Skylar!"

"Daddy," I scream just as I'm thrown to the floor and a knee presses into my lower back. My arms are yanked backward, and my wrists tied together with cable ties.

"Stop!" I cry as I try to wiggle free. "Oh Jesus…Jesus…Jesus." Frantic panic stuns me into a stupor, and I keep gasping the same word over and over.

The knee lifts from my back, and I'm hauled upright and shoved onto a seat.

With wide eyes, my gaze lands on a man I've never seen before. He has light brown hair and eyes that seem black. Tattoos cover his neck, making him look scary as hell.

My breaths explode over my lips, and my heart hammers in my chest as I stare at the man who just kidnapped me in broad daylight.

Before I can even think to ask what's happening, he levels me with a terrifying look that makes ice pour through my veins. He grabs an old rag from the floor, and leaning over me, he forcefully gags me before tying it behind my head. Distressing sounds spill from me, sounding muffled from the rag biting into my lips.

*What do I do?*

*Oh, God. What do I do?*

*Shit.*

*I don't know what to do!!!*

My eyes sting from unshed tears as shock keeps hitting me in tidal waves.

I try to figure out where the van is taking me and hope Dad's being taken to the same place.

*God, please don't let them hurt Dad.*

*Are they going to kill us?*

*Why?*

*Is this a kidnapping for ransom?*

*Shit!*

My mind reels, and panicked thoughts rush through me, making me dizzy.

The van keeps speeding, taking sharp turns that toss me around on the seat, and when it finally comes to a screeching stop, I fall forward.

The man catches me, and when the side door slides open, I'm forcefully shoved out of the vehicle.

Wildly, my eyes dart around, and it looks like I'm in some kind of warehouse. To my left is a wall of crates, and in front of me, I see an office space where a man's sitting behind a desk, his eyes on me.

There are groups of men gathering to my right, and some sit at tables covered with guns. There are also open crates filled with all kinds of weapons.

*Jesus.*

The other van pulls into the warehouse as I'm shoved forward. I keep glancing over my shoulder as the man grips my bicep, forcing me to walk as he drags me toward a set of metal steps.

I watch as two men pull Dad out of the van while he struggles against their hold, trying to break free. Seeing Dad fight, I rear back and manage to break loose. I run toward Dad, but a moment later, I'm grabbed from behind again, and my feet leave the floor as I'm lifted into the air.

My side is tender from all the exertion and manhandling, and I worry about my kidney. I'm not supposed to do anything strenuous for another three weeks, and this is as freaking strenuous as it gets.

I hear Dad's muffled shouts, his eyes wide on me with shock and worry.

We're hauled up the steps and shoved into a room. I stumble into a concrete wall, then Dad's thrown onto the stained floor.

A second later, the door shuts, and I gasp through the shock of the terrifying situation we find ourselves in.

I'm unable to process anything, and nothing makes sense.

My eyes lock on Dad as he struggles to his feet, and my breaths come faster and faster until my chest burns.

"Daddy," I whimper around the dirty rag that tastes like oil.

I glance at the steel table by the one wall, an empty stained bucket, and all the marks on the concrete floor. I think some might be from blood.

*Jesus.*

Dad moves his head from side to side, straining against the rag in an attempt to get it off his mouth. "Skylar."

He rushes to my side and glances frantically around the room before his fear-filled eyes meet mine.

A tear sneaks over my cheek until it disappears into the rag.

Suddenly the door opens, and my eyes grow twice their size as Dr. Bentall is shoved into the room.

Four men follow him inside, and one of them comes to grab my arm. I try to resist as he pulls me to the middle of the room, where I'm shoved down to my knees.

*Oh God.*

My heart beats so freaking hard I swear my chest shakes with every beat.

Dad is forced to kneel on my right side and Dr. Bentall on my left. I glance between them, seeing the same horror in their eyes that's filling every inch of my body.

One by one, they remove the rags from our mouths, and my tongue darts out to wet my dry lips.

The moment Dad can talk, he begins to plead, "Don't do this. Please. Let my daughter go. She's innocent."

Slowly, I turn my head to look at Dad because it sounds like he knows why we're here.

"Shut up," one of the men snaps as he slaps Dad against the side of the head.

Two of the men leave, and the remaining two pull guns from behind their backs, where they are tucked into the waistband of their pants.

"You'll remain kneeling and only speak when spoken to," one of them orders.

My knees begin to ache from digging into the cold concrete, and my body trembles like a leaf in a shit storm.

I hear calculated footsteps approach the room, and a moment later, a man walks in, his demeanor predatory.

Recognition has my eyes widening again, and I stare at the man who's been watching me. The one who cornered me in the restroom last night.

Today, he's wearing a pale green suit, and it makes the green ring around his irises pop. The brown almost looks gold, and once again, it reminds me of a tiger.

Immediately I know he's in charge from the power radiating from him.

My breaths keep bursting over my lips, my chest rising and falling rapidly.

A chair is brought in, and without even looking, the man takes a seat while casually undoing the buttons of his jacket.

*Jesus, he's terrifying.*

Slowly his eyes settle on me before moving to Dad and stopping on Dr. Bentall. There's so much rage in his gaze it makes my fear grow tenfold.

When his eyes flick back to me, I flinch from the startling impact of having them focused on me.

It feels like an eternity passes before he takes a deep breath and nods at one of his men.

One by one, we're searched. They take Dr. Bentall and Dad's phones and wallets, and tossing the wallets on the metal table, they hand the phones to the man who's in charge.

When his lips part, his voice is such a low and deep timbre it makes shivers rush over my skin.

"Do any of you know who I am?"

I instantly shake my head, my hair wildly flipping over my shoulders.

"Renzo Torrisi," Dad whispers, his tone drenched with fear.

My eyes flit between Dad and the man.

The man holds Dad's gaze as he demands, "Who did you buy the kidney from?"

*What?*

When I gasp, Renzo's eyes flick back to me, and I cringe again.

"Dr. Bentall made all the arrangements," Dad answers hurriedly.

Renzo keeps staring at me as he asks, "Who was your contact?"

I'm about to wet myself as I whisper, "I don't know."

Annoyance flashes over Renzo's face before he looks at Dr. Bentall, who quickly answers, "A man by the name of Manual Castellanos."

Renzo pulls his phone out of his breast pocket and makes a call.

A moment later, he murmurs, "I have a name. Find Manual Castellanos...no, I haven't killed them yet."

My body goes numb for a moment, and I sway forward before catching myself from falling face-first onto the concrete floor.

Terror keeps washing over me, prickling my skin and making my mind feel hazy.

I've experienced intense fear before when I was told I was going to die, but it's nothing compared to what I'm feeling right now.

# Chapter 14

## Skylar

A million questions bombard me, but I don't have the guts to ask any of them.

My knees ache, and my body feels weak. I sway again, and it brings Renzo's attention back to me.

"With you still recovering from the transplant, this must be taking a toll on your body," he says, his tone biting.

"She's innocent in all of this!" Dad suddenly exclaims.

Renzo's eyes flick to the man who's holding a gun. I assume he's a guard, and without a word passing between them, the man walks to Dad and slams the gun into the side of his head.

"No!" I cry desperately.

"Shut up," the guard hisses at me.

Whimpering, I scoot closer to Dad, but the guard aims the gun at me, and it has me instantly freezing.

"No, please," Dad begs as he quickly moves between the gun and me.

Tears spill over my cheeks, and a sob explodes from my burning chest.

"Enough!" Renzo's voice is like a whip tearing through raw skin, and I swear my bladder is a second away from failing me.

Giving Renzo a pleading look, I press my lips together to keep the sobs from escaping me.

There's no mercy on his face as he watches me cry, and I realize we're all going to die.

*After everything I've been through, I'm still going to die.*

Unlike before, when I had to face death, I don't have time to process it. There's no making peace with the inevitable.

The ringing of a phone startles the hell out of me, and Renzo answers the call. "What do you have for me?"

He listens for a while, then says, "Let me know if you find out where the fucker is."

When he ends the call, his enraged gaze settles on Dr. Bentall. "Tell me everything you know about the group who calls themselves The Harvest."

Dr. Bentall shifts on his knees as he hastily answers, "They operate worldwide. The few times I've needed an organ, I contacted Manual. That's all I know."

"Have you ever met him in person?" Renzo asks.

Dr. Bentall nods. "Twice."

"Can you arrange a meeting?" another question is fired from Renzo.

"He'll be suspicious if I ask him to meet, especially so soon after asking for a kidney."

Renzo stares at Dr. Bentall until there's so much tension in the room it's suffocating.

"Then I have no reason to keep you alive." The threatening words shudder through me, and my tears dry up as ruthless fear grips me in a chokehold.

Renzo nods his head, and when the guard closes in on Dr. Bentall, the doctor starts to ramble," No! Wait. I'll contact him. I'll find a way to set up a meeting."

Renzo doesn't stop the guard as he repeatedly starts to slam the butt of his gun into Dr. Bentall's face. The violence and horror have me falling to my side, and I try to scramble away from it.

Droplets of blood spray over my legs, and I feel faint.

Only when Dr. Bentall slips in and out of consciousness, and the left side of his face is bloody and swollen, does Renzo say, "Enough."

Instantly, the guard steps back and resumes his standing position near the wall.

*Holy shit.*

*We're going to die.*

*We're really going to die.*

I'm reeling in horror when Renzo stands up and orders, "Bring the woman."

Turning around, he stalks away while the guard comes to grab my arm, and I'm hauled to my feet.

"No! Please," Dad shouts as he struggles to his feet. "She's innocent. Take me."

I meet Dad's frantic eyes for a moment, then the guard shoves him hard, making him fall on the floor.

I'm dragged out of the room, and another man shuts the door and locks it.

"No! Please," I hear Dad shout.

His pleas die away when I'm shoved into a different room. Instantly, my eyes land on the table where various tools and knives are spread out.

Renzo shrugs off his jacket, revealing a vest that fits his muscled chest and trimmed waist like a glove.

*Oh, God.*

*No.*

*NoNoNo!*

I rear back, wanting to get out of the room. I struggle with all my might, but the guard shoves me to the floor.

I hear the door slam shut, and when I look at it, I see the guard standing in front of it with his gun still in his right hand.

My head swivels to where Renzo's picking a knife from the selection, and I start to stammer, "P-Please. D-Don't k-kill m-m-me."

When he walks closer to me, I swear I feel my brain trembling in my skull as the cold, hard fact that I'm about to die hits me.

I try to scramble to my feet, but when Renzo's fingers clamp around my arm and I'm hauled up, I can only make a squeaking sound.

Bracing for the sharp pain of being stabbed to death, I'm surprised out of my everloving mind when the cable ties are cut, and my wrists are freed before he lets go of me.

Spinning around, my hair flies through the air. I tilt my chin head back and stare up at the man who's put the fear of God in me.

The only expression in his eyes is rage.

Slowly, he tilts his head, and his gaze narrows on me, making a hard tremble wrack through my body.

Somehow, I manage to find my voice and ask, "Who are you? Why are you doing this?"

The flash of rage on his face is so freaking brutal I feel the force of it in my bones. Faster than I can process, he moves, and my feet are swiped from under me.

As I fall back, I see Renzo come after me, and when I slam into the floor, he's on top of me like a vicious animal. The knife presses into the skin beneath my chin, forcing me to tilt my head backward.

My hands fly up, and I grab his wrist, trying to pull the blade away from my throat, but he's incredibly strong, and all I can do is hold onto him.

His lips pull back in a sneer, and with his face right by mine, he growls, "I'm one of the heads of the Cosa Nostra, and the kidney in your body belonged to my little brother."

*Cosa Nostra.*

I've watched a documentary about the mafia and know just how ruthless the group of criminals can be.

Renzo leans even closer, and his words are haunting and ferocious as he says, "My little brother was killed so you could fucking live."

*Little brother.*

*Killed.*

Unshed tears blur my sight, and I can't think of a single thing to say as I try to make sense of what he's telling me.

Being face-to-face with this man and feeling his breaths on my skin is unnerving, making my mouth grow bone dry.

He tilts his head slightly. "Do you understand what I'm saying?"

Slowly, I shake my head.

The tip of the knife presses into my skin, and a petrified shriek escapes me. My nails dig into his skin, and I squeeze my eyes shut.

"They fucking killed my brother in an empty lot at the back of an alley. They gutted him open like an animal and ripped his kidney from his body." With every word leaving his mouth, I hear the incredible pain he's in. "He was only twenty years old."

*No.*

I shake my head and cringe when he shouts, "Open your fucking eyes!"

They pop open, and immediately, tears spiral into my hairline.

With his brutal gaze holding mine captive, he hisses, "Do you understand what I'm saying?"

This time, I nod.

As he stares at me, the intense rage returns until his features seem to be carved from stone.

"As long as my brother's kidney is in your body, you belong to me."

*No.*

*God.*

*No.*

When I start to shake my head, he suddenly pulls back, and the next moment, my dress is shoved up my body, and the knife is pressed against the red scar where I had surgery.

A desperate scream is torn from my soul as I try to grab hold of his hand while begging, "Don't. Please, don't!"

His eyes lock with mine again. "Your choice, *topolina.* Either you do exactly as I say, or I take the kidney back right now."

*Shit.*

*Shit.*

*Shit.*

"I…I…I'll d-do what you s-s-say."

Once again, he moves quickly and rises to his feet. His eyes burn over me, and I don't dare move a muscle to fix my dress so it will cover me.

"Take her back to the other room," he orders the guard before throwing the knife on the table and grabbing his jacket.

With terror vibrating through me, I watch as he shrugs the jacket on and walks out of the room.

I quickly sit up and pull my dress down while I climb to my feet.

The guard grabs my arm, and I'm hauled out of the room that's clearly used for torturing people, and taken back to Dad and Dr. Bentall.

I'm shoved inside before the door is shut behind me, and standing on shaky legs, my eyes find my father's.

"Are you okay? What did he do?" Dad asks as he rushes to me with his hands still tied behind his back.

*Cosa Nostra.*

*His little brother was killed.*

*He was only twenty years old.*

My voice sounds a million miles away as I ask, "Did you buy a kidney for me on the black market?"

Dad stands in front of me, and his features are torn between worry and guilt.

I'm bombarded with destructive emotions as I put all the pieces together.

"You had someone killed so I could get a kidney," I cry. "He was only twenty years old." I gasp for air as I wrap my arms around my middle. "I never wanted that!"

Giving Dad a heartbroken and incredulous look, I whisper, "How could you do that?"

Tears spiral down my cheeks, and knowing I have a kidney from someone who was murdered makes my heart shatter into a million pieces.

"I would rather have died a dignified death than be subjected to this horror."

Dad's face crumbles beneath the guilt he feels. "I didn't know they'd kill someone for it." He turns and levels Dr. Bentall with an enraged glare. "You said nothing would go wrong!"

"Seriously?" I shriek as I step away from my father. "That's what you're going with?" Leaning forward, I shout, "A man was killed! Do you get that? A man was freaking killed!"

*I'm going to lose my mind.*

*I can't deal with this.*

Sobs wrack from me as I say, "And that man was the little brother of a mafia boss! What were you thinking?"

*God, what were they thinking?*

Lifting my hands to my head, I grip fistfuls of my hair. "We're going to die. We're all going to die. He's going to kill us one by one. He's going to cut the kidney out of me. He's going to–"

"Skylar!" Dad shouts, his whole body vibrating from how upset he is. "Calm down."

"Don't tell me to calm down!"

Dr. Bentall takes a step closer to us. "All this shouting isn't helping."

"Shut up!" I snap at him.

My angry gaze snaps between Dad and Dr. Bentall, and then I'm hit with an unbearable wave of guilt.

*Because of me, a person was killed.*

I wrap my arms around myself again while a whimper ripples over my lips.

My rights were violated, and an innocent person died so I could live.

# Chapter 15

## Renzo

Watching Skylar scream at her father on the livestream from the camera in the room brings me a sliver of satisfaction.

It looks like she's losing her mind, and it's clear she had no idea where the kidney came from.

Not that it changes anything.

I'm still going to make her suffer for the rest of her life.

*The way I have to suffer every day I'm forced to live without Giulio.*

Skylar slumps down to her ass and leans back against the wall. She looks exhausted.

Not wanting her to die yet, I know I'll have to make her more comfortable.

"Carlo, put a bed in one of the empty offices," I order.

"On it, boss."

My eyes are glued to the screen as I watch Harlan stalk up and down like a caged animal while Bentall stands in a corner.

Skylar buries her face in her arms that are wrapped around her knees, the skirt of her dress pinned between her calves and the back of her thighs.

My phone vibrates in my pocket, and I quickly pull it out. Seeing Dario's name, I answer, "Did you find out anything else?"

"We officially have a photo of Manual Castellanos, and he's popped up on several CCTV cameras around the city."

"Send me the photo and places where he was spotted."

"Already did that." He yawns then asks, "How are things there?"

"Good. I have Davies and Bentall sweating."

"When are you killing them?"

"When I feel like it," I mutter.

"Do you need anything else?" he asks. "I have a ballet recital I don't want to miss."

Shaking my head, I let out a chuckle. "Go to your recital, and don't forget your tutu."

"Don't diss it until you've tried it."

"Enjoy the rest of the day, brother. Thanks for all the help."

"Anytime," he says, and I hear him moving. "I'll send you my invoice."

Chuckling, I mutter, "You do that."

Ending the call, my eyes return to the screen, but then Elio walks into the office, pulling my attention away again.

Opening my emails, I click on the one from Dario and forward it to Elio. "I've just sent you an email. We have a photo of Castellanos. Get the men to search New York and tell them the one to bring him in alive gets a fifty thousand bonus."

"They're going to tear the city apart," Elio mutters as he checks his email.

"That's the idea," I murmur as I look at the livestream from the room.

Skylar's now leaning her head back against the wall, looking deathly pale.

"What's Antonio's number?" I ask.

When Elio gives it to me, I quickly dial it.

"Hello," Antonio answers abruptly.

"It's Renzo."

"Yes, boss," he says, his tone instantly filled with respect. "What can I do for you?"

"Bring Bianca to the warehouse."

"Have you found the group responsible?"

"Not yet, but I need Bianca's medical skills."

"We'll leave as soon as possible, boss."

I end the call and keep staring at Skylar.

*Don't die on me, topolina. I need you to live a long and torturous life.*

Carlo comes into the office and gives me a chin lift. "The office is ready, boss."

"Come with me," I order as I walk toward the steps. Taking them up, I signal for Emilio to unlock the door, and when I step inside, Skylar's already scrambled to her feet and is darting to the back of the room.

Wanting to teach her that she has to obey my every command, I growl, "Come here, Skylar."

She shakes her head, her body plastered to the wall.

"If you make me ask you anything for a second time, I'll cut the kidney from you without any hesitation."

"Please. This is insane," Harlan cries as he moves between his daughter and me.

I hold out my hand, and a moment later, a gun is placed in my palm. My fingers close around the hilt and pointing the barrel at Harlan, I don't hesitate for a single second and pull the trigger.

The bullet tears through the sleeve of his dress shirt, and before blood can blossom on the white fabric, the bullet slams into the wall less than a foot away from Skylar.

"Daddy!" she screams as she darts toward him.

"Skylar!" I shout to get her attention.

Her eyes snap to me.

"Come. Here."

She hesitates, but now that she knows I won't hesitate to shoot her father, she walks to me.

When she tilts her head back to meet my eyes, I lean down until our faces are an inch apart.

"Don't ever disobey me again."

She swallows hard as she nods.

Turning around, I mutter, "Follow me."

I leave the room and hear Skylar's rapid breaths behind me. When I walk into the office that's now a makeshift bedroom, I use the gun to point at the bed.

"Get some rest," I order.

"W-What?"

My eyes flick to her face, and she recoils while wrapping her arms around her waist.

"Do you really want me to repeat myself?"

She quickly shakes her head and hurries to the bed. When she lies down, her body is ramrod straight, and tension comes off her in waves.

I walk closer and look down into her terrified eyes that sparkle like the ocean when the sun shines down on the water.

"Sleep, *topolina*. You're going to need your rest for what comes next."

Instead of begging for her own life, her voice trembles as she pleads, "Please don't kill my father."

"You're in no position to ask that of me," I remind her.

She sits up, and with a tear spiraling down her cheek, she says, "I'll do anything you want. Spare my father. Please."

I didn't plan on killing Harlan. Not soon, anyway. I want him to suffer knowing I have his precious daughter.

Bringing my right hand, which is still holding the gun to her face, I drag the barrel through the wetness left behind by her tears.

"Next time I give an order, you carry it out without hesitation."

She nods quickly.

When I turn around and walk away, she calls out, "Will you spare my father?"

I stop in the doorway and say, "That all depends on how well you behave."

When I step out of the room, Carlo pulls the door shut and locks it.

"Give me the key," I order while holding out the gun for him to take.

When I have the key, I shove it into my pocket and head back to the other room, where I'm met with a worried father and cowardly doctor.

"What did you do with Skylar?" Harlan asks, his voice hoarse from the hell I've put him through.

"I've made her comfortable on a bed," I answer honestly, knowing it's going to make him worry whether I'll have Skylar raped.

Much to my satisfaction, the air wooshes from Harlan, and his complexion turns a shade grayer.

"Please don't hurt her. I'm begging you. I'll give you everything I own."

My lips curve up as I let out a chuckle. Walking closer to Harlan, I lean in and hiss, "I'm going to make her wish she was never been born."

I watch as tears well in his eyes and unspeakable fear tightens his features.

I move even closer until we're almost nose to nose, then say, "I'm going to make you feel all the pain I feel and then some. Because of you, I have to live without my brother, so you'll live without your daughter, knowing I'll fuck her raw until she's nothing but a ghost of the girl you raised."

"Please," he breathes. "I'll do anything you want."

"You only have one thing I want, and I already have her." Pulling back, my smile widens. "Your precious little daughter now belongs to me."

His features crumble again, and seeing the unbearable pain my words are causing him fills me with satisfaction.

I tilt my head and breathe it in.

*I'll make them suffer, Giulio. I'll make them fucking pay.*

I stare at Harlan until he lowers his head, and silent sobs wrack his shoulders.

"I didn't know they would kill your brother," he cries.

I step closer again and whisper near his ear, "You would still have done it to save your daughter. You would've killed half of New York, if that's what it took to keep her alive, because you love her." I pull back and gripping his jaw, I force him to look at me. "I loved my brother, and you took him from me."

I move backward, and my eyes flick to where the doctor is cowering in the corner.

"Dr. Bentall," I say and wait for him to look at me before I continue, "Enjoy your last night. I'm killing you tomorrow."

The blood drains from his face, and I watch as he realizes there's nothing he can do to stop me.

Walking out of the room, I hear Emilio close the door before he locks it.

"Have men take turns to guard the prisoners," I say to Carlo, who's right behind me.

"Okay, boss."

We take the steps down, and as I head to the office, Carlo walks to where a group of my soldiers are gathering.

I find Elio behind the desk, and he lifts his eyes to me from where he's looking at the computer screen.

"Having fun?" he asks.

I slump down on the couch and mutter, "I need a drink."

Elio gets up and walks to the small liquor cabinet, where he pours some whiskey into a tumbler. He brings me the drink then sits down beside me.

"Thanks," I say before taking a sip.

Resting my head against the back of the couch, I close my eyes.

"The Mexicans are happy with the AKs."

"Good," I murmur.

"The Yakuza wants fifty full-auto Glock 17s. They have to be converted," he informs me.

"Do we have enough carbine PDW conversion kits?"

"Yes. The men can get it done quickly, and the shipment can leave by the end of the week."

"Good. Go ahead with the deal," I give my approval.

"Why don't you go home and get some rest?" Elio suggests as he gets up from the couch.

"I'm too hyped. It's taking all my strength not to kill Bentall right now."

"Kill him and go home. Why wait?"

Opening my eyes, I down the rest of the whiskey before saying, "I want him to suffer through the night."

# Chapter 16

## Skylar

I thought I wouldn't be able to shut an eye, but I ended up passing out. I slept like the dead before waking up in the dark room.

I have no idea what time it is, but seeing as I can't hear any noises, I assume it's the middle of the night.

Sitting up on the bed, I glance around the room, and my eyes latch onto a shadowy figure standing in the corner.

I stare at Renzo while draping the covers over my lap and legs.

I have no idea what the man plans to do with me, and it terrifies me.

"Sleep well?" his voice rumbles from the corner.

Unable to speak, I nod.

"Good."

Minutes of silence follow where he just stares at me, and it rattles the hell out of me.

"You have good instincts," he suddenly pays me a compliment. "Every time you were in the kitchen, or watching TV, or in your bedroom, and you glanced around thinking you were losing your mind, I was watching you."

My mouth drops open, and before I can stop myself, I mutter, "That's not creepy at all. "

He lets out a chuckle that actually sounds amused.

Taking a chance, I ask, "What are you going to do with me?"

I hear him take a deep breath then he moves, coming closer to me. I climb to my feet and shove the covers onto the bed.

When he stops in front of me, I can make out his features, and I hate that he's still attractive as hell and hasn't morphed into the hideous beast he is.

Lifting a hand to my face, he grips my jaw tightly before I can yank away. He leans down until the terrifying thought that he might kiss me zips through my mind, but he stops an inch from my mouth, his eyes boring into mine.

"I'm playing around with a couple of ideas. Want me to run them by you? Maybe you can help me decide what to do with you."

My body starts to tremble again, and I swallow hard on the fear this man makes me feel.

His thumb brushes over my jaw, then his hand slips down to my throat, and his fingers clamp tightly around my neck.

"At first, I fantasized about crushing your windpipe and watching you gasp for air until I squeezed the last air from your lungs."

*Jesus.*

"But that means you'll be dead. I won't be able to torture you anymore."

Again, I swallow hard, and I know he feels it.

He lets go of my neck and shoves his hands into his pockets. "I might keep you locked in this room for the rest of your life."

*That will be hell. I'd rather die.*

The corner of his mouth lifts. "What do you think I should do with you?"

My tongue darts out to wet my lips, and I shake my head. "You don't give a shit about what I think."

A smile spreads over his face, making him look devilishly attractive. "Actually, I do." A frown forms on my forehead, and it has him saying, "My little brother's kidney is keeping you alive. How do you suggest you repay me?"

143

The guilt and heartbreak knock the air from my lungs, and tears jump to my eyes. My voice is hoarse as I say, "I'm so sorry they killed your brother. I never wanted someone to die so I could live. I would never have agreed to the surgery if I had known."

He lets out a scoffing sound. "Do you expect me to believe you'd just go gracefully into the afterlife and give up the chance of getting a kidney?"

Without zero hesitation, I answer, "Yes."

Renzo stares into my eyes until I fist my hands at my sides to keep from squirming.

"If you could turn back time, would you die so my brother could live?"

Again, I don't hesitate. "Yes."

He takes a deep breath before letting it out slowly, then turning around, he walks to the door. "Follow me, *topolina*."

*What the hell is he calling me in Italian?*

I walk behind Renzo as we head back to the room where Dad and Dr. Bentall are. My stomach coils with dread, and when I follow him into the room, I see there's a bandage around Dad's arm.

*Surely Renzo wouldn't give Dad medical care if he was going to kill him?*

The thought has hope exploding in my heart, and I rush over to Dad, who's struggling to his feet.

I wrap my arms around him and give him a hug, whispering, "Are you okay?"

"Don't worry about me. What happened? Did he do something to you?"

"No. I just slept," I answer.

"Enough with the little reunion," Renzo says, his tone low and dark. "Get Dr. Bentall."

The same guard from yesterday walks to Dr. Bentall and forces him onto his knees. The doctor who's treated me for the past three years looks nothing like the educated and confident man I've gotten to know and trust.

His face is swollen badly from yesterday's beating, and I feel sorry for him even though he committed an unforgivable crime.

"Any last words?" Renzo asks.

My eyes grow wide as saucers when the question registers.

*No.*

Dr. Bentall looks at Renzo and says, "I've devoted my life to saving people."

"Yet my brother is dead," Renzo snaps. "How many times did you buy an organ off the black market?"

"Not many," Dr. Bentall answers. "Maybe seven or eight times."

Renzo shakes his head. "Do you know they kill healthy children in Mexico for organ trafficking?"

Dr. Bentall remains quiet.

*I didn't know that.*

Renzo reaches behind his back and pulls a gun from where it was tucked into the waistband of his pants. His fingers flex around the handle before he walks closer to Dr. Bentall.

I shake my head wildly as I shriek, "Don't! Please, don't kill him."

Renzo's eyes snap to me, and the next moment, the gun is trained on Dad. I dart in front of my father, keeping my arms wide open as if it would make me bigger.

"No! I'm begging you." I shake my head again.

"Choose." The single word from Renzo falls heavy in the room. "Your father or your doctor."

Horrified, I can only stare at the cruel man.

His arm swings back to Dr. Bentall, and he presses the barrel right against his forehead. "Consider this a mercy death, Doctor. I could've torn you limb from limb."

Dr. Bentall squeezes his eyes shut.

"Thank me for showing you mercy," Renzo demands.

*Dear God.*

"T-Thank y-y-you."

The bang is so loud I jerk, and my ears ring as Dr. Bentall falls to his side, and blood seeps from the bullet wound to his head.

I stare as a puddle of blood spreads over the floor, my body shuddering as if I'm convulsing. I'm gasping for air, but it doesn't feel like it's reaching my lungs.

My legs give way, and I sink to the floor, my vision going spotty from the unbearable shock of seeing Dr. Bentall die.

"Skylar," Dad cries, and he falls to his knees next to me. "Breathe, sweetheart."

"Clean the mess," I hear Renzo order.

Men come into the room, and when they drag Dr. Bentall's body out, it leaves a streak of blood in his wake.

Tears wet my cheeks, and I continue to gasp like a fish out of water.

"Skylar, look at Daddy," I hear Dad, but I can't do anything but gasp through the horror.

Renzo walks closer and crouches in front of me. Gripping my chin with his forefinger and thumb, he pushes my face up so I'll meet his eyes.

His expression is grim and unforgiving as he orders, "Breathe, *topolina*. I don't want you dying on me yet."

I continue to gasp as tears spill down my face.

"Breathe!" he snaps angrily.

Terrified, I try to suck in a painful breath, causing a strangled sound to come from my throat.

"Please untie me so I can hold her," Dad begs. "She needs to calm down, and shouting at her won't stop the panic attack."

Renzo shoves Dad away, and then I'm in for the shock of my life as the merciless mafia boss wraps his arms around me, pulling me to his chest.

Lowering his mouth to my ear, he brushes a hand over my hair as he whispers, "Breathe, or your father dies."

Another strangled sound is torn from my chest, but I manage to get air into my lungs.

When I take another breath, Renzo says, "You'll never comfort your daughter again, Harlan. She's mine."

I try to pull back from his embrace, but he tightens his arms around me until I'm squashed against his chest.

I smell his woodsy aftershave.

I feel his strength.

I hear his steady heartbeat.

That's when I realize just how much trouble I'm in. Where my heart is fluttering like a caged bird's, Renzo's is steady.

Not even killing a man can get his heart rate up.

# Chapter 17

## Renzo

As I rise to my feet, I pull Skylar up until she's standing on shaky legs.

I let go of her and gesture to her father as I order, "Untie him."

Carlo comes closer, and pulling a pocket knife out, he flips it open and crouches behind Harlan, cutting the cable ties.

When Harlan climbs to his feet, rubbing his swollen wrists, I say, "You have five minutes to say goodbye to your daughter."

"What?" he gasps, his eyes flicking between me and Skylar. "Why? What are you going to do?"

Not answering the man, I cross my arms over my chest and mutter, "Your five minutes has already started."

With panic blooming over his face, he grabs Skylar to him and holds her tightly.

"No matter what happens, I love you, sweetheart."

She begins to cry harder and clings to her father.

*I didn't get to say goodbye. Christ. I'd give everything I have to hug Giulio one last time. To tell him I love him.*

My grief spirals until the deadly rage that was soothed by killing the doctor returns with a vengeance.

"D-Daddy," she sobs. "I love y-you."

"I'm so sorry for this mess I've caused," he whispers to her. "I just wanted to save you. Please forgive me."

When she nods, my blood runs cold and I snap, "Time's up."

My eyes flick to where Carlo and Emilio are standing, and they jump into action, pulling Harlan and Skylar apart.

"You will be dropped off at your house, Harlan. If you call the police, Skylar dies. If you try to help her in any way, she dies. You die. Your fucking housekeeper dies. Understand?"

He nods frantically. "What are you going to do with my daughter?"

The corner of my mouth lifts. "I'm taking Skylar to her new home, where she'll serve me on her hands and knees."

His features tighten, and I drink in his distress like the sweet nectar it is.

I lift my hand and wrap my fingers around the back of Skylar's neck, tugging her to my side. "If she's a good servant, I might give her visitation rights every once in a while."

"Please. Don't do this," Harlan begs.

Letting out a sigh, I mutter, "Christ, I'm getting tired of hearing those words. Say them again, and I'll kill you for annoying me."

Skylar surprises me by murmuring, "It's okay, Daddy. Go home."

I tilt my head as I stare at Harlan, taking in every second of his pain. "I won't repeat myself," I warn him.

"Go, Dad! Please," Skylar begs him. "Just go."

"Carlo, make sure Mr. Davies takes his phone and wallet," I order as I let go of Skylar. Turning around, I walk to the doorway. "You better follow me, *topolina*."

"Bye, Daddy. I love you," she says quickly before I hear her hurried footsteps behind me.

"Skylar!" Harlan cries before a grunt comes from him.

Carlo probably shut him up with a punch.

When I take the steps down, Skylar's still behind me.

The woman surprised me, but then again, she's trying to save her father's life.

*The things we do for love.*

I stop by the office and say, "I'm heading home. Let me know when you find Castellanos."

Elio's eyes move between Skylar and me before he says, "Get some sleep."

When I glance to my right, I see Bianca talking to Antonio, and I head toward them. As soon as Bianca notices me, her spine stiffens, and she lowers her eyes.

Stopping by the cousins, I say, "Bianca, you'll work at our clinic from now on. You'll be paid well."

"Thank you, Mr. Torrisi."

My eyes flick to Antonio. "Bring Bianca to my place tomorrow so she can do a checkup on Skylar."

"Yes, boss."

With that out of the way, I walk to the exit and signal with a chin lift to Vincenzo and Fabrizio that we're leaving.

Fabrizio sets his coffee cup down on one of the tables, and both my men give Skylar a wary look as they walk to where the Bentley is parked.

When Vincenzo opens the backdoor, I step to the side and gesture for Skylar to get in.

She glances over her shoulder, probably hoping to see her father one last time. She climbs in, and I follow, which has her pressing her body to the other door in an attempt to put some distance between us.

"Where to, boss?" Fabrizio asks.

"Home."

Skylar turns her face away from me and stares out of the window as we drive away from the warehouse.

I hear her suck in a shaky breath and realize she's silently crying.

I roll my shoulders to ease the tension in my neck as I glance out of my own window.

My phone starts to vibrate, and when I pull the device out of my pocket, I see Franco's name.

"Morning," I mutter, exhausted from the long night.

"How are you holding up?"

I close my eyes and let out a sigh. "I'm fine. How's the family? Are you getting any sleep?"

Franco lets out a chuckle. "Remind me what sleep is again? Just as we get the one settled, another one starts to fuss. I'm about to hire a group of nannies."

"Why don't you?"

"Samantha doesn't want to. And honestly, I'm not going to trust a stranger with my kids."

"Dario's bored. You should get him to babysit so you can get some rest."

Laughter explodes over the line. "Hell will freeze over. Every time he comes over, he looks at the triplets like they're a bomb that's about to detonate. He's shit scared of them."

A chuckle escapes me, then I say, "I'll make some time to visit over the weekend."

"You better, or I'm coming to your place with the triplets, and you can babysit them while I take a nap in one of the guest rooms."

"Don't you dare." My eyes flick to Skylar, who quickly turns her face away again. "I have a guest. Don't bring the kids around."

"Who's the guest?"

Lifting my hand, I rub my palm over my face before replying, "The woman who got Giulio's kidney."

"Christ, Renzo," Franco snaps. "You're taking her to your penthouse? Why?"

"I'll tell you when I see you," I say, not wanting Skylar to hear that part of our conversation.

"Okay. Be careful."

"I will." Ending the call, I tuck the device back into my pocket.

Minutes later, Fabrizio parks the Bentley in the designated spot, and I push the door open. Climbing out, I bark, "Come, *topolina*."

Skylar hesitates before she gets out, and halfway to the elevator, she stops.

I press the button, and when the doors open, I scan the keycard and order, "Vincenzo, shoot her if she's not inside the elevator when the doors shut."

"Yes, boss."

Skylar hurries inside and wraps her arms around her middle.

The silence is thick between us as we go up to the top floor, and when the doors slide open, I walk to the living room and pick up the remote. Switching the TV on, all the livestreams from the cameras in the Davies house appear.

The housekeeper is in the kitchen, but there's no sign of Harlan. Pulling my phone out, I dial Carlo's number.

"Yes, boss?" he answers before the third ring.

"Where is he?"

"We had to rough him up a little. We're five minutes from the house."

"Did he get the warning?"

"Yes, boss."

"Good."

I end the call, and while I wait for Harlan to get home, I glance at Skylar, who stares at the TV with a horrified expression.

"Welcome to your new home," I say, my tone promising nothing good.

Her eyes flit to my face. "This will never be my home."

I let out a dark chuckle. "We'll see about that."

# Chapter 18

## Skylar

*Holy shit.*

There's a camera showing my bedroom.

My mouth grows dry when I think Renzo probably watched me get dressed.

*Has he seen me naked?*

*Shit.*

My fear spirals a little as the question teeters on the tip of my tongue.

As Renzo drops the remote on the coffee table before shrugging off his jacket, the question bursts from me, "Did you watch me get dressed?"

His eyes touch on me for a second, then he casually takes his phone from the inside pocket before draping the jacket over the back of a couch.

He sets the device down next to the remote, and only then does he look at me again. I can't place his expression, but the longer he just stares at me, the faster my heart beats.

His gaze burns down my body and stops on my bare legs, where there are still droplets of dried blood.

Finally his lips part, and he says, "I suppose we have to get you something clean to wear."

He's not answering my question. That has to mean he did see me naked. Right?

He grabs his phone again and dials a number. A moment later, he says, "While you're dropping off Davies, pack Skylar's clothes and toiletries and bring them to my place."

He ends the call, and his eyes settle on the TV screen again.

"You didn't answer me," I whisper, my heart in my throat and my hands fisted at my sides.

I watch as the corner of his mouth lifts, his gaze still locked on the screen. "Mmh...wouldn't you like to know."

My eyebrows draw together, and just as I begin to feel utterly violated, his eyes meet mine. He tilts his head, taking in my reaction as if he finds it fascinating.

Lifting my arms, I wrap them tightly around my waist, and I hunch my shoulders while lowering my eyes to the gleaming tiles beneath my feet.

"No. I have zero desire to see you naked."

My gaze flies to his, and intense relief shudders through me. That means he won't force himself on me.

*Thank God.*

I glance around the living room, that's decorated in light gray and cream tones. A stylish glass partitioning gives me a view of the state-of-the-art kitchen and a dining room.

This penthouse must easily cost ten times more than our mansion, seeing as it's situated in Manhattan.

The TV screen draws my attention, and when I see Dad being forcefully shoved into the foyer of our home, my hand flies up to cover my mouth.

His eye is swollen shut, and blood trickles from a cut above his eyebrow. He looks disheveled and nothing like the strong man who raised me.

Louisa comes out of the kitchen, and shock registers on her face when she sees Renzo's men and the state Dad's in. A couple of the men head up the stairs to my bedroom, while two stay in the foyer.

"So what do you think, *topolina*? Is your father going to run to the police and risk your life?" Renzo tilts his head, his eyes locked on the livestream. "Or maybe the housekeeper will be the one responsible for your death."

My voice is nothing more than a hoarse whisper as I say, "They won't do anything to risk my life."

"You sound so sure," he murmurs. Letting out a sigh, he adds, "It's going to be fun watching it all unfold."

Turning to face me, his predatory gaze locks on me. "I'll leave the TV on so you can watch your father from your tower, *principessa*. If you turn up the volume, you'll be able to hear them."

*At least I'll get to see Dad.*

He pushes his hands into his pockets, and even though his stance is casual, it doesn't fool me. I know he's capable of great violence at the drop of a hat.

"You'll stay in the penthouse. Men will guard it around the clock, and if you try to leave, your father will die." His eyes narrow on me. "And I won't give him a quick death. I'll fucking dismember him right in front of you."

Horror shudders through me because I know he will carry out the threat.

He lets his terrifying words sink in before he continues, "You are not my guest. You'll prepare every meal. You'll keep the place spotless. If your health deteriorates, your father dies. If I see you crying, your father will pay for each tear you spill." He takes a few steps closer to me, and I have to tip my head back to keep eye contact. "Do you understand?"

My dry lips part, and the single word trembles between us. "Yes."

"Don't get in my way, and you might survive living here," he murmurs darkly.

*I seriously doubt that.*

He begins to walk, and his arm brushes against mine as he passes me.

"Come, *topolina.*"

My eyes flick to the TV, and I see Louisa cleaning Dad's face. They're quiet, and she keeps glancing nervously at Renzo's two men, who are still watching them.

I wonder what Dad's going to tell her. How will he explain why I'm not home?

Again, I'm struck hard with the realization that Dad bought a kidney on the black market. Renzo's little brother was killed so I could live.

*And now I'm a prisoner of a deranged man.*

*God help me.*

"Skylar!" Renzo's voice cracks like thunder in the air.

I jerk with fright and quickly rush to catch up to him, where he's already halfway up the stairs.

*At this rate, I'm going to die of a heart attack.*

I follow Renzo to a bedroom that's more luxurious than mine at home.

*Crime must really pay well.*

There's a king-sized bed with light gray and cream bedding and pillows. A window and sliding door give me a stunning view of a balcony where potted ferns surround an outdoor lounge suite. I see skyscrapers and can only imagine how beautiful the view must be at night.

The wall behind the bed is made of slated granite, and to my left is a spacious walk-in closet that doesn't look like it's been used before.

I see another door, and cautiously moving closer, I peek into the ensuite bathroom, fitted with a shower and a tub that can easily pass for a jacuzzi.

*Not bad for a prison cell.*

"Your belongings will be here soon," Renzo mutters before he steps away from the open door and disappears down the hallway.

I walk to the doorway and watch as he enters the room at the end of the hallway, which I'm guessing is his.

Letting out a sigh, I step back into the bedroom and shut the door. I dart to the bathroom to relieve my poor bladder that's been put through the wringer.

163

While I wash my face, my eyes lock on my disheveled reflection, and all the hell I've been forced to endure the past twenty-four hours floods back like a destructive tsunami.

*He shot Dr. Bentall as if it was nothing.*

*Renzo just killed him.*

I squeeze my eyes shut as tears threaten to fall.

I'm a prisoner in a cold-hearted monster's penthouse.

*God! After surviving the past three years and getting a second chance at life, this madness happens?*

I hear movement in the bedroom and suck in a deep breath of air before I go to check who it is.

Men throw trash bags filled with my clothes and belongings on the floor. They don't glance in my direction once, and when they leave, they don't bother shutting the door.

Staring at my clothes, I realize this is really happening. It's not a nightmare I'll wake from. It's not my imagination playing tricks on me.

I've been taken captive by a ruthless mafia boss who kills without blinking an eye.

# Chapter 19

## Renzo

*I lied.*

I've seen every fucking bare inch of Skylar's delectable body.

I lied because I didn't want her to have that kind of knowledge. If she finds out I've seen her naked, she might get it in her head to seduce me in an attempt to gain her freedom. It's the last thing I need. She's my prisoner, and that's the extent of our relationship.

After I've showered, I change into black suit pants, a crisp white dress shirt, and a vest. I don't bother with a jacket as I don't plan to leave the apartment.

Tucking my Glock behind my back into the waistband of my pants, I let out a sigh as I leave my bedroom.

When Carlo dropped off Skylar's shit, I told him to go shopping so the woman will have ingredients to cook with. I've watched her long enough to know exactly what she needs to prepare a five-star meal.

Dario will finally get his wish for me to eat healthier. That should put a smile on his face.

Passing the guestroom where Skylar is, I notice the door's shut, and I don't hear anything.

I take the stairs down, and when I reach the living room, my eyes scan over every live feed from the Davies mansion. I grab the remote and turn up the sound.

"...can't go to the police," Harlan snaps at his housekeeper, who has tears running down her face. "We can't do anything that will risk Skylar's life."

"How did this happen?" Louisa asks. "Just as things were finally returning to normal and Skylar wasn't sick anymore. This isn't right, Mr. Davies."

"You think I don't know that?"

*The man's losing his cool. Good.*

"Skylar is my entire life! She's my daughter," he continues to shout, the unrelenting worry on his face giving me great satisfaction.

"We have to do something," Louisa exclaims.

Watching the Davies household spiral is exactly what I wanted.

*Now they'll feel the pain I have to live with.*

As the memory of Giulio calling me an old man flits through my mind, my eyes snap shut from the intensity of the grief hitting me.

It feels like, with every passing day, it's getting worse. It still feels like he'll walk into the room at any moment. I expect to hear his laughter.

Then the emptiness sets in, and once again, my heart's shredded to pieces.

I feel Skylar before I hear her soft footsteps as she comes down the stairs.

My eyes open and flick to her, seeing that she's cleaned herself up. She's wearing another dress, this one cream with a big black flower over half the skirt.

Her features are tense with a cautious expression, and her eyes still tremble with horror and fear.

Even though my little mouse is shit scared, she lifts her chin and looks at me.

"You said I have to keep the place clean, but there are certain things I won't be able to do for the next four weeks."

*Right. She's still recovering.*

When I just stare at her, her tongue darts out to wet her lips. She glances at the kitchen before meeting my eyes again.

"Cooking isn't a problem. I can sit while doing most of the prep work."

Again, I don't answer her, but my gaze leaves hers to travel up and down her body.

Skylar starts to fidget with the skirt of her dress and eventually wraps her arms around herself in an attempt to keep still.

My eyes flick back to the TV screen, and I see the housekeeper sobbing her little heart out in the kitchen. There's no sign of Harlan.

My gaze moves from one livestream to the next until it stops on Skylar's empty bedroom.

I finally have the little mouse. I no longer have to watch her from a distance.

I turn my attention back to Skylar, whose breathing has sped up. Sweat beads on her forehead, and she's back to looking pale as fuck.

"Sit," I bark.

She darts forward and, a second later, takes a seat on the couch farthest from me.

"A nurse will continue with your follow-up checkups." My eyes lock with Skylar's again. "Until Bianca's cleared you, you'll only cook."

I'm surprised when my little mouse is brave enough to ask, "What am I supposed to do with the rest of my time?"

The corner of my mouth lifts, and I almost let out a bark of laughter.

"You're not here to be entertained, *topolina*."

She tilts her head slightly, then asks, "What does the Italian word mean?"

A smirk forms on my face before I murmur, "Little mouse."

Climbing to my feet, I walk closer until I'm towering over her and she has to look up at me. I bring my hand to her face and watch as she flinches when I brush a finger along the curve of her jaw.

"Have you ever seen a cat play with a mouse?" The question is a low rumble from my chest.

Skylar shakes her head, her eyes sparkling with terror.

I have to be careful because I'm actually starting to like it.

"They don't kill the mouse instantly. They'll torture it for hours..." my finger moves down Skylar's neck to her racing pulse. "Taking a bite here..." I clamp my hand around her throat and only use enough force to make her gasp. "Taking a bite there..."

When I pull her to her feet by her neck, Skylar grabs hold of my wrist with both her hands, her lips parting as her breaths burst over them.

I lean in close until her terrified breaths hit my lips, then I whisper, "When the mouse finally begs for death, the cat rips its head off."

The elevator doors open, and I let go of Skylar. Turning around, I see Carlo coming in with the shopping. Bianca follows him into the penthouse, carrying a medical bag.

"I think I got everything you asked for, boss," Carlo says before taking the shopping to the kitchen.

"Just leave it on the island," I order. My eyes flick to Bianca, and I say, "You can check her here in the living room."

Bianca's face remains neutral when she approaches Skylar, who's still trembling in fear.

"Are you taking your medication?" Bianca asks.

"No." Skylar's eyes flit to me. "It's in the kitchen at my house."

"Carlo," I bark.

He comes rushing back into the living room. "Yes, boss?"

"Go to the Davies mansion and bring Skylar's medication."

"Yes, boss."

"I'm going to draw some blood," Bianca informs Skylar.

I watch as the blood is drawn and her vitals are checked.

Bianco glances at me, then murmurs, "I have to check the surgery cut."

"Then check it," I mutter.

Bianca's eyes dart to Skylar's before she says, "Please lift your dress."

I give them zero privacy and almost smile when I see Skylar's wearing black panties again.

Bianca inspects the scar, then says, "It's healing nicely. You can cover yourself."

Bianca packs everything back into her bag, then glances at me again. "In two months, she'll have to come to the clinic so they can do a kidney biopsy. I can't perform the procedure here."

"We'll deal with it when the time comes," I reply.

"Her vitals are normal... under the circumstances," the nurse informs me. When I lift my eyebrow, she explains, "Her heart rate is fast, and her blood pressure is low. She needs to eat and get rest."

I can see Bianca wants to say more, so I mutter, "What else?"

"Her mental health is just as important as her physical health, Mr. Torrisi. This is a critical period after the surgery, and with too much distress, her body can reject the kidney."

*So basically, I can't torture Skylar in any way for the next three to six months? Fuck that shit.*

I stare at the nurse until she starts to squirm, then she whispers, "It's just a clinical opinion, sir."

"How long before she can do basic things like household chores?" I ask.

"Oh, she can start with light duties, and after four weeks, she can resume most activities."

Nodding at the elevator, I say, "Thanks, Bianca. Let me know the results of the blood tests."

"I will." She glances at Skylar, who's still sitting on the couch with her head slightly bowed.

I watch as Bianca leaves the penthouse, then my eyes flick to Skylar, and I order, "Make something to eat."

She meets my gaze for a moment before she gets up and walks to the kitchen. I hear as she opens and closes cupboards, probably familiarizing herself with where everything is.

Turning my head, I see her pull a couple of knives from a block, and she stares at the one that could easily slice through my neck like butter.

Letting out a chuckle, I walk closer.

Skylar startles at the sound, her eyes flying to me.

My voice is low, but a hint of amusement trickles through the words as I ask, "Thinking of killing me, *topolina*?"

"Would it make any difference to my situation?" she asks bravely. "Your men would still kill us. Right?"

The corner of my mouth lifts in a smirk as I stop within striking distance of her. "Oh, little mouse..."

Before she can take her next breath, I grab her wrist and twist her around so her back slams into my chest. The sharp blade of the knife presses against her fluttering pulse.

Leaning my head down, I whisper, "You couldn't kill me even if you tried."

# Chapter 20

## Skylar

It's difficult focusing on cooking with Renzo sitting by the island and watching me like a hawk.

I'm in a constant state of fear, and whenever I manage to calm down a little, Renzo does something to terrify the hell out of me.

I've never encountered anyone like him – a monster with no humanity at all.

Just as I think the thought, I hear the elevator doors open, and a moment later, an attractive man with light brown hair and brown eyes, the color of melted chocolate, walks into the kitchen.

When his eyes land on me, he comes to a stop, and pushing his hands into his pockets, he just stares at me.

My eyes dart between the man and Renzo, then Renzo mutters, "Smile, fucker. I'm finally going to eat healthy."

Again, my eyes dart between them, every muscle in my body on high alert while I grip the knife tightly.

"Yeah, this is not what I meant when I said you need to eat healthier," the man says as he turns his attention from me to Renzo. "You seriously brought her to your penthouse?"

"Don't look surprised, Dario. I said I would," Renzo answers.

Dario lets out a sigh before heading in my direction. My eyes widen, and my heartbeat speeds up dangerously fast, but then he walks past me and makes his way to the fridge where he helps himself to a can of soda.

He leans back against a counter as he opens the can, and only after taking a sip, he says, "I hope she's making enough for three. I'm dying to taste her cooking."

"She's the one holding the knife." Renzo's eyes settle on me. "You better ask her."

Dario pushes away from the counter, and his gaze flicks to the knife in my hand before locking with mine, then he says, "Hi, *bellissima*. I'm Dario La Rosa, someone who's unfortunate enough to call Renzo my friend."

When he reaches a hand out and waits for me to shake it, I just stare at him.

If he's Renzo's friend, then I'm going to assume he's just as dangerous.

"Dario is one of the heads of the Cosa Nostra," Renzo informs me.

*My assumption was right.*

I grip the knife even tighter because having two ruthless mafia bosses with their attention focused on me is twice as terrifying.

Dario's mouth curves into a hot smile with a hint of playfulness. "Relax, *bellissima*. I'm the nice one."

"Stop calling her beautiful," Renzo suddenly growls, something possessive in his tone.

Dario lets out a burst of laughter before moving away from me and taking a seat at the island. His eyes settle on Renzo, a mischievous expression making him seem friendly.

"Hmm...Possessive much?" he taunts Renzo.

I hold my breath with growing apprehension as I watch the interaction.

"Fuck off," Renzo growls, then he levels me with a threatening glare. "You should be cooking."

My eyes snap back to the chicken breast I'm slicing into thin strips to make a chicken salad with a drizzled honey and mustard dressing.

"You're going to give the woman a heart attack long before she dies of kidney failure," Dario drawls as if he's mentioning the weather.

"Is there a reason for your visit?" Renzo snaps angrily.

*Jesus. Don't poke the beast when he wants to rip my head off.*

My hand trembles as I continue slicing the chicken breast. Not paying attention to what I'm doing, there's a sharp sting as the knife nicks my finger.

"Ouch," I whisper before I can stop myself and quickly move to the sink to hold the bleeding cut beneath cold water.

"Now look what you've done," Dario mutters.

When I hear him moving closer, my heart jumps to my throat, and my breathing becomes rapid puffs of hot air.

He reaches for my arm but stops when Renzo barks, "If you touch her, we're going to have a problem."

"Then you better take care of the cut," Dario snaps. "Or I will. She can't get an infection. It will jeopardize the transplant."

The air tenses, and I close my eyes, waiting for the bomb to detonate.

"You're testing my patience," Renzo mutters.

I hear his chair scrape over the tiles, and a moment later, I'm grabbed by my arm and yanked to the side. I almost lose my balance from the sudden movement, my eyes popping wide open.

Renzo drags me up the stairs, his steps much larger than mine.

From all the tension and fear, tears burn my eyes and threaten to fall, but I bite them back, remembering he said he'd make Dad pay for each tear I spill.

By the time he drags me into the bedroom I assume is his, I'm a second away from having a panic attack.

Where my room is decorated in light gray and cream, Renzo's is all black.

*Just like his heart.*

I'm yanked into the ensuite bathroom that's twice the size of the one in my bedroom and brought to a jarring stop by the counter.

The scent of his woodsy cologne is much stronger in the bathroom, making me overly aware of the powerful man as he shoves my hand beneath a cold spray of water.

While my blood spirals down the drain, Renzo takes a first aid kit from the cupboard and opens it.

He manhandles my hand as he dries the cut before cleaning it with an antiseptic wipe. My eyes are locked on his fingers as he removes a Bandaid from its packaging.

I'm losing my mind because noticing he has attractive hands is definitely not something I should be doing right now.

He wraps the bandaid around the tip of my finger, then his eyes snap to my face, and I feel a gut punch from him looking at me while there's so little space between us.

"Slow your breathing," he orders in a biting tone.

It's only then I realize I'm practically hyperventilating.

My vision grows spotty from all the unbearable tension, and I struggle to calm down.

He lets out an annoyed sigh, then his fingers wrap around the side of my neck, and I'm tugged against his chest.

I'm so freaking stunned by the act of kindness it rattles the hell out of me. And it doesn't help one bit to calm me down, but instead, it has the opposite effect on me.

*You can't cry! He'll hurt Dad.*

My eyes are on fire, and my body shudders from the effort it's taking to keep the tears back.

When I feel his thumb brush against my skin, it makes shivers spread through me. I try to pull back, but it only makes him wrap his other arm around my back, and I'm squashed to his chest.

He lowers his mouth to my ear, then whispers, "Calm your breathing, Skylar."

I desperately suck in breaths, and pinching my eyes shut, I do my best to calm down so he'll let go of me.

*This isn't comforting at all. I wish he'd let go.*

*God, I wish I'd never gotten the transplant. I'd rather die than live every day with this kind of torment.*

"Shh…" he breathes against my ear.

Goose bumps erupt over my skin.

Somehow, I manage to regain control over my breathing, even though my emotions are spiraling into a hopeless pit filled with despair.

When Renzo seems to be satisfied that I'm calmer, he pulls back, but then his fingers grip my chin, and my head is forced back so I'll look up at him.

Our eyes lock, and I see zero compassion and kindness in his predatory gaze. "Do you get panic attacks often?"

*No, it's a special effect you have on me, asshole.*

I shake my head, pulling my chin from his hold.

He nods to the doorway. "Finish preparing the food so you can eat and get some rest."

Without a word, I spin around and rush out of the bathroom. I don't glance around Renzo's bedroom, but hurry into the hallway. When I reach the top of the stairs, I remember Dario's in the apartment, and I'm not sure I want to be alone with the man.

Suddenly Renzo passes me, once again startling the living hell out of me because I didn't hear him approaching.

I quickly follow him down the stairs and into the kitchen, where Dario's reading something on his phone. He's sitting at the island again, and his head lifts when he hears us.

"Happy?" Renzo growls at him.

Dario's eyes touch on the bandaid around my finger before he smiles. "Yes. It wasn't that hard, was it?"

"Shut up," Renzo mutters, but the brutality he has when speaking to me is gone from his tone. "Let's sit in the living room. I don't want Skylar losing a finger."

When the men leave the kitchen, I suck in deep breaths, and closing my eyes, I place my hand on the tense ball of nerves that used to be my stomach.

*Jesus. How am I going to survive this nightmare?*

# Chapter 21

## Skylar

While I continue to slice the chicken and fry it in a pan, I hear the two men talking in the living room.

I add garlic and herbs to the pan as Dario says, "You missed a good ballet performance." There's pride in his voice. "The company I bought will soon be the best in the country."

*He owns a ballet company?*

It's hard to think a mafia boss cares about arts and culture.

"Watching a bunch of women twirling around on a stage to some boring opera piece is the last thing I'm interested in," Renzo replies, his tone surprisingly humorous. "I'm more interested in your hacking skills. Have you found out anything new about Castellanos?"

I actually manage to relax a little now that the atmosphere is less tense.

When the chicken is ready, I remove it from the hot pan.

Finding three plates, I arrange sliced avocado, cherry tomatoes, and cucumber slices on a bed of Boston lettuce. I plate the grilled slices of chicken carefully before I return to the pan to fry some corn, which I then sprinkle over the salad.

I'm so focused on what I'm doing I'm no longer listening to the men's conversation as I make the honey and mustard dressing from scratch.

When it's ready, I drizzle it over the salad before I wipe the sides of the plates so the presentation is perfect.

"Not bad," Dario suddenly says from behind me.

He scares the living hell out of me, and I stagger a couple of steps to the side while my hand flies to my thundering heart.

"Jesus," the word bursts from me, my eyes wide on the men who must've returned to the kitchen while I was deep in thought.

"Sorry. I didn't mean to scare you," Dario actually apologizes.

Renzo lets out an annoyed huff while he walks to the drawers to grab cutlery before he moves past me, slamming the knives and forks down on the island.

"Let's eat," he orders.

He takes a seat, and Dario joins him. When I remain standing, he gives me a look of warning.

I quickly sit down and grab a knife and fork. Pulling my plate closer, I cut into the avo, and take a bite.

I keep my eyes focused on my food while the two men's dangerous and powerful presence makes it hard to enjoy the meal.

Dario lets out a groan, then he says, "The dressing is delicious. How did you get it sweet and tangy?"

"Honey and mustard," I murmur, not looking up.

"I need you to make me a whole bottle so I can have it at home."

This time, my eyes flick to Renzo's face, and he nods.

"Should I make it now?" I ask, not wanting to anger Renzo.

"No. Finish your food."

I continue to eat and steal glances at the men. For the first time since I was thrown into this hellish nightmare, there's a tiny burst of warmth in my heart when I see how much they enjoy their salads.

As soon as I'm done eating, I get up and retrieve a mixing bowl from the cupboard. When I start to make the dressing, Dario gets up from his chair, and bringing his plate along, he continues to eat while watching what I'm doing.

"Do you love being a chef?" he asks between bites.

"Yes," I murmur softly.

"You used to work at *Dame*, right?"

I nod, not offering any details.

"I read the restaurant got a Michelin Star while you worked there."

I nod again, my heart pinching because I don't know if I'll ever be able to work in a restaurant again.

Realizing Renzo might keep me captive for the rest of my life, a gloomy emotion fills my chest.

All my hopes and dreams slip through my fingers and my hands still while my eyes drift shut from the pain of losing them again.

"Are you okay?" Dario asks.

When he places his hand on my lower back, I instantly jerk away from him and almost drop the bowl.

"I said don't touch her," Renzo snaps at Dario before saying to me, "Finish the dressing."

Doing my best to ignore my breaking heart, I quickly add herbs and spices to the mixture and stir it. When it's ready, I set the bowl down on the counter and start to search through the cupboards for something to pour the dressing into.

"What are you looking for?" Renzo asks.

"A bottle or something I can use for the dressing," I answer.

He gets up and walks to the fridge, where he takes a bottle of water out. Emptying it in the sink, he holds it out to me.

I carefully pour the dressing into the bottle then place it on the counter near Dario.

When I gather the dishes, Renzo snaps, "Leave it and go get some rest."

Not waiting for him to change his mind, I rush out of the kitchen. When I head up the stairs, I hear Renzo say, "Stop trying to get to know the woman. She's a fucking prisoner."

"*Your* prisoner," Dario mutters. "I'll be friendly with her if I want to."

"You're looking for shit," Renzo warns him.

"Brother, you know how I feel about all of this. Skylar did nothing wrong. You're torturing an innocent woman."

Hearing Dario's words, I stop halfway up the stairs.

"Giulio's kidney is in her fucking body," Renzo growls angrily, intense pain shimmering in his tone.

"That's not her fault. Kill her fucking father and let the woman go."

Renzo's quiet for a moment, then he says, "Don't interfere in my business, or we're going to have a problem."

Too brave for my own good, I quietly take a couple of steps down and peek toward the kitchen, where I see the two men practically standing toe-to-toe.

Dario lets out a sigh, a worried expression on his face. He places his hand on Renzo's shoulder, then says, "I don't want you doing something you'll regret. I'm looking out for you, brother."

"I know what I'm doing. Stop worrying," Renzo replies, his tone no longer harsh.

When he turns around, I dart up the stairs and rush to my bedroom.

With Dario's visit I've seen a different side to Renzo. Even when he gets angry, he reins it in around his friend.

Closing the door behind me, I stare at the floor.

Dario thinks I'm innocent and doesn't agree with Renzo holding me captive.

*Holy shit. Dario might be my way out of this mess.*

# Chapter 22

## Renzo

The past three days it's taken some getting used to having Skylar in my place.

Mostly, she's quiet like the little mouse she is. She only leaves her bedroom when she has to make food, and I've noticed she'll spare the TV screen no more than five minutes a day. As soon as she gets a glimpse of her father, she'll return to her room.

She never talks unless I demand a response from her, and dark circles have formed beneath her eyes which have lost their sparkle. Even when I threaten her, they don't shimmer with fear anymore.

It's supposed to fill me with satisfaction. This is what I wanted. The Davies family is suffering for the part they played in Giulio's death.

Still, as I watch Skylar prepare some kind of Asian dish, the thick silence grates against my ears.

The sound of Skylar chopping vegetables is all I hear for a while, and with every passing second, I grow increasingly agitated.

My knee starts bouncing, and my shoulders tense, my eyes following the elegant movement of my little mouse's hands while she tosses the vegetables into some kind of watery soup.

My gaze creeps over every inch of her, the dark blue dress she's wearing today looking beautiful on her body.

*I love that she wears dresses.*

The intrusive thought has a frown darkening my forehead.

Skylar drops a spoon, and I notice she's started trembling. When she knocks over the salt, she whispers, "Can you stop staring, please?"

The agitation I've been feeling morphs into something unknown, and before I know what I'm doing, I lunge from the chair and grab hold of Skylar. I shove her against the counter, and when her hand slaps against the granite top, she knocks an onion to the floor. I hear it roll a few feet away while my eyes lock with her terrified ones.

*Still no sparkle.*

Gripping her hips, I feel a tremor wrack through her.

There's no reason for the sudden burst of anger, and I have no words to lash out with.

We just stare at each other for a tense minute.

I feel her breaths explode over my face, her body pressed to mine as I keep her imprisoned against the counter, her chest desperately rising and falling.

When I realize my heart is hammering against my ribs, I yank away from her and stalk out of the kitchen. Reaching the elevator, I slam the button, and the moment the doors slide open, I step inside.

With my hands fisted at my sides, I take the elevator down, and when I step out, Vincenzo and Fabrizio's heads turn in my direction from where they're sitting in the Bentley.

"Going out?" Vincenzo asks when I climb into the back of the car.

"Yes. Take me to Franco," I mutter. "Fabrizio, stay here and keep an eye on the woman."

As he shoves the door open, he says, "Yes, boss."

Vincenzo starts the engine and steers us out of the basement and onto the street.

I know my friend has his hands full with the triplets, but I need to see him.

Resting my elbow against the door, I rub my fingers over my mouth, the scene in the kitchen replaying in my mind.

I don't know why I lost my shit. It's unlike me. Usually I'm the calm one out of the five heads of the Cosa Nostra.

I'm the chilled and funny friend between Franco and me.

But with Skylar in my personal space, I'm finding it hard to control my rage. One look at the woman has me on the constant brink of losing my shit.

*It's because you're faced around the clock with the woman who has Giulio's kidney in her body.*

Maybe I should just kill Skylar and Harlan and be done with it.

When Vincenzo pulls into the driveway at the back of the house, I see Marcello and Milo, Franco's right-hand men, having a cigarette on the patio.

I throw the door open as Marcello kills the cigarette in an ashtray. His eyes lock on me, "This is a surprise."

I can't exchange pleasantries right now. "Where's Franco?"

Marcello gestures to the sliding doors. "Probably in the kitchen or nursery."

I walk into the house and check the kitchen, where I find Franco downing a cup of coffee.

His eyebrows fly up when he sees me, then his features tighten. "What's wrong?"

"I just needed a break from my place," I reply as I lean back against the island, crossing my arms over my chest.

"The woman?" he asks.

I just nod.

We're quiet for a moment, then he asks, "Want to talk about it?"

I let out a sigh before muttering, "I'm thinking maybe I should just kill them and be done with it."

"If that's what you want to do," Franco says, his eyes locked on my face.

"Dario will be pissed off," I mention.

"Why?"

"He feels the woman is innocent in all of this," I explain.

"But you don't feel the same," Franco states the obvious.

He sets the coffee cup down, and walking out of the kitchen, he calls out, "Follow me."

Letting out another sigh, I follow my friend to the third floor and into a nursery that's decorated with baby animals.

The light is dimmed. Two of the triplets are fast asleep, while the third is making baby sounds. From the blue onesie the baby has on, I know it's Augusto, Franco's son.

Franco reaches down and picks up Augusto, then comes closer to me. There's a proud smile on his face as he stares down at his heir, then his eyes flick to mine.

"Hold him," he whispers.

I shake my head and take a step back.

Franco gives me a look of warning. "Hold my fucking son, Renzo."

Reluctantly and very fucking awkwardly, I take the baby, instantly anxious I'll drop him.

Augusto makes a cute gurgling sound, and it looks like he's smiling at me.

Weirdly enough, I begin to feel calmer. When I aim to touch his chubby cheek, he grabs hold of my finger. Seeing his tiny hand holding mine, my fucking heart melts.

"You're their godfather. You should bond with them," Franco says.

"I know. They just terrify the fuck out of me," I admit with a soft chuckle.

"You just needed a little oxytocin to make you feel better," Franco murmurs.

I glance at my friend. "Oxytocin?"

"Love hormones. They release when you hold babies or puppies. Why do you think I'm so much calmer? I'm constantly high on the shit."

I let out another chuckle and have to admit, I feel better.

When Augusto starts fussing, I hand him back to Franco, who makes it look like it's the most natural thing for him to hold a baby.

"Being a father looks good on you," I say.

"I totally agree," Samantha suddenly says behind me.

Glancing over my shoulder, I smile at the woman who brought my best friend to his knees. "Hey."

When she comes into the room, I move out of the way. Samantha might have gotten used to me, but I still keep my distance from her so she won't feel uncomfortable.

Franco told me some of the shit his wife went through before they met, and the last thing I want to do is trigger a panic attack in her.

"Let me take him so you can visit with Renzo," she tells Franco.

He hands their son over to his wife then nods at the door.

I follow him to the living room, where he pours two tumblers of whiskey. Handing one to me, he says, "Take a seat."

Sitting down on one of the couches, I sip on the drink while glancing around the room. There's baby shit everywhere.

"Have you found that guy you were looking for? Castellanos."

I shake my head, frustration flitting through my chest. "Not yet. He's all over New York, scurrying around like a fucking rat."

He takes a sip of his whiskey, then says, "So the woman." Shaking his head, he mutters, "What are you doing, Renzo? It's clearly fucking with your head and not good for you to have her around."

I suck in a deep breath and stare at the amber liquid in my tumbler.

"I get Giulio's death hit you hard, and you need to deal with it, but is this really the way to do it?" he asks.

Lifting my eyes to his, I mutter, "How would you deal with it if someone killed me for my kidney."

He thinks for a moment, then lets out a heavy sigh. "I wouldn't take anyone captive. I'd just fucking kill them all."

"The woman included?"

Again, he thinks about it before he answers, "No. I'm going to side with Dario on this one. Her only crime is

195

being the recipient of the kidney. She wasn't the one who killed Giulio, and her father bought the kidney. From what I understand, she was completely unaware of what was happening behind the scenes."

He sets his tumbler down on the coffee table, and leaning forward, he rests his forearms on his thighs. "I get it must be hard knowing Giulio's kidney is in her body, but maybe you should rethink what you're doing."

I don't respond immediately as I think about the past five weeks.

The excruciating pain of losing Giulio. The rage. The men I've killed and the ones I plan to torture to death. Harlan. Skylar.

"If Harlan Davies didn't order a kidney, Giulio would still be alive," I say.

"Then kill him." Franco picks up his drink again. "Kill him and let the woman go."

*No.*

"Because of her, I have no heir," I mutter. "Because of her, Giulio's dead. It starts and ends with Skylar Davies."

Franco lets out a sigh. "What do you want me to say, Renzo? Do you want my blessing to kill the woman? Fine. Off her. It makes no difference to me. I just fucking hate seeing you like this."

I down the rest of the whiskey, letting the alcohol burn down my throat.

*Do I really want to kill her?*

*No.*

*Am I going to keep her locked in my penthouse for the rest of her life?*

*That means I'm stuck with her forever, and that's a fucking long time.*

*Fuck.*

"Or…" Franco lets the word hang in the air until I look up to meet his eyes, then he continues, "You could always marry her, and she could give you the heir you lost."

"What. The. Fuck," I practically gasp.

He shrugs. "Just saying. It's another way for this thing to play out, and you'll get an heir from it."

"Hell no," I growl, not even willing to consider it as an option.

"Dario says Skylar Davies is beautiful and talented," Franco mentions. "Isn't there any attraction?"

I give my friend an incredulous look. "Whether a woman gives me a hard-on doesn't qualify her to be my wife."

"Most relationships start with attraction, brother. You just need to get it up to make a baby."

197

"You really think an arranged marriage is the way to go?" I chuckle, my tone still incredulous because this conversation is absurd.

"Take a page out of Angelo's book. It will be a forced marriage because from what you and Dario have told me, Skylar won't be saying 'I do' out of her own free will."

"Raping a woman just to have an heir is not exactly my style," I growl. "Just because we'll be legally married won't change shit. She's not just going to lie back like a good little wife and take it."

Franco shakes his head. "Yeah, you're right." He finishes his drink. "Forget what I said. It was a stupid idea."

We both lean back against the couches and let out sighs.

"So I'm back to square one. I'll continue to keep her captive."

# Chapter 23

## Skylar

Sitting out on the balcony, I stare at the city lights.

I'm only wearing a pair of shorts and an oversized T-shirt, and it's starting to get chilly.

Rubbing my hands up and down my arms, I think about the past five days.

I'm starting to get used to the new routine. I prepare three meals every day, even when Renzo's not home. When I'm alone, I watch the livestream, taking every chance I get to see Dad.

He's not doing well. He hasn't shaved and spends a lot of time in my bedroom, just staring at the floor.

My heart breaks seeing him like that, but part of me is angry because he bought the kidney on the black market, and now I'm a deranged mafia boss' prisoner.

I understand why Dad did it, but I still feel it was my choice to make and not his. It's hard to accept a man died because of me.

If I could turn back time, I would've chosen death instead of getting the surgery because the torment I'm forced to endure in this penthouse is no life at all.

Knowing all my hopes and dreams are once again out of reach is a hard pill to swallow.

*It's much more difficult than the first time I had to give up on them.*

The skin at the back of my neck prickles, and my body instantly tenses.

Not once since I got here has Renzo come into my room. Feeling his eyes on me, my heartbeat speeds up, and I swallow hard on the fear tightening my throat.

After he suddenly lunged at me two nights ago, he hasn't spoken a word to me, and I've only seen him at dinner.

A drop of rain splats on my knee, and I glance up at the dark sky. A flash of lightning strikes in the distance, and another drop lands on my forehead.

Knowing I can't afford to get sick, I reluctantly get up and walk back into the bedroom. When I pull the sliding door shut, I still feel Renzo's eyes on me.

Sucking in a deep breath, I turn around and see him leaning against the doorjamb, his arms crossed over his chest.

I have zero intention of being the first to speak, and copying his stance, I lean against the wall and cross my arms.

The stand-off lasts for unnervingly long minutes before he murmurs, "I'm surprised you haven't tried to escape."

I shrug. "I'm not going to risk my father's life. You've made it pretty clear you'll kill him if I try anything."

"So you're just going to lie back and take it?" he asks. "I was under the impression you're a fighter and not someone who gives up so easily."

His words have anger exploding in my chest, and pushing away from the wall, I walk in the direction of the bathroom so I can get away from him before I say something that will get Dad and me killed.

Before I can make it past the bed, Renzo grabs hold of my arm and tugs me closer until my shoulder presses against his solid chest.

His tone is low as he asks, "Do you think you're innocent in my little brother's death?"

I close my eyes as the guilt rears in my heart.

Not looking at Renzo, I answer, "It wasn't my choice."

"What would you have chosen?"

I suck in a deep breath of air as the days before the surgery ghost through my mind.

My voice is soft as I say, "I made peace with dying. I wouldn't have agreed to the surgery had I known they'd kill someone for the kidney." Turning my head, my eyes lock with his. I don't know where the bravery comes from as I whisper, "There's only one murderer in this room, and it's not me."

His lips curve up in a dangerous-looking smile, and a burst of laughter escapes him.

Letting go of my arm, he lifts his hand to my face, and when he aims to touch my jaw, I jerk my head away.

His eyebrow lifts. "Suddenly, you're brave, my little mouse."

Lightening flashes right outside the windows and lights up the room for a split second. I see the cold and unforgiving look in Renzo's eyes and remember what he's capable of.

He killed Dr. Bentall without showing any emotion.

The heavens open up, and rain pours down in a thick curtain, the sound filling the room.

"Maybe you are innocent," Renzo murmurs. For a moment, I wonder if I heard right, then he continues, "I thought about killing you and putting an end to this...situation."

My heart squeezes in my chest, and my eyes flit back to his face.

"But some of my friends are rooting for your survival."

*Dario?*

*He said friends, so there's more than one. Right?*

This time, when he lifts his hand to my face, I keep still. His fingers brush along my jaw and down the side of my neck, leaving a trail of goosebumps in its wake.

I hate that his touch affects me and ignore the fluttering sensation in my stomach.

"You don't get as scared anymore," he mentions. "Which means you're getting used to living here, and soon it might not be torture anymore."

*I doubt that. This place will never be my home.*

I continue to just stare at him, refusing to play into his mind games.

"I'll have to think of a creative way to get my pound of flesh. Maybe Franco was right after all."

I begin to frown because I don't know what he's referring to.

Suddenly, Renzo moves away, and a second later, he switches the light on. Standing near the door his eyes sweep over my body, then he smirks.

"Yeah, I'm starting to think Franco's onto something."

*What?*

Not explaining himself, he walks out of the room, leaving me feeling confused as hell.

Shaking my head, I replay the conversation we just had while walking to the closet and pulling on a sweater.

It's the first time Renzo's bothered to ask me how I feel.

*It's weird.*

*Who's Franco, and what is he right about?*

Walking to the doorway, my teeth tug at my bottom lip. There's no reason for me to leave my bedroom. We've already had dinner.

*Still, Renzo seems calm and willing to talk.*

Maybe I can reason with him, and if not, I might be able to plant a seed of doubt by adding to what Dario said to him last week. It's clear it bothers him, or he wouldn't have asked me whether I think I'm innocent.

Leaving my room, I glance at the closed door at the end of the hallway before I head toward the staircase.

Halfway down the stairs, there's a loud crack of thunder before the penthouse is plunged into darkness.

A peep escapes me as I jerk with fright. "Crap."

I don't hear anything but the rain and wait a moment for my eyes to adjust to the darkness.

The eerie sensation creeps down my spine, and I glance over my shoulder. Seeing Renzo's silhouette, I say, "I'm here. Just in case you don't see me."

His tone is a low whisper that sends shivers racing over my body. "I see you just fine, *topolina*."

My muscles instinctively tense as if they recognize the predatory tone before my brain does.

When Renzo prowls toward me, I take another step down and almost lose my footing from not being able to see shit. His arm wraps around my side, and I'm kept in place as he moves in front of me.

Renzo's right. I'm becoming used to my new circumstances because my heart doesn't race like crazy with fear anymore. Even though my breathing speeds up, there's no threat of me hyperventilating.

Instead, I'm overly aware of his powerful presence as the scent of his woodsy cologne fills the air I breathe.

I'm beginning to think the man has excellent night vision because he grips my jaw and tips my head back without any effort on his part. There's a glint of light in his eyes that makes him look even more predatory.

He presses closer to me, and with his face an inch from mine, he says, "The last thing we need is you breaking your neck on the stairs."

In the moment that follows his words, a weird tension fills the air around us. It sizzles with electricity as if a lightning bolt is about to strike.

His head begins to lower, and I suck in a shocked breath before holding it.

*What's he planning to do?*

*Surely...no, he wouldn't.*

*Would he?*

The warm air of his breath fans over my lips, making them tingle. My stomach does a somersault, and my brain struggles to think of how I should react.

The air around us tenses even more. His arm holding me to him tightens. His body presses closer to mine.

*Holy shit.*

Suddenly, the lights come on, and seeing how close Renzo's face is to mine has my heart instantly beating like a wild horse trying to get out of a burning barn.

Before another second can pass, Renzo lets go of me and takes the stairs down before walking to the living room.

Stunned out of my ever-loving mind, I remain standing in the middle of the staircase.

I place a hand over my fluttering stomach and suck in deep breaths of air.

*Did that just happen?*

*Was he about to try and kiss me?*

*But why?*

I should be terrified if that's really the case.

Turning my head, I stare at Renzo as he pours himself a tumbler of whiskey.

*Maybe…*

*Just maybe…*

*Did Dario get through to him, and he's softening toward me?*

My heart starts to race for a whole different reason.

*If I can make Renzo care about me, he might spare Dad's life. Maybe he'll give me my freedom.*

With my chest rising and falling and the idea taking root, I watch as the hot-as-hell mafia boss takes a sip of the whiskey while staring out at the city lights beyond the window.

# Chapter 24

## Renzo

It's been two weeks since I took Skylar, and as I watch the livestream on the TV screen, it's clear Harlan Davies is losing his mind.

Unshaven, disheveled, and losing weight, the man looks like death.

My eyes flick to Skylar where she's cleaning the kitchen after we just had dinner.

With an annoyed sigh, I pull my phone from my pocket and dial Carlo's number.

"Yes, boss?" he answers.

"Take two men and bring Harlan Davies to the warehouse," I order.

"On it, boss."

I end the call and walk to the kitchen. Ripping the dishcloth from Skylar's hand, I grab her wrist and pull her toward the elevator.

I hear her startled gasp and how her breaths speed up, but she doesn't ask what's happening.

We step into the elevator, and when the doors close, I press the button for the basement. Without thinking my hand slides down her wrist until my fingers wrap around her slender ones.

I feel her hand tremble in mine and mutter, "I'm taking you to see your father."

Her head snaps up, her eyes widening with disbelief.

"You'll have thirty minutes to visit with him while I take care of some business. Fuck up, and I won't allow another visit."

She nods quickly, her eyes still wide on me.

"I'm doing this so you don't fucking die of depression," I add so she doesn't make the mistake of thinking I care about her.

During the power outage last week, I almost fucked up. I was a second away from kissing the woman just because Franco and Dario got into my head.

*Fucking little shits.*

Still, Franco's words keep popping into my mind at the most random times, and I find myself thinking more and more of Skylar as a woman and less as a prisoner.

*My little captive might just turn out to be my downfall if I'm not careful.*

The elevator doors slide open, and I tug Skylar out of it. Vincenzo and Fabrizio quickly get out of the Bentley, giving me questioning looks.

I open the back door and don't even have to give an order for Skylar to get in. She pulls her hand from mine, and while she climbs into the back of the car, I glance at my men and say, "We're going to the warehouse."

I get in beside Skylar and don't miss the emotional smile wavering around her lips.

When Vincenzo starts the engine, Skylar whispers, "Thank you."

Turning my head, I stare at her beautiful face. There are still dark circles beneath her eyes. I was getting worried, but Bianca assured me after the last checkup that Skylar's doing well and the kidney is functioning as it should.

Her eyes meet mine, and we stare at each other for a moment before I glance away.

I become aware of my heart beating a little faster and try to ignore the fucking organ.

The ride to the warehouse is filled with silence, but I feel the excitement coming in waves from Skylar and soon find myself looking at her again.

Her bottom lip is being tortured by her teeth, and her eyes are shimmering with unshed tears. Her hands tremble where they're clasped together on her lap.

When Vincenzo brings the Bentley to a stop, Skylar's eyes turn to me. She hesitates for a moment, then says, "You said if I cry, you'll make my father pay for each tear."

I forgot I said that to her.

Her tone is soft as she pleads, "I'm not sure I can hold back the tears when I see him. Please don't hurt him."

Fuck, she's asking permission to cry, and it hits me square in the chest.

Unable to speak, I just nod before I shove the door open and climb out of the car.

Skylar's right behind me as I walk into the warehouse. I glance around the open space that's slowly filling with crates as we get ready for a shipment that's due for Somalia.

Walking into the office that's become Elio's second home since I took Skylar, I find my right-hand man hard at work.

"Do you ever go home?" I ask.

His head snaps up, then he leans back in the chair and sighs. "I didn't expect to see you tonight."

His eyes move between Skylar and me.

"I'll only be here for half an hour or so."

Skylar keeps glancing at the entrance to the warehouse, her breaths already coming fast.

"Give me ten minutes, and I'll be back so we can talk business," I say to Elio before I take Skylar's hand and pull her toward the steps.

As I head to the room we usually use to torture some poor fuck for information, I suddenly change direction and take her to one of the empty offices.

Pulling her inside the dusty room, I don't let go of her hand and tug her closer. Her head tilts back, her eyes sparkling like they used to.

Just the thought of spending time with her father is enough to breathe life back into her gaze.

*I've missed that fucking sparkle.*

The thought catches me off guard and I quickly let go of her hand.

I sound agitated as fuck when I say, "Wait here."

Skylar nods, and her eyes follow me out of the office.

Walking toward the steps, I stop by the metal railing and placing my hands on it, I stare down at the lower floor where my men are hard at work.

I hear a car pull up, and turning my attention to the entrance, I watch as Carlo and Emilio pull Harlan from the vehicle before shoving him into the warehouse.

My eyes follow the man as he's forced through the warehouse and up the steps. Carlo brings him to a stop a couple of feet away from me. Letting go of the railing, I turn to Harlan and take in his sorry state.

"You have thirty minutes," I mutter.

Harlan's eyes snap to my face, and I see the hatred burning in them.

*He wishes he could kill me.*

I let out a chuckle. "Don't fuck this up for Skylar. She's really looking forward to seeing you." Unable to resist fucking with the man, I add, "I'd hate to see *my woman* upset."

Harlan's eyes widen with a mixture of rage and disbelief.

I nod toward the office, and Carlo shoves Harlan so he'll move.

The moment Harlan enters the office, I hear a strangled sob from Skylar. "Daddy!"

I walk closer to the door, and locking eyes with Carlo, I say, "You can leave."

213

As Carlo heads back to the steps, I watch Skylar and Harlan hugging each other. They're just crying, not saying a word.

I leave the door open, and walking a couple of feet away, I lean back against the wall so I can listen to their conversation.

For the longest moment, all I hear is Skylar crying. My heart squeezes in my chest, and I lower my head and stare at the metal landing beneath my feet.

The uncontrollable rage I felt toward Skylar has faded over the past two weeks, but the sight of Harlan still pisses me off.

"Are you okay?" I hear Harlan ask.

"I'm fine, Daddy." She takes a shuddering breath. "You don't look okay. I never see you eating."

"What do you mean?" he asks.

"I can see and hear you on a livestream. Renzo somehow planted cameras in the mansion. The kitchen, living room, my bedroom, and by the staircase. I get to see you and Louisa."

There's a moment's silence again, then Skylar whispers, "You need to eat. Stop sitting in my bedroom. It breaks my heart seeing you like that."

Harlan doesn't respond to what his daughter just said but instead asks, "Has he hurt you?"

"No. Not once. I spend my days cooking and watching the livestream."

*Oh, so my little mouse has been watching the livestream more than I thought.*

"He also has a nurse come over to give me my regular checkups. Considering I'm being held captive, it isn't so bad."

Her words should upset me because I want her to suffer, not feel like she's on some fucking vacation.

Instead, the corner of my mouth lifts.

A commotion downstairs pulls my attention away from the reunion, and I quickly walk to the metal staircase.

# Chapter 25

## Renzo

Halfway down the steps, I see Antonio and Roberto dragging a man who's been beaten up toward me.

"Boss!" Antonio says, excitement in his tone. "We found him. I was just about to call you."

The man is forced up the steps, and when I get a good look at his face, rage detonates in my chest.

"Castellanos," I growl. "Finally we meet." My eyes flick to Antonio. "Take him to the room."

As they force him past me, I glance over the warehouse floor until I see Carlo and Emilio. I gesture for them to come.

It's only when I walk to the room where they took the fucker the realization that I finally have Castellanos registers.

I have one of the men directly involved with Giulio's death.

As I enter the room, I shrug my jacket off and toss it to the side. Antonio and Roberto have a tight grip on the man as my arm swings back, and my fist connects with his already busted jaw.

The satisfaction I feel is fucking intense, but it does nothing to lessen my need for vengeance.

I hit him twice more before Carlo and Emilio join us.

Taking a step back, I unbutton my cuffs so I can roll up my sleeves.

"Good job, guys. You can leave," I say to Antonio and Roberto. "Go to Elio so he can pay you."

"Yes, boss," Antonio replies before they leave.

I need to promote Antonio. He's become a valuable asset.

"Strip the fucker," I order.

Carlo and Emilio get to work while my eyes burn on the man who belongs to The Harvest.

When he's as naked as the day he was born, I signal for my men to force him to his knees.

"You supplied a kidney to Dr. Bentall," I say to bring him up to speed in case he has no idea why he's here.

Castellanos' eyes snap to my face.

"The faster you tell me everything I want to hear, the quicker this is over," I lie because I'm going to fucking make him pray for death before I kill him.

"I don't know a Dr. Bentall," he mutters.

My chest rises and falls with heavy breaths as my focus zooms in on the fucker, and unable to stop myself, I repeatedly kick the fucking shit out of him.

Before I kill him too fast, I manage to pull back and roll my shoulders to ease the tension building in them.

"Let's try this again," I say. "You supplied a kidney to Dr. Bentall."

"So fucking what?" he spits as he moves back into a kneeling position, his face torn with pain. "Hah? What does it have to do with you?"

I crouch down until I'm at eye level with him. "Who grabbed Giulio Pirrotta? Who cut him open?"

A bloody smile pulls at Castellanos' busted lips. "Oh, you mean the boy who cried like a baby? Why do you care?"

"He was my little brother," I grit out between clenched teeth.

Castellanos' eyes widen as he realizes he's not getting out of this alive.

"Your brother?" He shakes his head. "You have no siblings."

"I fucking adopted him. He was my heir, and you fucking gutted him." Rage flays me to the bone and strips me of all my self-control. Lunging at the fucker, I force him onto his back and shout, "Hand me a fucking knife!"

Emilio acts quickly, and when he places the knife in my hand, I order, "Hold the fucker down."

They grab his shoulders, and I move off Castellanos. Pressing the tip of the blade against his side, I shove it slowly into his abdomen.

He lets out an agonizing cry, and with a cruel smile on my face, I say, "Look who's crying like a baby now, bitch."

His body trembles from the shock, and his eyes are wide as he finally has the common sense to fear me.

Keeping the blade embedded into his abdomen, I growl, "Who grabbed Giulio?"

"I did," he hisses. "I fucking gutted him like a meatbag."

*He's pushing me, so I'll just kill him.*

"Where does The Harvest operate from?" I demand.

Another bloody smile stretches over his face. "We're everywhere...move from city to city...never in one place... longer than three months."

219

Using force, I cut a deep line down to where his pubic hair starts.

The fucker howls like an animal, the sound making a powerful wave of satisfaction fill my soul.

"Who's your leader?" I ask through gritted teeth.

A humorless chuckle ripples from him. "Montes."

"Montes fucking who?" I shout.

Castellanos' eyes lock on me. "Servando...Servando Montes. He's a...ghost. You'll never...find him."

The corner of my mouth lifts. "Don't underestimate me."

Pulling the knife out, I shove my fucking hand into his abdomen, grab a fistful of whatever fucking organs I touch first and yank it right out of his body.

His agonizing cry is cut short as his body starts to convulse.

I rise to my feet and watch as he goes into shock, and with his blood dripping from my hands, I savor his last breaths.

---

# Skylar

After reassuring Dad for the hundredth time I'm okay, I take a step away from him and cross my arms over my chest.

"Why did you do it, Dad? Why go to such extreme measures for a kidney?"

"I couldn't lose you, sweetheart," he whispers.

"I made peace with dying," I say, my voice still thick with tears.

"I wasn't…I couldn't just watch you die!" he exclaims.

"So you got a kidney on the black market? Surely, you know how they get most of the organs. Innocent people suffer and die to supply the market."

"I didn't think about that," he admits. "Dr. Bentall told me he could get a kidney, and I didn't ask any questions. I just wanted to save you."

"At the expense of a twenty-year-old man! His life had barely started." I suck in a breath to try and calm down.

Finally, being able to express my anger and heartache, it's hard to keep my temper under control.

"What is done is done," Dad says, making my eyes widen on him.

"It's far from done," I almost shout. I slap my hand against my chest. "I'm a freaking prisoner. For the rest of my life."

Dad's face crumbles under the strain of knowing he failed me as a father.

"I'm trying to think of a way to get us out of this mess."

"Us?" I hiss. "There's no us. I'm the one spending day in and day out in that penthouse with a monster."

I move farther away from Dad and close my eyes as I suck in deep breaths so I can calm down. I don't have long before I have to return to the penthouse, and who knows when I'll see Dad again.

"I'm sorry," I whisper.

"It's okay, sweetheart. I deserve your anger."

Suddenly, a man screams in pain, and the sound has me jerking with fright.

Dad and I stand frozen, staring at each other with wide eyes.

*That did not sound good at all.*

A howl of pain fills the air, and I quickly move to Dad's side and grab his arm.

Dad shakes his head before looking at me again with urgency filling his eyes. "I'll find a way to get you back. I promise."

"I think I have a way, but it's risky," I whisper, scared someone will overhear us.

"What?"

"I think I can make him care about me."

Dad immediately shakes his head. "No! No, don't do that. It's too dangerous. A man like him will rape you if he thinks you're interested in him."

Yeah, I've thought about that as well, and honestly, I'm willing to sleep with Renzo if it means I'll get my freedom.

"I'll be careful," I say. When Dad shakes his head again, I remind him, "Renzo hasn't hurt me, Dad, and I don't think he'll force himself on me. He seems to be softening toward me. I really think my plan will work."

An excruciating, pain-filled wail tears through the air, making us freeze again.

*Someone's being killed.*

*Jesus.*

The air fills with tension, and before I can catch my bearings, Renzo stalks into the room. His hands are bloody, and the rage on his face is so dark it makes my soul cower back in an attempt to escape him.

*Dear God.*

Without saying a word, Renzo grabs my forearm, and I'm ripped away from Dad.

Glancing over my shoulder, I hurry to say, "Bye, Daddy. I love you. Don't worry about me. Remember, I can see you on the livestream."

"I love you, sweetheart!" Dad's face crumbles as he watches me being dragged away by Renzo.

As we pass an open door, I make the mistake of glancing inside, and horror crashes over me. A naked body of a man lies on the concrete floor. He's been brutally beaten and disemboweled.

*Jesus.*

I've never seen such a level of violence in my life.

The air is knocked from my lungs as I'm reminded who Renzo really is. The past two weeks I've forgotten what he's capable of.

He drags me down the stairs to the lower floor while my mind reels with terror.

I'm pulled into the office, where Renzo addresses the man behind the desk with rage simmering in his tone. "We're looking for Servando Montes. He's the leader of The Harvest. Have every available man look for the fucker."

"Will do, boss," the man replies, not at all bothered by the blood on Renzo's hands.

The blood that's now on my arm.

*Oh God.*

My stomach churns as I glance down to where he's holding me.

My breaths become audible, drawing Renzo's attention to me. When he notices what I'm staring at, I'm pulled out of the office and taken to a restroom. My arm is shoved beneath the tap, and Renzo rinses the blood off my skin.

The moment he lets go of me, I pull my arm away and take a couple of steps backward.

I watch as he washes his hands and how the blood-stained water swirls down the drain.

He just tortured a man. He pulled his freaking insides out with his bare hands.

Jesus, what was I thinking? I'll never be able to make this man care about me. Someone like him isn't capable of feeling love.

Renzo dries his hands, and his eyes settle on my face. "Did you enjoy your visit with your father?" he asks.

"W-W-What?" I stutter as I struggle to switch gears from being engulfed in terror to answering such a simple question.

He moves closer to me, and taking hold of my jaw, his eyes sweep over my face. "Another panic attack, *topolina*?"

I quickly shake my head and suck in a deep breath of air so he'll see I'm breathing just fine.

"Didn't you enjoy the visit?" he asks, his eyes sharpening on my face.

"I did," I whisper. "Thank you."

He tilts his head. "Then why do you look shit scared right now?"

*Seriously?*

My eyebrows pinch together, and I pray to all that's holy I don't piss him off as I say, "You j-just killed a man w-with your bare h-hands." I pause, and my tongue darts out to wet my dry lips. "You disemboweled h-him. The blood…t-t-the blood…"

Once again, this man surprises the hell out of me when he suddenly pulls me against his chest. His arms lock around me, and his hand settles against the back of my head.

A tremor wracks through my body from feeling his powerful body against mine.

*Maybe he does care? Why else would he try to comfort me?*

"He deserved to die," Renzo whispers, his voice still laced with darkness but also carrying an undertone of sorrow. "He's the one who killed Giulio."

I nod quickly to show I'm listening.

"My little brother was my heir. There was no one I loved more than him," he admits.

Realizing Renzo is actually opening up to me has my lips parting with shock. This is a side of him I haven't seen before.

Silence falls around us, and I become overly aware of how it feels to be held by this man. Whether he's holding me to offer some comfort or because he's playing with my emotions is unclear, though.

Turning my head, I rest my ear against his chest, and my face goes slack when I hear how fast his heart is beating.

*Is it racing because of me?*

*Do I dare get my hopes up?*

Not wanting to miss my chance, I pull my arms free from between us and wrap them around his waist.

My heartbeat speeds up dangerously fast when his body curves around mine, and he presses his mouth to my hair.

*Holy. Freaking. Shit.*

Suddenly, he lets go of me, and walking past me, he mutters, "Let's go home."

I quickly follow him out of the restroom while my mind races a mile a minute to process what I just learned.

*Renzo has to care about me to react like that. Right?*

# Chapter 26

## Renzo

Feeling a hell of a lot better since I killed Constellanos, I'm calmer when it comes to Skylar.

With Dario and my men searching the globe for Servando Montes, I took some time to check on my mother before she left to visit her cousins in Sicily.

Standing in the living room with a tumbler of whiskey in my hand, I stare out the floor-to-ceiling window, not actually taking in the scenery of the city skyline.

I hear Skylar's soft footsteps as she comes down the stairs, and turning around, my eyes follow her to the kitchen.

I finish the last of the whiskey and set the glass down before I head to the kitchen. She's busy taking ingredients from the fridge.

I sit down on one of the chairs by the island so I can watch her cook. No amount of torture will have me admitting out loud that I like watching her prepare food for us.

"What are you making for lunch?" I ask as I rest my forearms on the granite top.

"Lamb rib eye with garlic and sage roasted potatoes," she replies. She sets the meat down on the counter then looks at me. "It was my mom's favorite."

A smile tugs at her mouth, and as I stare at her like a dumbstruck idiot, it widens.

Her tone sounds friendly when she adds, "I hope you'll like it."

Seeing her smile does weird things to my insides. Especially my heart.

*'You could always marry her, and she could give you the heir you lost.'*

Franco's words shoot through my mind, making a frown form on my face.

Skylar's smile disappears, and suddenly looking nervous, she focuses on prepping the meat.

Realizing I'm not happy because she's back to being nervous, the frown on my face darkens.

*The fuck?*

*Why do I care whether she smiles or not?*

It's that fucking thought Franco planted. Since then, I've been struggling to remember Skylar's my prisoner.

My eyes follow every movement from her. I take in the pink dress she's wearing, and my gaze stops on her bare feet.

*She looks like she belongs in my kitchen.*

Suddenly, Skylar says, "Is there something you don't like to eat? Any allergies?"

I let out a chuckle. "Why? So you can make sure to feed me whatever I'm allergic to?"

She shakes her head and glances over her shoulder. "I'd never do that. I just want you to enjoy the meals."

The corner of my mouth lifts. "No allergies."

I watch her work for a while, then she asks, "So, what do you like to eat?"

*Is the sudden interest because I hugged her last week?*

I've been ignoring the elephant in the room since it happened, especially how good it felt when she hugged me back.

"Don't get Stockholm syndrome," I mutter.

"What?"

"It's when you show affection or attachment to your kidnapper," I explain.

"I know what it means," she replies. "And just because I want to make something you'll enjoy eating doesn't mean I'm growing attached. I'm not stupid."

My eyebrow lifts, and I'm not happy when there's a sense of disappointment in my chest.

*Why does it matter whether she grows attached or not?*

While I watch her peel potatoes, my heart begins to beat faster as I process what's happening.

*Fuck.*

*Don't, Renzo.*

Lifting a hand, I wipe my palm over my face as I suck in a deep breath.

Do I like the woman?

*No, why would I?*

Needing to test the unwelcome theory, I get up and move around the island. Skylar's eyes dart to me, and she sets the potato and knife down on the counter.

She doesn't take a step back when I stop in front of her.

Staring at her, I focus on how she makes me feel while taking in every single inch of her beautiful face.

The first thing I notice is the current of attraction running between us.

*Is it one-sided?*

The attraction is quickly followed by an urge to touch her.

Lifting my hand, I brush my finger along her jaw. Her lips part in response to my touch, but I can't read her eyes.

Do I like this woman?

*Yes.*

The realization has me pulling my hand away from her.

Her voice is soft as she asks, "Is something wrong?"

*Yes. Something is very fucking wrong. This was not supposed to happen.*

"Fucking, Franco," I mutter.

This is because of the seed he planted when he mentioned I should marry her.

She shakes her head, a frown forming on her forehead. "I don't understand."

Moving away from her before I do something I'll regret, I walk out of the kitchen and head to my bedroom.

I slam the door shut behind me, and pushing my fingers through my hair, I suck in a deep breath.

*What the fuck do I do now?*

I begin to pace up and down in front of the bed while I process my newly discovered feelings.

Sure, I've liked a woman before, but never one I planned to keep for the rest of her life.

Do I take Franco's advice and marry her? A forced marriage worked for Angelo, and Vittoria learned to love him.

Yeah, but he didn't make her life a living hell. Angelo did everything in his power to win over his wife.

"Fuck," I mutter, my heart beating faster and faster. "I have to stop caring about her."

It's still in the early stages. I can just stop liking her.

I hide in my bedroom until I'm sure she's done cooking and eating, and by the time I open the door, I'm dead sure I'm in control of my emotions.

*You're her kidnapper and nothing more.*

*You've got this.*

I continue my little pep talk as I head down the stairs, and when I reach the kitchen, a breeze draws my attention to the open sliding doors in the dining room.

Seeing Skylar leaning over the glass railing of the balcony, my heart stutters in my chest, and I lunge into action.

I grab her from behind before she can even try to climb over and haul her away from the railing.

"Jesus!" she gasps.

It takes no effort from me to force her down to the floor while making sure I don't hurt her in the process.

My fingers wrap around her neck to hold her in place, and with my heart hammering in my chest, I growl, "What the fuck are doing?"

Her hands fly up to grip my wrist, her eyes wide with shock. "Nothing!"

My voice is hoarse as I say, "If you think jumping will resolve everything, you're very wrong."

"I wasn't going to jump," she rambles. "I was just looking at the traffic below. Twenty-seven! There were twenty-seven yellow cabs."

*Fuck. My heart.*

The wind catches her dress, blowing it up her body and giving me a perfect view of her black panties.

I sink back on my ass and suck in a deep breath while my eyes burn on her.

Skylar sits up and pushes her dress down, her face pale from the fright I just gave her.

When her eyes meet mine, her tone is soft as she says, "I'm sorry. I didn't mean to scare you. I'd never do something like that."

My heartbeat doesn't slow down but instead continues to hammer against my ribs.

My breaths explode over my lips, and before I can stop myself, I dart forward again. Grabbing Skylar by her shoulders, I force her backward. My hand moves behind her head so she doesn't bump it against the floor, and a second later, my mouth slams into hers.

# Chapter 27

## Skylar

I'm still recovering from the heart attack Renzo just gave me when he suddenly darts forward again. I'm shoved back down, and before I know what's happening, his mouth slams into mine.

My mind comes to a screeching halt, and I don't even have the capacity to gasp.

I wanted to make him care about me, but I never expected my plan to work so quickly. Hell, all I did was smile at him and show a little interest.

His lips move hungrily against mine, and it feels unbelievably good.

*Shit. No feelings, woman. This isn't a romance. It's your ticket out of here.*

It takes a hell of a lot of effort to remember my plan, and keeping with the act, I wrap my arms around his neck.

Renzo tilts his head, and as his teeth tug at my bottom lip, the kiss spirals into a wild force that threatens to overwhelm me.

*Holy shit. Focus.*

His tongue sweeps through my mouth, and my abdomen clenches hard while my stomach erupts with a kaleidoscope of butterflies.

Instead of having to put in effort to return the kiss, it just happens, and before I know it, I'm lost. His body presses against mine, and it makes anticipation and need build within me.

*This man is like the apple in the Garden of Eden, and just like Eve, I'm tempted to take a bite.*

My teeth tug at his bottom lip, and my tongue wars with his.

His addictive scent fills the air I breathe.

His hard cock presses against my thigh.

His mouth casts a spell over me until my plan is nowhere in sight, and I'm solely focused on how good it feels to kiss him.

With his one hand clamped around my neck, his other moves down the right side of my body until he reaches the bare skin of my outer thigh.

His touch has tingles racing over me, and I move my hands to the sides of his jaw. Our lips knead, and our tongues taste, creating so much friction I'm not sure I can remember my name right now.

His hand moves up, and when his fingers brush over the surgery scar, he pulls away as if I just burned him.

It happens so fast. One second he's devouring me, and the next, he gets up and stalks away.

I'm left lying on the balcony floor, blinking like an idiot.

*What the hell was that?*

I'm not talking about him walking away. I'm referring to the way I returned his kiss. The way I freaking loved it.

*Holy shit. No.*

Renzo is a killer. A criminal. A freaking mafia boss.

He kidnapped me and hurt Dad.

He killed Dr. Bentall.

Pressing my hand to my stomach, I suck in desperate breaths.

*Renzo is your enemy. Never forget that. You're just making him care, so he'll let you go. This is all part of the plan.*

Feeling calmer, I get up off the floor and head inside. I shut the sliding door, and when I walk past the living room, I find Renzo taking a sip of whiskey.

I stop and stare at the man who just kissed the ever-loving hell out of me. My eyes glide over his muscular body, the impeccable three-piece suit, and his ruffled hair, which normally doesn't have a hair out of place.

His features are drawn tight, and the air around him feels tense.

Renzo's eyes flick to me, and I consider running to the safety of my bedroom.

*That would defeat the purpose. Stay right where you are.*

His gaze remains locked on me as he takes a sip of his drink, the sight hot and a little unnerving.

Damn, the man is heartbreakingly attractive.

And he just kissed me.

*Stick to the plan. It doesn't matter how hot he is.*

He tilts his head, his eyes narrowing on me as if he knows I'm up to something.

I take a step forward and gesturing in the direction of the dining room, I say, "Thanks for that." Realizing it sounds like I'm thanking him for the kiss, I quickly add, "For saving me even though I wasn't planning to jump."

His voice is low and deep when he murmurs, "Twenty-seven yellow cabs?"

I shrug and take another step closer to him. "There's not a lot for me to do here. I was just passing the time."

When I take another step, the corner of his mouth lifts as if he's amused. "What are you doing, *topolina*?"

I shake my head and feign innocence. "What do you mean?"

He takes another sip of his drink, just staring at me as I slowly inch closer as if I'm approaching a wild animal.

My stomach is a ball of nerves, but I don't stop until I'm standing right in front of him.

*I suck at flirting, but here goes nothing.*

Reaching for the glass in his hand, I take it from him and help myself to a sip before handing it back. I need the alcohol to be brave.

Giving the man my best provocative expression, I say, "You kissed me."

He's still watching me with amusement as he murmurs, "I did."

Lifting a hand, I run a finger over the buttons of his vest. "Want to continue what you started?"

Suddenly, laughter bursts from him, and he sets the tumbler down before shoving his hands into the pockets of his pants.

"I'm curious to see how far you'll take this," he says as he looks at me again.

*Crap. He's not falling for the act.*

Changing tactics, I let out a sigh, and crossing my arms over my chest, I force myself to think of Dad and the state he was in so the memory will bring tears to my eyes.

With my chin trembling, I say, "Can you blame me, Renzo? I'm lonely. Is it so hard to believe I crave human interaction?"

The amusement vanishes from his face, and his breathing actually speeds up.

*Did the threatening tears actually work?*

He stares at me for a moment, then whispers, "That's the first time you've said my name."

*It is?*

"I'm sure I've said it before."

He shakes his head. "No, you haven't."

I take in his strong reaction to hearing his name and wonder why it matters.

"Renzo," I say it again. "Renzo Torrisi."

His expression grows serious, and his eyes sharpen on me. "That's enough mind games for one night."

Lifting my chin, I say, "I'm not playing mind games." When he walks past me, I hurry to add, "I'm stuck here forever. The least you can do is let me get to know you better."

He stops walking, and standing with his back to me, he asks, "What do you want to know?"

"Anything."

"I'm thirty-five, can't cook to save my life, and love long walks on the beach." Turning around, he gives me a mocking smile. "My favorite color is blue."

Letting out a sigh, I lift my hand and push some hair behind my ear. "You're being impossible."

His expression darkens as he takes a step back toward me. "What do you want to hear, *topolina*? I've killed eighty-seven people. Some quicker than others." He takes another step, and it feels like I'm being hunted. "I smuggle illegal arms and deal with people who would leave you traumatized for life if you ever met them."

Another step brings him almost toe-to-toe with me.

He leans down a little. "And right now, I'm thinking about forcing you to marry me so you can give me the heir

I lost. After all, I'm stuck with you for life. I might as well get something out of it."

*Jesus.*

I'm so rattled the only thing I can say in my defense is, "I have to wait a year before I can have children."

For the second time tonight, he lets out a burst of laughter before saying, "Thanks for the heads-up. I'll make sure to buy condoms when I go to the store again so I don't get you pregnant before the year is up."

Not winning with this man, anger starts to bubble in my chest, making me stupidly brave.

"Good. Make sure you stock up. I haven't had sex in years," I snap.

The man gives me whiplash as his expression turns serious again. "How many years?"

Frowning at him, I mutter, "Seriously?"

"How many fucking years?" he barks.

"Five."

His eyebrow lifts. "Want me to rectify that problem right now?"

*What?*

I move backward until I'm out of his reach. "It's not a problem, and no thanks, I'll pass."

When he comes closer, desire tightens his features, and while I'm stunned by the sudden change in his mood, he lifts his hand to my face. His thumb tugs at my bottom lip as he leans closer, and I find myself holding my breath.

Instead of kissing me, his lips brush along my jaw until he reaches my ear. "Careful, my little mouse. Two can play this game, and I'm much better at it than you."

"I'm not playing a game," I whisper as I bring my hands to his sides.

He pulls back until our eyes meet. "I deal with thieves and murderers on a daily basis. I can smell a lie a mile away."

*Crap.*

The corner of his mouth lifts. "You don't really want to get to know me."

*Damn, he's good.*

I swallow hard because I'm all out of ideas.

*What do I do now?*

He tilts his head, and this time, when he leans forward, his mouth brushes against mine. "But I do want to get to know you."

That means he's definitely attracted to me. I just have to find a way to use it to my advantage.

"What do you want to know?" I ask.

His tone is downright predatory as he whispers, "Everything."

Giving him a taste of his own medicine, I say, "I'm thirty, excellent at cooking, and beach sand makes me itch. My favorite color is green."

A genuine smile spreads over his face, and it leaves me a little breathless because he looks way too freaking hot for me to handle.

"Is ginger your natural color?"

"Yes."

He moves away from me and takes off his jacket. My eyes lock on the gun tucked into the waistband of his pants before he takes a seat on one of the couches. He rests his arm on the back of the couch, then gestures with a jerk of his head for me to take a seat.

Only when I sit down on one of the other couches does he ask, "Have you always wanted to be a chef?"

A smile tugs at my mouth. "Yes. My mom taught me how to cook, and I always found it relaxing."

"Were you planning on working at a restaurant again?"

"Yes. I had a list of four restaurants I was going to visit so they'd know I'm available as a sous chef." Scrunching my nose, I correct myself. "Make that three. The one reminds me too much of you, which is a pity. It was one of my favorites."

He lets out a burst of laughter. "How the fuck do I remind you of a restaurant?"

"La Torrisi," I say.

Again, he laughs, and it makes me smile.

"If you'd walked into my restaurant, I would've given you the job."

"Pity you don't own one," I mutter.

"I do."

Actually feeling relaxed, I ask, "Yeah? Which one?"

His expression turns playful. "Take a wild guess."

The list of restaurants in New York runs through my mind until I stop on one. My lips part, and my eyes widen. "Are you serious? La Torrisi?"

When he nods, I can only shake my head. "I don't believe you." My mind races, then I say, "The manager is Viviana Corso."

"Elio's wife."

Not remembering the name, I ask, "Elio?"

"My right-hand man. You've seen him at the warehouse."

"The one always sitting behind the desk in the office?"

When he nods, I'm still skeptical. There's no way he owns one of the best restaurants in New York.

"You still don't believe me," he murmurs.

"No."

He gets up and grabs the remote from the coffee table. Switching on the TV, he searches for a folder out of the many ones on the screen and clicks on it.

Come to think of it. I've never seen Renzo watch regular TV. He just uses it as if it's an oversized computer screen.

The next moment, there's a livestream of the restaurant on the TV, and my lips part in another gasp.

Renzo takes his phone out of his pocket, and as he dials a number, he says, "Keep your eyes on the screen."

A second later, he says, "Hi, Viviana. I can see you're busy. I just need you to wave at the camera."

I watch as the manager waves, a smile on her face.

"I'll drop by tomorrow," he tells her before ending the call.

*Holy shit.*

I can't stop staring at the screen, and Renzo has to switch off the TV before I turn my attention back to him.

"Your father's house is not the only place I watch. I like to keep an eye on all my businesses."

*Renzo owns La Torrisi.*

I blink at him for a solid minute before I ask, "Why be a criminal if you have such an amazing restaurant?"

"Being a criminal is my birthright. I was born into the Cosa Nostra and took over when my father died."

"Still. Can't you just leave?"

A smirk forms on his face. "The Cosa Nostra is my family, *topolina*. They come first." He waves at the TV. "My other businesses are purely a source of income."

He leans back against the couch again and watches me, the playful expression still on his face.

Today, I've seen a side of this man that's left me speechless.

This mafia boss who kills without blinking an eye and kisses like the devil is also a businessman with a playful side.

And I get the feeling I haven't even scratched the surface. There's a hell of a lot more to learn about him.

# Chapter 28

## Renzo

Leaning my shoulder against the doorjamb with my arms crossed over my chest, I watch Skylar as she sleeps.

The events of yesterday keep replaying in my mind.

Kissing her was not planned, and it only left me wanting more.

Remembering how she melted beneath me and kissed me back with a fuck ton of passion, the corner of my mouth lifts.

*She might not like me, but she sure as fuck is attracted to me.*

Talking with her until late into the night was also not planned, but I enjoyed every second of it.

The act she was putting on to flirt with me fell away, and I got to see her real smile and talk about something she's passionate about.

Does it bother me that she's trying to flirt with me in the hopes that I'll free her?

*Not one bit. It's entertaining.*

But this isn't some Beauty and the Beast fairytale where she'll get to return to her father. She belongs to me.

*Forever.*

Pushing away from the doorjamb, I walk closer to the side of the bed and stare down at the sleeping woman I was never supposed to fall for.

It's only been three weeks, and I no longer have the desire to torture her.

I take in her slightly parted lips, her hands that are tightly fisted beneath her chin, and her body that's curled in a fetal position.

Even while sleeping, she's tense.

When I watched her in her bedroom at the Davies mansion, she used to sleep on her back with her fingers relaxed.

Sitting down on the side of the bed, I bring my hand to her hair, and pull my fingers through the strands.

*They're as soft as they look.*

Letting out a sigh, I whisper, "What am I going to do with you?"

When I mentioned marriage to her last night, I saw the shock on her face. Skylar isn't from my world, and she won't just be a good little girl and say her vows.

*If I threaten her father's life, she will.*

Remembering the attitude she gave me last night makes a smile tug at my lips.

*She has some fight in her, after all.*

As I continue to look at her, I become more and more curious. I want to see what she's like when she's happy.

Leaning over her, I press a kiss to her jaw before saying, "Wake up, *topolina.*"

Her breathing changes, and her eyelashes flutter open. When she sees me sitting next to her, fear flashes over her face, and she quickly sits up.

Her tone is cautious as she asks, "What? Why did you wake me?"

"Get dressed," I say as I get up. "We're leaving in fifteen minutes."

"It's still dark. What's the time?"

"Four am."

Walking to the door, I say, "If you want a chance to cook at La Torrisi, be downstairs in fifteen."

As I leave the room, I hear her footsteps hurrying in the direction of the bathroom.

Letting out a chuckle, I head to the kitchen to pour myself a cup of coffee. I only get to drink half of it before

Skylar comes into the kitchen. Her hair's tied back in a ponytail, and she's wearing a black and white dress.

I hand her my cup. "Drink some."

She doesn't hesitate and takes a couple of sips before handing it back to me.

When her eyes connect with mine, a smile spreads over her face. "Are you really going to let me cook in your kitchen?"

"The kitchen belongs to Chef Alain," I say. "But he won't be in until eleven, so you'll have plenty of time to make breakfast for me."

Her smile widens even more, and I find myself staring at her with wonder.

"Prepare to have the best breakfast you've ever tasted," she says, excitement coming off her in waves.

I drink the last of the coffee before putting the cup in the sink. When I walk toward the elevator, Skylar's right behind me.

Once we're in the elevator, I turn my head and stare at her. There's no tension on her face, and she seems genuinely excited.

The doors slide open, and stepping out, I walk toward the Bentley. I didn't bother calling Vincenzo and Fabrizio, leaving my men to get a good night's sleep.

"No guards?" Skylar asks when I open the passenger door for her.

"No. It's just us." I don't elaborate why.

She climbs inside, and while she tugs on the safety belt, I shut the door and walk around the front of the car.

Sliding behind the steering wheel, I adjust the seat before starting the engine.

When I pull out of the basement and steer the Bentley onto the quiet streets, I feel Skylar stealing glances at me.

"Sooo, last night was nice," she murmurs. "We should do that again."

Letting out a sigh, I mutter, "I'll make you deal. Just for today, I won't be an asshole, and you'll drop the act."

"What act?"

"The one where you think flirting with me will make me care enough to let you go." My eyes flick to hers. "I'm not that kind of man. If you make me love you, there's no fucking way I'll let you go. You're fighting a losing battle."

"Are you saying there's a chance you might fall in love with me?"

My hand grips the steering wheel tighter as I clench my jaw while growling, "Don't make me regret bringing you along to La Torrisi."

She drops the subject instantly and turns her attention to the window.

"I just want one day where we're not kidnapper and captive. Just one fucking day where I can be myself around you, and you can show me what you're like when you're actually happy," I admit.

Her tone is soft as she whispers, "Okay." I hear her taking a deep breath, then she adds, "It will be a nice change of pace."

I park the Bentley in my designated spot, and getting out, my eyes scan our surroundings for any threats.

Skylar climbs out of the car before I reach the passenger's side. She follows me to the back door that's used for deliveries and staff.

I search for the right key, and unlocking the door, I walk inside and flick on the lights as we move through the hallway and past my office.

When we reach the kitchen, I glance at Skylar. Her lips are parted with a look of awe as she slowly moves forward.

"Holy crap, you really own La Torrisi," she murmurs as she trails her hand along one of the counters. "This is surreal."

I walk to the freezer, and opening it, I say, "You'll find everything in here." Noticing stacks of fish, I mutter, "The fucker once again ordered trout. I'm going to kill him."

Skylar comes to stand next to me and peeks inside. "Does Chef Alain love using trout in his dishes?"

"Yes, but it's not the most popular dish on the menu. Last time he fucked up, more than half went into the trash."

Her eyes flit to me, a flash of worry on her face. "Are you really going to kill him?"

Letting out a chuckle, I shake my head. "That would draw attention to me, but at this rate, I'm going to fire his ass."

"And kidnapping me doesn't draw attention to you?" she asks as she moves deeper into the freezer.

"You weren't connected to me when I took you," I explain.

"Right." Her eyes meet mine. "What do you want for breakfast?"

"Whatever you feel like making," I say as I pull my phone from my pocket. "Just not trout. I'll be in my office if you need me." Walking away, I call out, "Don't burn down the kitchen."

I hear her chuckle as I dial Elio's number while heading to my office.

256

"Yes, boss?" his sleepy voice comes over the line.

"I'm taking the day off. Make sure everyone reports to you, and don't call me unless you find Servando Montes."

"Okay. You going to get some rest?"

"Something like that," I mutter before ending the call.

Taking a seat at my desk, I switch on the computer so I can get all the work out of the way.

It only takes me fifteen minutes to check everything because Viviana does a good job of running the restaurant.

When I head back to the kitchen, I pause by the arch leading from the hallway to the workspace and stare at Skylar.

She's busy frying something that looks like a vegetable pancake.

When I move closer, her eyes dart to me before returning to the pan as she flips the pancake without any effort.

"I'm making Asian food," she informs me. "Korean pancakes, egg fried rice, and grilled mackerel."

"I'm looking forward to it, Chef."

Her eyes dart to me again, and I see the surprise in them because I called her chef. It's followed closely by a confused expression before she focuses on the hot pan again.

257

"What was the confused look for?" I ask as I lean against one of the counters and cross my arms over my chest.

"It was just weird when you called me chef," she replies. "You almost sounded like a normal person."

She slides the pancake onto a plate, and using a pizza cutter, she slices it into triangles.

"It's difficult to process you're the owner of La Torrisi and a ruthless mafia boss." She holds a tray out to me and says, "I've taken the liberty of setting one of the tables."

Skylar grabs another tray with the rice and mackerel, and I follow her to the table.

When we take our seats, I notice she's placed chopsticks on the table. She picks up her pair, and as if she's used them a million times, she places a slice of the pancake and some of the meat from the mackerel on my plate.

We each have our own bowl of fried egg rice, and she smiles as she says, "I hope you enjoy the meal, Mr. Torrisi."

It almost feels like an interview.

"Why is it difficult to accept I own this restaurant while being a part of the Cosa Nostra?" I ask to bring us back to our earlier conversation.

She picks up her glass of water and takes a sip before she answers, "This restaurant is a place where masterpieces are created."

"And?" I take a bite of the pancake, loving the texture and flavor.

Her eyes meet mine. "Last week, I saw the body of a man you disemboweled with your bare hands."

I stare at her as I suck in a deep breath of air.

It wasn't my intention for her to see Castellanos.

"How do you straddle the light and dark? How can you create a place like this," she waves over the tables, "and at the same time, you kill without blinking?"

"Easy," I murmur. "Just because I don't hesitate to kill anyone who crosses me doesn't mean I can't enjoy the beautiful things in life." I keep her gaze imprisoned as I continue, "You've seen the worst of me. I lost my brother, the person who I loved more than anything. You're seeing the pain, the rage, the fucking relentless thirst for vengeance."

The air vibrates with my sorrow, and I take a couple of breaths in an attempt to calm down before I say, "Giulio was full of life. He always had an infectious smile on his face. Everyone loved him."

I close my eyes as a wave of pain washes over me. It's not as intense anymore, but it still packs a punch.

*Christ. I miss him.*

When I open my eyes again, it's to see Skylar's chin trembling.

My voice is hoarse when I say, "I loved him so fucking much, and every day without him is hell."

A tear spirals down her cheek, and as she wipes it away, she whispers, "I'm so sorry for your loss."

Reaching for my glass of water, I take a few sips while gathering my thoughts.

"I'm actually the calm and funny one between my friends." My eyes meet hers. "That's why I was so close with Giulio." I glance at the empty tables, the food forgotten between us. "A week before Giulio's murder, I told him I was going to train him to take over when I retired. I've never seen him work so hard. Up until then, he gave me shit because he wanted to become one of my guards, and I wouldn't let him."

*Talking about him isn't as hard as I thought it would be.*

My gaze flicks back to Skylar's when she wipes another tear from her cheek.

"Why are you crying?" I ask with zero harshness in my tone.

She sucks in a trembling breath before she answers, "Because I feel so freaking bad that he was killed because of me."

"Giulio," I murmur. "You've never said his name."

She lifts her chin, and looking me in the eye, she says, "I feel horrible for being the reason Giulio's dead. If I could, I'd swap places with him in a heartbeat."

I let out a humorless chuckle. "The fucked up part is he wouldn't have wanted that. He had a soft heart and probably would've donated his kidney if he had known he could help."

Skylar covers her face with her hands as a sob escapes her.

With all the raw pain out on the table between us, I stare at her as she cries for my brother.

*Giulio would've loved her.*

He would've comforted her and said something funny to make her laugh.

Climbing to my feet, I move around the table. I take hold of Skylar's arm, and pulling her up, I wrap her in a tight embrace against my chest.

"I'm s-so sorry, Renzo," she cries.

*Yeah, so am I, my little mouse.*

*So am I.*

# Chapter 29

## Skylar

Renzo's not supposed to be the one comforting me. It should be the other way around.

I wrap my arms tightly around his waist, wishing I could take away his pain.

His grief is something I've never considered, but after seeing how much losing Giulio's hurt him, I can't ignore it.

Renzo's human, after all. He's capable of loving someone so much that losing them turns him into a monster.

For the first time since he kidnapped me, I put myself in his shoes. If someone had killed Mom or Dad to steal one of their kidneys so a stranger could live, I'd be angry.

*I'd be inconsolable.*

Pulling my arms back, I move them up, and wrapping them around Renzo's neck, I hold him to me as I admit, "I wish I could take away your pain."

When he turns his head, and his lips brush over my jaw, I don't pull away. Not because I'm playing some game, but because I really want to comfort him.

Right now, he's not my kidnapper, and I'm not his captive.

He pulls slightly back, and his eyes lock with mine. There's no brutality or anger. All I see is a man who's in indescribable pain.

Bringing my hands to the sides of his jaw, I push myself up on my toes and press my mouth to his. My lips taste his, and when my tongue brushes over his bottom lip, his arms tighten around me and he takes over.

Just like yesterday, the kiss goes from zero to a hundred real fast, and Renzo all but devours me.

His kiss is forceful and hungry, his lips and teeth branding mine.

When a moan drifts from me, Renzo suddenly breaks the kiss. I'm lifted from my feet and sat down on the nearest empty table. He shoves my legs open, and moving between them, his palms grip the sides of my face before his mouth comes down on mine again.

The man kisses me like the devil attempting to possess my soul. I can't hold back or stop myself from being swept up by him.

His hands move down my body, and I lose his mouth as he breaks away so he can pepper kisses down the side of my neck.

*Damn, it feels good.*

It's been so long since I've had a man kiss me. His mouth feels heavenly on my skin.

He keeps moving down, and when his teeth tug at my hard nipple beneath the fabric of my bra and dress, I let out a needy moan.

Renzo pulls away again, and I watch as he grabs a chair, the legs scraping on the floor, before he positions it in front of me.

He sits down on the chair, and when his hands settle on my knees, pushing them wider apart, I have a fleeting thought that I should put a stop to this.

His eyes burn on my face as he pushes my dress up, then he takes hold of my panties and tugs them down my legs.

"Hold onto the table, *mia topolina*," he warns before he moves forward, and his face disappears between my thighs.

*Oh God.*

He spreads me with two fingers, and when his tongue swipes over my clit, I lie back while grabbing the sides of the table.

He begins to feast on me as if I'm all that stands between him and starvation.

*Oh. My. God.*

My hips swivel, and it has Renzo sucking my clit into oblivion, making an orgasm hit me out of left field. My back arches as whimpers spill over my lips and lights explode behind my eyelids from the intense pleasure seizing me.

My heart races wildly, and my breaths are nothing but quick bursts over my lips.

When my clit becomes sensitive, my body jerks, but Renzo doesn't stop, and instead, he increases the potency he's eating me out with.

"Crap," I gasp. "Too sensitive."

He pushes a finger inside me, and flicking his tongue over the bundle of nerves, he forces another orgasm to crash through me.

"Oh God," I cry, my body wound tight as the ecstasy hits hard.

Rising to his feet, he massages my pussy with his palm, a satisfied expression on his face. He leans over me, and wrapping his other hand around the back of my neck, he tugs me up from the table.

His mouth meets mine in a fierce kiss, and tasting my arousal on his lips feels downright sinful.

When the last of my pleasure ebbs away, his hand stills between my legs, and he ends the kiss. Opening my eyes, I'm face-to-face with Renzo, the green ring around his irises darker than ever.

"Just one taste," he growls.

*That was way more than just a taste.*

"That's all it took." His expression turns grim as he pulls his hand from between my legs, then he says, "Careful, *mia topolina*, you're making me fall in love with you."

*'If you make me love you, there's no fucking way I'll let you go.'*

Remembering his warning from earlier, my heartbeat speeds up again.

I can't think of anything to say, and the moment he takes a step backward, I slip off the table and grab my panties from the floor. Rushing to the restroom, I close myself in one of the stalls, and quickly pull on my underwear.

The realization of what just happened pours like scalding lava through me.

"Shit," I whisper as I untie my hair and push my fingers through the strands.

*Why did I let it happen? Why didn't I stop him?*

My breathing speeds up and embarrassment fills my chest.

How the hell am I going to look at Renzo again? It's not like I have feelings for him. Even though we shared a moment, he's still my enemy.

He's still the man who's put me and Dad through hell.

*Shit, I screwed up badly.*

When the initial shock passes, I open the door and walk to the basin where I splash some water onto my face.

While I'm patting my skin dry with a paper towel, Renzo comes into the restroom. I look at every inch of the counter so I don't have to meet his eyes.

"The staff are coming in soon, *mia topolina.* We should leave."

My voice is filled with embarrassment as I reply, "I'll be right out."

Instead of leaving, he stalks to me, and taking hold of my chin, he forces me to look at him.

His features are cut from stone as he says, "Don't you dare make this awkward. I made you come, and you loved it. Own it."

*Jesus.*

My neck goes up in flames, and cursed just like every other ginger out there, I blush hard.

Suddenly, he lets out a chuckle. "You're cute when you blush." Pulling me against his chest, he places a hand behind my head. "Don't make a big deal about it. Okay?"

The embrace feels different from the others. He holds me tenderly, his body not tense at all.

He lets go of me a moment later, only to take my hand and weave our fingers together. I'm pulled out of the restroom and toward the back of the restaurant.

We didn't even eat the food I made, and we didn't clear the table.

*None of that matters! You let your kidnapper go down on you.*

As we leave the building and walk to the Bentley, I refuse to think about how amazing the two orgasms were.

I don't think about how his kisses drugged me.

And I definitely don't inspect my emotions, fearing what I'll find.

Renzo's a brutal and unforgiving man. He's my kidnapper and nothing more.

# Chapter 30

## Renzo

Since I fucked up at the restaurant two days ago, things have been strained between Skylar and me.

Her walls are back up, and she only speaks when I demand a response from her.

In my defense, she could've stopped me, but she didn't.

I'm at the warehouse because I figured Skylar could do with some alone time.

Elio's taking a nap on the couch while I check that all the shipments are on schedule.

It's been a while since I heard from Dario, and pulling my phone from my pocket, I dial his number.

"Hey, brother," he answers, "you still alive?"

"Why wouldn't I be?"

"I figured you and Skylar would've killed each other by now," he chuckles.

"We had a close call, but we're both still breathing," I say, a smile curving my lips.

"What's up?" he asks.

"I'm just checking in with you. You've been quiet."

He lets out a sigh. "I figured you didn't need me around making things harder for you, so I'm in Spain busy tracking Montes."

"You left without telling any of us?" I ask, surprised to hear he's halfway across the world.

"I told Damiano. The rest of you are a little preoccupied lately."

"Sorry, brother," I say while relaxing back in the chair. "No matter how busy I am, I always have time for you."

"I know." I hear him move, and the wind whistles over the line. "How are things with Skylar? You haven't changed your mind about keeping her captive?"

"No, I haven't," I reply, and knowing it will make Dario stop worrying about her, I admit, "I've actually grown fond of the woman. She's not so bad once you get to know her."

"What?" he gasps. There's a few seconds of silence, then he asks, "Are you fucking with me?"

"Not at all. Franco planted the damn seed, suggesting I should marry her so she can give me an heir. Since then, I started seeing her in a different light."

"And how does Skylar feel about all of this?"

"I'm not sure," I answer honestly. "We're getting to know each other, but she's got a ten-foot wall around her emotions."

"I don't blame her. You've put the woman through all kinds of hell."

Glancing up at the ceiling, I let out a sigh. "I know."

"Want my advice?"

"Sure, why not?" I mutter, already knowing I'm not going to like it.

"Let her go. She won't give you a snowball's chance in hell unless you let her go free."

"Not happening," I mutter.

"Good luck winning her over then," Dario says. "I have to go. I'll be in touch if I find Montes."

"Okay. Be careful."

Ending the call, I suck in a deep breath before letting it out slowly.

I'm dead sure if I let Skylar go, I'll never see her again. She might be attracted to me, but it doesn't mean shit. In her eyes, I'm the villain.

I have to somehow change her opinion of me. I have to make her see I'm not just a killer and capo.

*Fuck knows how I'm going to do that.*

# Skylar

Sitting on the couch with my arms crossed over my chest, I watch the livestream from my house.

Dad's in the kitchen with Louisa, and they're eating a meatloaf she threw together.

*If I ever get out of here, I'm teaching Louisa how to cook.*

"The food's good. Thanks, Louisa," Dad murmurs before he shovels a bite into his mouth.

*At least he's eating.*

He looks much better since we got to see each other.

"It's not Skylar's cooking, but it will have to do," Louisa replies while she loads dishes into the dishwasher. "Do you think she's watching right now?"

"I don't know." Dad glances around the kitchen, everywhere but in the direction of the camera.

"I'm here, Daddy," I whisper.

"We miss you, Skylar," Louisa says, assuming I can hear her. "The house is quiet without you, and I might poison your father before you get back."

I let out a chuckle, a smile spreading over my face.

"Hopefully, we'll see each other again soon," Dad says.

*I hope so, too.*

Maybe I can ask Renzo? Things aren't as bad as they used to be, and he might let me see Dad once or twice a week.

They stop talking to me, and while Dad continues to eat, Louisa wipes down the counters.

Watching them, my thoughts turn to my problem.

While Renzo's out, probably killing someone, I'm trying to figure out what I'm going to do.

Honestly, I'm pissed off with myself. I initiated the kiss, and I didn't stop him when he took things further.

Nope, I laid back and enjoyed the orgasms.

He didn't even get off.

I screwed up, and now I don't know what to do. I feel like shit for leading him on.

I just wanted to make him care enough to let me go. The last thing I want is for him to fall in love with me and get hurt.

*Yeah, let's ignore your emotions because this is all one-sided from Renzo, right?*

I try to shove the thought away, not wanting to inspect my feelings because they don't matter. I'm not going to be that insane captive who falls for her kidnapper.

I hear the elevator doors open, and when I get up so I can go to my room, Renzo snaps, "Sit your ass down."

I do as he says and keep my eyes on the TV screen.

When I hear him go up the stairs, my gaze darts to his back, and I watch him until he disappears down the hallway.

There's an unwelcome emotion in my chest, a mixture of strong attraction and sadness, and once again, I ignore it with all my might.

"Who could that be?" I hear Dad say from the livestream, drawing my attention back to the TV.

I watch as he leaves the kitchen and pops up on the other camera with a view of the foyer.

He opens the door, and I don't recognize the men.

"Can I help?" Dad asks.

"Yes." One of the men pushes his way into the foyer, and glancing around, he asks, "Are you alone?"

"Hey, you can't just barge into my house," Dad snaps.

The man signals with his hand, and two other men head toward the kitchen.

*What the hell is happening?*

275

When the man suddenly punches Dad, I jump off the couch and scream, "Renzo!"

"We're here because you can't keep your mouth shut," the man sneers.

"What?" Dad gasps.

Louisa's dragged into the foyer by the other men, and a fourth one blocks the front door.

My hand flies up to cover my mouth, and when Renzo comes flying down the stairs, I point at the TV. "They're at my house! The men you're looking for are hurting my dad!"

His eyes flick to the screen while he pulls his phone out to call someone.

I cover my mouth again when I see the man hitting Dad repeatedly.

*God. No!*

"Elio, take a group of men and get your asses to the Davies mansion. The fuckers from The Harvest are going to kill Harlan and get away. Move!" Renzo orders.

When the man climbs off Dad, I suck in a relieved breath, but then he pulls a gun from behind his back, and my legs go numb.

"No!" I cry as he points the barrel at Louisa.

"You and that fucking doctor couldn't keep your mouths shut, and now Renzo Torrisi and Dario La Rosa are fucking searching the city for us," the man says, his tone threatening and dark. "Where's the doctor?"

"Dead," Dad answers, his voice shaky. "Renzo already killed him."

"This is what happens when you fucking talk," the man says, the gun still trained on Louisa.

"Wait! Wait!" Dad shouts.

Renzo grabs me, and as a blast comes from the TV, he squashes my face against his chest.

*No.*

"Jesus fucking Christ," Renzo growls right before he lets go of me and grabs my hand.

I'm yanked toward the elevator and when he presses the button for the doors to open, I glance over my shoulder. I see Louisa lying on the floor with a pool of blood forming around her head while the one with the gun stands in front of Dad.

"I love you, Skylar," Dad shouts. "It's been an honor to be your father. I'm so proud of you, sweetheart."

"Renzo," I shriek, my face crumbling as tears start to stream down my cheeks.

"Don't look," Renzo snaps as he turns to me.

There's another gunshot, and I see the bullet hit Dad in his chest, and then I'm staring at Renzo's dark blue vest and white dress shirt.

I just watched Louisa and Dad being killed.

*They're dead.*

*No.*

*NoNoNoNoNo.*

My breathing hitches repeatedly, no air making it past my throat.

"Fuck, Skylar!"

I'm forced into the elevator, and Renzo's hands frame my face, forcing me to look at him. "Breathe, *mia topolina*. Come on, breathe."

I can only shake my head as the horrifying images of Dad and Louisa being killed keep replaying in my mind.

Renzo's expression turns to the brutal one that always puts the fear of God in me, then he growls, "Breathe!"

I jerk as I suck in air, and then the trauma of what I just saw hits me so hard, it rips a scream from me.

I'm pulled to his chest again, and the next moment, I hear him say, "Elio, I'm on my way. Have the men spread out around the neighborhood and surrounding areas. I want them fucking caught."

The elevator doors open, and I'm pulled out, agonizing sobs shuddering from me.

"The fuckers killed Harlan," Renzo informs Vincenzo and Fabrizio.

I'm ushered into the car, and when Renzo slides in beside me, I get a glimpse of his phone. He has the livestream footage paused on the man who killed Dad and Louisa. He takes a screenshot, then opens a different app where he pastes the photo.

When he makes another call, the trauma pours into me until it feels like it's suffocating me.

"I just sent you a photo. I want a name."

After the call ends, his fingers take hold of my chin, and my face is turned toward him.

"Fuck, *amo*," he whispers while pulling me against his side. His arms wrap around me, and with his mouth by my hair, he says, "I never wanted this. I'm so fucking sorry."

The same men who killed Giulio just murdered Dad and Louisa in cold blood.

As the unbearable sorrow rips through me, I realize how Renzo must've felt.

I realize why he's been so ruthless in his pursuit of finding those who played a part in his brother's death.

The same destructive rage and pain that fueled his thirst for vengeance creeps into every part of my soul.

"They killed them," I whisper, my voice hoarse.

"I'll find them, *amo*. I'll fucking hunt down every last one of them."

I never thought I'd condone violence. Less than thirty minutes ago, I was entirely against everything Renzo stood for.

*But now…*

"Please," I whimper as I burrow closer to him, then sobs shudder through me again. "It h-hurts so m-much, Renzo."

"I've got you, *amo*," he murmurs before pressing a kiss to the side of my head. "Just let it out."

Shaking my head, I can't break down. Everything is still too raw, and the shock has a merciless hold on my mind.

There's nothing I can do but feel as my heart shatters.

# Chapter 31

## Renzo

Vincenzo checks with Elio to make sure it's safe before he gives Fabrizio the go-ahead to steer the car up the driveway of the Davies mansion.

"Stay in the car, Skylar," I order.

She shakes her head slowly as if she's stuck in a trance.

*I know that feeling well.*

"I don't want you to see the bodies. It will make it much worse," I explain.

Again, she shakes her head, then she whispers, "It's my choice."

*It is.*

I open the door, and keeping a tight grip on her hand, I get out of the car. Seeing Elio as he comes out of the mansion, I walk toward him.

"Any sign of the fuckers?" I ask.

"Two were stopped just down the street. They've already been taken to the warehouse."

"Good. Have the men continue searching for the other two," I order.

Elio nods as his eyes move between me and Skylar. "The bodies are still inside. We haven't moved them."

Nodding, I say, "Keep everyone out of the house until I give the clear."

I suck in a fortifying breath as I lead Skylar up the porch steps. When we walk into the foyer, she starts to shake her head wildly and pulls her hand free from mine.

I look at Harlan, where he lies in a pool of blood with a gunshot wound to his chest.

"Daddy," Skylar whimpers as she slowly moves closer to his body.

She drops to his side, not caring about the blood, and the sight takes a swing at my heart.

Her lips part with a silent cry as she frames his jaw with trembling hands.

*Christ.*

She sucks in a harsh breath, then screams, "Daddy!"

Unable to just stand still and watch her break, I move forward, and sinking to my knees behind her, I wrap my arms around her.

The cries tearing from her break my fucking heart, and all I can do is hold her.

Where I once wanted her to feel the same pain as me, I'd now do anything to be able to take it from her.

Skylar turns in my arms, and gripping hold of me, she falls apart.

Her sorrow fills the air and finds an echo in my chest.

My voice is hoarse as I promise, "I'll find every last one of them."

*I need to be stronger than ever now. This isn't just about my pain and thirst for revenge any longer.*

Moving my arms beneath her back and knees, I hold her bridal style as I climb to my feet. I carry her up the stairs to her old bedroom and into the bathroom. Setting her down on the counter, I reach for a facecloth and wet it beneath the cold water tap.

I start to clean her father's blood from her legs, and when I'm sure I didn't miss a single drop, I toss the facecloth in the tub.

Placing my hands on either side of her neck, I say, "Look at me."

She lifts her eyes to mine, and I see all her pain.

They might not be the words she wants to hear right now, but I need to say them. "You have me, Skylar."

A sob sputters from her, and she lifts her arms, wrapping them around my neck. When I hold her to me, she breaks down again.

I brush my hand repeatedly over her hair, wishing there was a way to stop her pain.

But there isn't.

"You have me, *amo*."

It's only then I realize what I'm calling her. *Love.* It came so naturally I didn't even notice.

In Skylar's darkest moment, I realize I've fallen for her.

Hopelessly, irrevocably, madly in fucking love.

I hold her tighter and press another kiss to her hair while she struggles to regain control over her emotions.

"I n-now understand why you w-wanted everyone involved with G-Giulio's death dead," she whispers. "I understand b-because it h-hurts so much."

Lifting Skylar bridal style to my chest again, I carry her out of her old bedroom so we can get out of the fucking mansion.

When I reach the stairs, I whisper, "Don't look, *amo*."

She buries her face against my neck as I carry her past the bodies, and when we leave the mansion, I head toward Elio.

"Call our guy to take care of the bodies. Let me know when everything's ready for the funerals."

"On it, boss," he replies.

"Give me an hour, and I'll meet you at the warehouse. I just want to take Skylar home."

"No," she says as she lifts her head. "I'm going with you."

I glance at her, and when I see the rage starting to burn in her eyes, I say, "Okay."

I set her down on her feet, then look at my right-hand man again. "I'll see you at the warehouse."

Elio nods before he walks back to the front door while pulling his phone out of his pocket to make the call to the coroner.

Placing my hand on Skylar's lower back, I nudge her to walk toward the Bentley.

When we climb inside, Vincenzo and Fabrizio join us.

"We're sorry for your loss, Skylar," Vincenzo says as he glances over his shoulder at her.

Keeping her head bowed, she only nods.

"Where to, boss?" Fabrizio asks.

"The warehouse."

He starts the engine, and when he steers the car off the property, I dig my phone out of my pocket, and dial Dario's number again.

"Third call today," he answers. "Admit it, you can't live without me."

"Yeah-yeah," I mutter. "The fuckers took out Harlan Davies."

"Fuck. How's Skylar doing?"

"Not well. Did you look at the photos I sent you?"

"Yeah. I've managed to identify one out of the four. Enrique Valverde. He actually flew in from the UK two days ago under a different name. I'm still running the facial recognition for the others. Oh, hold on, I just got a hit."

I wait as Dario checks the information, and a minute later, he comes back, "The one who stood by the door is Alberto Gonzalez. By the way, both these men are wanted by Interpol, so I'm assuming they're high on the totem pole."

*Christ, I hope they were the ones taken to the warehouse.*

"Thanks, brother. I owe you," I say as I glance at Skylar, who's still sitting with her head bowed and her eyes closed.

"Don't worry. I'll send you the bill once I'm back tomorrow."

I'm relieved to hear he's coming home. "Call me when you land in New York."

"Will do. Tell Skylar I'm sorry for her loss."

"I will."

We end the call, and putting my phone away, I take hold of her hand. "Dario said to give his condolences."

She lifts her head and looks at me, her eyes dull as if all life has been drained from them. "Did he find out anything?"

I nod. "He managed to identify two of the men."

"Good," she whispers, then she leans her head against my shoulder. "I hope you find them all and make them suffer."

"I will," I promise.

———

When Fabrizio brings the car to a stop in front of the warehouse, we get out, and taking Skylar's hand, I weave our fingers together as we head inside.

When I spot Antonio, I signal for him to come to me. He jogs across the open stretch of concrete floor, then says, "Yes, boss?"

"Have Bianca come here. She needs to bring something to help Skylar deal with shock."

"I'll be fine," Skylar mutters.

Ignoring Skylar, I add, "I also want Bianca to do a full checkup."

"Okay, boss."

When we continue to walk, I glance at Skylar. "You're not fine, and I want you checked out. If your body rejects the kidney because of this, I'll fucking burn the world down. Think of having the checkup as you saving mankind from extinction."

An emotion I can't place flits over her face, and when we head up the steps, she pulls her hand free from mine.

The moment we reach the landing at the top, she breaks out into a run.

Skylar checks the first room before running to the second one, where she stops in the doorway.

As I come up behind her, I hear one of the men chuckle, "Hey, pretty mamma."

His words are followed by a grunt, then Skylar walks right up to him and punches the fucker.

"Oww!" she hisses as she cradles her hand against her stomach.

I move forward and pull her away from the men Carlo and Emilio have kneeling on the floor.

I check her hand, and seeing her red knuckles, I mutter, "Leave the torturing to me, *amo*. I don't want you touching the scum."

"Make them suffer," she whispers, the words burning with her anger.

I shrug off my jacket and hand it to her. "Stand back."

When Skylar moves to stand near the door, I turn my attention to the kneeling men. A smile spreads over my face when I see Enrique Valverde is one of the men.

His eyes are glued to me, and I see the fear he's trying to hide.

Walking closer, I crouch in front of him, and tilting my head, I stare him dead in the eyes.

"We didn't know the man was your brother. I would've stopped it. We're not looking for trouble with the Cosa Nostra," he says, an authoritative tone to his voice.

"Then you shouldn't have set foot in our city," I murmur. "That was your first mistake."

Rising to my feet, I look at the other man. He glances at Enrique as if the man can help him.

"What's your name?" I demand.

"Miguel," he whispers.

"He's just a soldier," Enrique informs me.

Taking my gun from behind my back, where it's tucked into my waistband, I move closer to Miguel and press the barrel hard against his forehead.

"Where's Servando Montes?"

Miguel's eyes fill with tears as he says, "I don't know."

Seeing the truth on his face, I pull the trigger, giving the man a merciful death. Soldiers do as they're told, and his crime was working for the wrong organization.

"Move him to the side," I order.

Emilio grabs Miguel beneath his shoulders and drags him to the back of the room so the body's out of my way.

"If I tell you where Servando is, will you promise to give me safe passage to India?"

"Why India?"

"The country's big enough for me to disappear."

"Okay. Tell me, and I'll make sure you get to India in one piece."

"Renzo!" Skylar gasps.

When I hear her move closer, I glance over my shoulder and snap, "Stay back!"

She freezes in her tracks, her eyes filling with tears and a look of betrayal on her face.

While I tuck my gun back into the waistband of my pants, I turn my attention back to Enrique. "Where is Servando?"

"He moves between Spain, Peru, and Alaska under the alias Gilberto Varela. He just left Spain and should already be in Peru. He only stays two weeks in one place before moving to the next."

Dario was actually right behind Servando. Sometimes, my friend manages to amaze me with his skills.

Holding out my hand, I only wait a couple of seconds before Emilio places a knife in my palm.

Enrique's eyes go wide as saucers, "We had a deal!"

The corner of my mouth lifts in a smirk. "Yes. I agreed to make sure you get to India in one piece. I didn't say whether you'd be dead or alive."

"No! I told you where Servando is."

"I appreciate the information," I mutter before I order, "Strip him down to his underwear."

"No!" He shouts, struggling against Carlo and Emilio as they rip his clothes off his body.

When they have him kneeling again, I say, "Not only did you gut my brother open like a bag of meat, but you once a-fucking-gain pissed me off by going after my woman's father."

Enrique shakes his head wildly, fear trembling in his eyes.

I move fast and slam the fucker down onto his back while pressing my knee hard into his groin.

"She had to watch as you killed him," I hiss as I hold the knife ready over his stomach. "And I had to watch as she fucking broke."

I slam the knife into his gut, ripping an agonizing wail from him.

"I want you to see what I saw when I found my brother," I growl as I hack the knife through his skin, all the way to his pubic hair. His screams fill the air until they become incoherent whimpers, his body shuddering from the pain.

Just like I did with Castellanos, I shove my hand into his open gut, and gripping whatever I feel first, I rip it out of him, making sure he's able to see his own intestines and organs as he goes into shock before dying.

Rising to my feet, I drop the already lukewarm intestines and shake the blood off my hand.

"Put everything back, close him up, and ship him to India," I order before I turn around.

My eyes land on Skylar, who has a strange look on her pale face. It's a mixture of disgust, horror, and relief.

Walking closer to her, I hold my clean hand out to her.

She stares at it for a moment, then surprises the fuck out of me by coming to take hold of my bloody hand. Lifting her head, her eyes are still dull when they meet mine.

Weaving our fingers together, I pull her out of the room and head down to the restroom so I can wash the blood off our hands.

I don't think Skylar fully understands what she just did.

By taking my bloody hand, she stepped into my world and left her own behind.

# Chapter 32

## Skylar

After Bianca gave me a complete checkup, assured Renzo I was physically okay, and reminded us of my biopsy next week, he brought us home.

Somehow, I managed to take a shower and put on a clean dress before heading down to the kitchen.

I remove all the vegetables from the fridge and pantry and set them down on the island. I pull all the plastic containers from the cupboard and set them down in a neat row.

Grabbing a cutting board and chopping knife, I start with the spring onions, chopping them fine before placing them in a container.

I pull the pack of carrots closer and get started on slicing them.

The nightmarish day replays on a constant loop in my mind.

I see Louisa and Dad being shot...their bodies at the mansion.

Watching Renzo kill two of the men...how he disemboweled Enrique.

Even though it was sickening, it also gave me some sense of relief. I should feel bad, but I don't.

*I feel nothing.*

"What are you doing?" Renzo suddenly asks.

"Prepping," I murmur, my tone emotionless.

He comes to pull the knife from my hand, and taking hold of my shoulders, he turns me so I'll face him.

Leaning down, he catches my eyes and stares at me for a moment before he pulls me into a hug.

"I know it's tough right now, but it will get better," he murmurs as he brushes his hand over my hair.

"Will it? Really?" I whisper. "Because it doesn't look like it's gotten any better for you."

"The pain lessens. It's not as bad as the first week after Giulio's death."

I shake my head, not believing him. I saw his raw heartache at the restaurant. He's lying to make me feel better.

"Once the bodies are ready to be buried, I'll help you with the funeral arrangements," he says.

"The funerals. Plural," I correct him. "I have to bury Louisa and my dad." My breathing hitches, and destructive emotions return with a force that knocks me off my feet.

I sway in Renzo's hold before my legs go numb. His arms tighten around me, and a second later, I'm airborne as he picks me up.

My breathing hitches in my throat as painful sobs shudder from me.

Renzo sits down on one of the couches and cradles me like a baby while he presses kisses to my forehead and hair.

*'Honey, I want you to meet someone very special,'* Mom says.

*I watch as a man comes to crouch in front of me, a kind smile on his face.*

*'Hi, Skylar. My name is Harlan Davies. I'm a friend of your mommy's.'*

I bury my face against Renzo's neck and cry my heart out as the memories start to bombard me.

*'Where could she be?' I hear Uncle Harlan call out.*

*Hiding behind the curtains, I let out a chuckle. Suddenly, the curtain's swept out of the way, and he lifts me into the air.*

*'Gotcha!' He gives me a hug, then taps his cheek. 'Where's my prize for finding you.'*

*I plant a wet kiss on his stubble, then wipe my mouth with the back of my hand.*

"Renzo," I groan, the pain too much for me to handle.

Wrapping his hand around the back of my neck, he pulls me away from his neck until our eyes meet.

"Tell me what to do, *amo*," he says, his tone hoarse. "How can I help you get through this?"

*I don't know.*

I grip the fabric over my heart as I struggle through the sobs, and Renzo squashes me against his chest again, rubbing his hand up and down my back.

"T-They killed my d-d-dad," I cry through broken sobs.

"I'm so fucking sorry," he whispers. "I'm here, *amo*. You're not alone."

"I am!" The words sound devastating to my ears. "I have n-no one l-left."

"You have me," Renzo assures me.

"You're my k-kidnapper," I argue.

"No. We both know that's no longer the case." He presses another kiss to the side of my head. "That ship sailed at the restaurant."

Somehow, his words manage to calm me down enough that I'm able to stop crying. I rest my head against his shoulder and suck in deep breaths as the storm inside me quiets until everything feels empty again.

"When I say you have me, I mean it, Skylar," Renzo murmurs. "No more kidnapper and captive bullshit."

"Will you let me go?" I whisper.

"Where? Back to the mansion?" He lets out a sigh. "No, it's too dangerous. You're staying with me so I can protect you."

I let out a hollow chuckle. "I've gone from captive to roommate. I guess I should count my blessings."

"Fuck no, you're not my roommate," he mutters. "Far from."

Lifting my head, I look into his eyes as I ask, "Then what am I?"

He stares at me for the longest moment before he says, "Mine." Lifting a hand to my face, he brushes his fingers over my jaw before cupping my cheek. "You're mine."

I don't have to ask him to elaborate. I know exactly what he means.

He's fallen in love with me. God only knows why, but it happened, and Renzo warned me he'd never let me go.

*Do I even still want to leave?*

What's there to go back to…an empty mansion where the memory of Louisa and Dad's murders will haunt me?

A life where I have no family.

My entire world has been shredded to pieces, and I have no idea how to put it back together again.

Nothing will be the same as before.

With my eyes still locked on Renzo's face, I try to come to terms with everything that's happened.

Slowly he leans forward and presses a gentle kiss to my mouth. Pulling back, his gaze drifts over my face, checking my reaction.

How did I manage to make this ruthless man fall for me?

Can I love him back after everything that's happened between us?

I remember the terror the first week after he took me. The fear of God this man instilled in me. His brutality. The hopelessness of having him keep me imprisoned in his penthouse.

Can I move past it all?

Can I forgive him?

*I don't know.*

Nudging me to rest my head against his shoulder, he murmurs, "Get some rest, *amo*."

I close my eyes and focus on the feel of his arms around me. I know firsthand how strong he is, and having him be gentle with me makes me feel safe.

It's been a long while since I felt this way, and it soothes my aching soul.

I let out a deep breath and place my hand against his chest as I press my face into the crook of his neck.

*How the tables have turned between us.*

# Chapter 33

## Skylar

I can't believe Dad's gone.

Sitting in the living room, I stare at the livestream of the mansion.

Renzo's men cleaned the foyer, and it's hard to believe it's been less than twenty-four hours since Dad and Louisa were killed.

Suddenly, the TV screen goes black, and it's only then I notice Renzo as he sets the remote down on the coffee table.

Taking his phone from his pocket, he dials a number, and a moment later, he says, "Go to the mansion and remove the four cameras I planted. The one in the kitchen is by the vent. There's another beneath the railing at the top of the stairs, one by the TV stand in the living room, and you'll find the last one by the dressing table in the second bedroom on the left."

When he ends the call, he looks at me with worry in his eyes.

Funnily enough, he doesn't ask me how I'm holding up, but then again, it's because he knows exactly how I feel.

It was probably worse for Renzo. A child expects their parents to die first, but Giulio was only twenty.

*'I want you to see what I saw when I found my brother.'*

I remember what he said yesterday before he killed Enrique, and it brings fresh tears to my eyes.

I wet my lips with my tongue before I say, "Yesterday you said you found Giulio, and you mentioned before it was in an empty lot."

He nods as he sits down on one of the other couches. Resting his forearms on his thighs, he glances at the floor-to-ceiling windows.

"I got the call early that morning, probably around the same time you were in surgery," he replies. He keeps his eyes trained on the window and continues, "He was in a mobile surgical unit. Bianca had already stitched him up, but his organs were in containers, ready to be transported."

*God. It was a million times worse for him. No wonder he lost his mind.*

"The evening before he was killed, he was smiling and giving me shit before leaving to go to a nightclub, and the next time I saw him…"

He doesn't have to finish the sentence. I get the picture.

Getting up, I walk to where he's sitting and take a seat next to him. I lift his arm around my shoulders before I wrap both of mine around his waist and give him a hug.

He leans back against the couch and holds me tighter.

The elevator doors open, and Renzo keeps an arm around me as he glances over his shoulder.

"Hey," I hear a familiar voice, then Dario walks into my line of vision.

When I try to pull away, Renzo tightens his hold on me.

Dario's eyes are filled with compassion as he looks at me. "I'm sorry about what happened." He shakes his head, then asks, "How are you holding up?"

I don't know how to answer his question because I have no idea how I'm doing. The pain comes in crushing waves.

"She'll be okay," Renzo answers on my behalf. "Things are a little tough right now."

"It's understandable."

"Did you find anything in Spain?" Renzo asks.

Dario shakes his head. "Montes stayed a step ahead of me. What happened with the two men you caught."

"The one was just a soldier, but the other was Valverde. He said Montes uses an alias to move between Spain, Peru, and Alaska. Gilberto Varela. He should be in Peru right now if what Valverde said was the truth."

"I'll check it out. Are they dead?"

Renzo just nods, then says, "Don't go after the fucker alone again. Something could've gone wrong."

"I wanted to travel light," Dario chuckles.

"Next time, I'll go with you," Renzo mutters. "Apparently, Montes only stays put for two weeks before he moves again. Keep that in mind."

"I'll watch all three countries just in case he switches things up."

"Thanks, brother."

Dario's eyes move between Renzo and me, then he says, "Something's changed between the two of you."

"Renzo doesn't want to kill me anymore," I answer.

Dario lets out a chuckle. "That's good to hear." He glances between us again. "Seems the saying is true, there's a fine line between love and hate."

"Don't you have work to do?" Renzo asks as he pulls his arm away from me and climbs to his feet.

"Yeah, but I can always spare some time for you."

I get up, and without saying a word, I head up the stairs so the men can catch up without me.

I walk into my room and head straight for the sliding doors. Opening them, I step out on the balcony and glance up at the sky.

*There's a fine line between love and hate.*

Is that what's busy happening between Renzo and me? Are the lines blurring?

---

# Renzo

When the Bentley comes to a stop at the cemetery, I open the door and climb out. Glancing at the line of cars as they pull up behind us, I walk around the back and open the other rear passenger door so Skylar can climb out.

"Stay next to me, *amo,*" I murmur before I head to the back of the hearse.

Everything feels eerily familiar as I open the rear doors and look at the black casket that holds Harlan Davies' remains.

I glance at the other hearse holding Louisa's casket and wait for my men to join me before I split them into two groups.

I take the lead with Harlan's casket, and when we start to walk toward the grave, Skylar falls in beside me.

There's no one else at the funeral. Just Skylar, me, and my men.

When I asked her why she didn't want to invite anyone else, she said it was because there was no one.

She has no living relatives, and she didn't want anyone from the business world to attend. After the funeral, a press release will be issued, saying her father passed away from a heart attack.

I've taken care of the death certificate, and the coroner on our payroll filed the cause of death as a heart attack, so no one will question the story Skylar tells the press.

So it's just us. A group of criminals and Skylar.

We position Harlan's casket over the grave, and I watch as my men gently set the other casket down. Skylar wanted Louisa close to her parents' graves.

My men move back to keep an eye on the surrounding area while Skylar says goodbyes to her father and Louisa.

My gaze settles on the headstone next to the open grave.

**Sadie Davies.**

Hoping it will make Skylar feel better, I say, "Your dad's been reunited with your mom. Try to think of them happily together again."

She nods, her face way too fucking pale.

The past few days, she's been through a rollercoaster of emotions, and I pray to God the funerals will give her some closure.

There's no priest to say any final words because the Davies family wasn't religious. It's something I learned about Skylar when I asked her whether I should arrange for Father Parisi to attend.

Feeling someone has to say something, I clear my throat and murmur, "Harlan Davies was a good man. I've never seen a father love his daughter the way he loved you, Skylar. I respect the lengths he was willing to go through to keep you alive."

A soft sob comes from Skylar, and I wrap my arm around her shoulders.

"If you can hear me, Harlan, know I'll keep her safe. I'll give her the life you wanted for her." I have to clear my throat again before I say, "I'm sorry we couldn't part on better terms."

Silence falls over us, and minutes pass before Skylar walks closer to the grave. She kisses the tips of her fingers and presses her hand to the casket.

"You were the most amazing father, and every day will be less colorful with you gone, Daddy." She has to pause as her voice threatens to disappear. "It was such an...honor to be your daughter."

Sobs overwhelm her, and my fucking eyes begin to burn from hearing her heartbroken words.

It takes a moment before she's able to speak again. "I'll miss you so much. Say hi to Mom for me."

When she turns around and walks back to me, I take hold of her arm and pull her against my chest. Engulfing her with my body, my eyes rest on Harlan's casket, and I nod so they'll lower it.

I press a kiss to her forehead before I lead her to Louisa's grave a few feet away.

"What about her family?" I only think to ask now after the crazy few days we've had.

"We were her family," Skylar murmurs.

She stops in front of the grave and stares at Louisa's final resting place, then says, "Thank you for being a second mother to me, Louisa. I'm sorry you died because of me."

Hearing the guilt in her voice pours ice through my body. Grabbing Skylar by her shoulder, I turn her so she'll face me, and leaning down, I meet her eyes.

"You are not responsible for anyone's death. Do you hear me?"

She shakes her head, her face threatening to crumble.

"Giulio died because he was O-negative. Your father and Louisa died because I put pressure on the fuckers. If anyone's to blame, it's me." I lean even closer so I have her full attention. "Lay it all on me, *amo*, but don't for one second blame yourself."

"If I hadn't needed a kidney –"

I shake her lightly, stopping her sentence dead in its tracks before moving my hands to the sides of her neck.

"You had no choice in the matter. Everything that's happened is because of decisions made by your father and me."

When she just stares at me, I demand, "Do you understand?"

She nods before pulling away from me.

As I follow her back to where the Bentley's parked, I let out a deep breath.

How the fuck am I going to undo all the trauma Skylar's suffered because of Harlan and me.

*Mostly me.*

For the first time since I've fallen head-over-fucking-heels for Skylar, fear creeps into my heart.

Before this moment, I would've taken Skylar any way I could have her, but now I want her love.

I want her to want me, and I'm not sure that will happen.

We climb into the back of the car, and I let out a sigh, my mind racing to come up with a way to win her love.

Fabrizio steers the car toward the cemetery gates as Skylar looks out the window to where her parents' and Louisa's graves are.

I notice her hands are fisted on her lap, and reaching for one of them, I pry her fingers open before weaving mine through hers.

Lifting our joined hands, I press a kiss to her knuckles.

The only plan I can come up with is showing her everything I have to offer.

*I'll love her so fucking hard she'll have no choice but to love me back.*

Turning my head, my eyes settle on her face, and I stare at her until she glances at me and asks, "What? Why are you looking at me like that?"

It's not the time or place, but there's no stopping the words.

"I love you."

Her lips part and surprise fills her eyes.

Shaking my head, I add, "Don't say anything back. I just want you to know you're loved."

She sucks in a deep breath, then giving my hand a squeeze, she leans her head against my shoulder.

I press my mouth to her hair and close my eyes.

# Chapter 34

## Skylar

Sitting out on the balcony, I pull the blanket tighter around my shoulders as I stare at the city lights.

It's been a week since I laid Dad to rest and had my biopsy. The results came back, and somehow, despite all the shit I've been through, the kidney is working perfectly.

When I think about everything, I can only shake my head because it sounds like something out of a movie.

The wind picks up, blowing my hair all over the place.

Suddenly, Renzo comes around the side of the outdoor couch and scoops me into his arms. Without a word, he carries me through the bedroom and heads downstairs, where he plants me on one of the chairs by the kitchen island.

My eyes widen when I see all the food spread out over the granite top.

"I didn't know what you'd be in the mood for, so I had Viviana send over an assortment," he says as he takes a seat next to me. "What do you want to try first?"

I let go of the blanket and answer, "I'll have the salmon, please."

Renzo dishes up for me, and I watch as he even cuts the salmon into bite-size pieces.

Not once since Dad's death has this man lost his temper with me. Instead, he's carried me more than I've ever been carried in my life, made sure I don't skip meals or my medication, and hovered obsessively around me.

He's been so caring and attentive I'm struggling to keep him out of my heart.

Renzo holds a fork out to me, and when I take it, he says, "You have more color in your face."

"It's from sitting outside in the cold," I reply before taking a bite of my food.

"Do you like the cold?" he asks.

I nod and swallow before I say, "Winter is my favorite season. Dad always took me –"

The pain is instant and sharp as it cuts through my heart.

Renzo places his hand on my back, his touch comforting.

I clear my throat. "He always took me ice skating."

"I went ice skating once and fell so fucking hard my ass was sore for a week," Renzo mentions.

The corner of my mouth lifts. "I'd have paid to see that."

"We can go this winter, and I'll fall just to make you laugh."

Glancing at him, I take in the soft expression in his eyes.

Since he told me he loved me, he hasn't said it again. He also hasn't tried to kiss me or push for more.

Well, except for all the forehead kisses. Those I get in spades.

Even though he seemed to fall in love with me at the speed of light, it's going to take me some time to return his feelings.

It's something I've tried to focus on instead of letting my grief consume me – whether I can love Renzo.

Yes, he can be brutal and unforgiving, but he's also gentle and understanding.

I stare at the man who's swept through my life like a tornado. Just as I think I've figured him out, I see a new side to him. He's bad, good, and everything in between.

Understanding why he did the things he did when we first met makes what I'm about to say easier.

"I forgive you."

I watch as the words hit him, and relief washes over his face.

"If I had the power you have, I would've done the same thing," I admit. "I don't know if I have it in me to kill a person, but I've fantasized about it a lot since Dad died. I've killed those bastards, over and over."

I suck in a deep breath and let it out slowly. "So, I forgive you for everything you've done to me and Dad because I understand the pain you felt when you lost Giulio."

Renzo lifts his hand to my face and tucks some hair behind my ear, and it causes tingles to rush over my skin.

His voice is soft as he says, "Thank you."

With our eyes still locked, I can finally admit I'm attracted to him, and it's no longer a bad thing.

Where I did everything to ignore the attraction before, I now let it in because I desperately need to feel something good.

I'm keeping a tight grip on my heart, though, not ready to let him in yet.

Leaning forward, I press a soft kiss to his mouth, then pull back and spear a piece of salmon with my fork.

Renzo doesn't make things awkward by asking why I kissed him, and instead, helps himself to a piece of steak and sautéed vegetables.

We eat in silence, and every now and then, he adds something to my plate, asking me to tell him what I think of it.

By the time we're done with dinner, there's a flicker of happiness in my chest. Forgiving Renzo was not only for his sake. I had to do it for myself.

Getting up, I help put the leftovers in the fridge and clear the dishes from the island. When his phone begins to ring, I walk to the stairs and head back to my room.

The curtains billow into the room from the wind blowing through the open sliding doors, and I step out onto the balcony again.

As I rub my hands up and down my arms to ward off the chill in the air, all the good feelings I shared with Renzo vanish, and the sorrow creeps back.

*Renzo makes me feel better.*

"Come inside, *amo*. I don't want you catching a cold," he suddenly says behind me.

Turning around, I look at the man who's all I have left in this life. Without him, I'd be completely alone.

He could've sent me to the mansion and forgot I ever existed.

He could've continued hating me.

He could've made my life hell until the day I died.

But he chose not to.

He chose to love and take care of me.

My breathing begins to speed up, and not wanting to dwell on everything that's happened any longer, I rush to him.

As Renzo grips hold of my hips and his head lowers, I place my hands on the sides of his neck, and press my mouth to his.

This isn't a 'I forgive you' kiss. It's filled with desperate need, and neither of us has any control over it as the kiss takes on a life of its own.

Our tongues move together as if we've kissed a million times, and it makes the need for more rush through my body.

My fingers find the buttons of his vest, and as I begin to undo them, Renzo lets out a groan and breaks the kiss.

He pushes me backward and shakes his head. "You're not ready."

Breathless and stunned, I watch him walk out of my room, and then anger explodes in my chest.

Going after him, I follow him into his bedroom. I've only been in here once, and again, I don't look around.

My eyes burn on his back as I snap, "Stop taking my choices away from me. I get to decide when I'm ready."

Pulling his vest off, he tosses it on the floor as he turns around, a look of warning darkening his features.

"Give me one good reason I should let things go further between us," he demands.

I take a few steps closer to him, then admit, "Because we want each other." I suck in a breath. "Because I need you." When he walks toward me, I whisper, "I need you."

His mouth slams down on mine, and I quickly wrap my arms around his neck so he won't be able to pull away again.

This time, I kiss Renzo with everything I feel. He pulls me toward his bed, our mouths claiming and devouring each other.

His hands move down to my outer thighs, and gripping hold of my dress, he drags the fabric up. We have to stop kissing so the fabric can pass over my head, and the moment I'm free of the dress, I start on the buttons of his shirt while my mouth finds his again.

When I push the fabric of his dress shirt off his shoulders, and I feel his warm skin beneath my fingers, I pepper kisses down his neck and over his chest.

*God, he feels so good.*

His hands move up and down my sides before he unclips my bra, then taking a step back, his eyes drift over my breasts.

"You're fucking beautiful," he breathes while he undoes his belt and the zipper of his pants.

I close the distance between us again, and our mouths fuse together while I help him shove his pants and boxers down.

"Condom," he murmurs against my lips, and it has me quickly pushing my panties down my legs while he walks to the bedside table.

When he takes a condom from the drawer and tears the foil open, my eyes take in every naked inch of him.

*Sweet Jesus.*

Renzo is pure muscle and blessed in ways no man should be blessed. He has abs for days, and the curve of his hips has my abdomen clenching hard.

"I want you," I whisper, my heartbeat speeding up and my breaths coming faster from how perfect his body is.

Walking closer, I take the condom from him and sink to my knees. I wrap my hand around his hard cock, loving the velvety feel of his skin. Sucking him into my mouth, I moan while I lubricate his thick hardness before I roll the condom on.

"Christ, woman," he hisses, hunger tightening his features. "If you do that again, this is over before we can get started."

He grabs hold of my arms, and hauling me to my feet, he shoves me back onto his bed. A chuckle escapes me as I bounce on the covers, and with his eyes on my body, I open my legs for him.

"Fuck, I'm going to come the instant I'm inside you," he mutters as he crawls over me.

He presses kisses over all my surgical scars before sucking my nipple into his mouth and letting out a groan.

My palms brush over his shoulders, loving the feel of his warm skin and the power rippling beneath it.

Renzo frees my nipple, and covering me with his body, he looks deep into my eyes. I feel his hard cock press against my slit, making tingles rush over my body, and my need for him skyrockets.

"Are you sure?" he asks.

I nod quickly while my fingers wrap around the back of his neck. "Yes." When he continues to stare at me, I ask, "What's wrong?"

"Nothing," he whispers. "I'm just taking in this moment."

My heart melts, and I try to ignore how close I am to falling head over heels for this man.

Slowly, he lowers his head and nips at my mouth a couple of times before he deepens the kiss.

I expected hot and heavy, but instead, Renzo kisses me as if I'm precious to him. I feel his love for me, and it makes me so emotional I struggle to keep from crying.

*God, will I make the biggest mistake of my life by letting him into my heart?*

The moment becomes so intense I feel it in my soul, and our mouths move as one.

By the time he frees my lips and moves down to my breasts, I'm completely focused on him.

There's no room for our pain, and the tight grip on my heart starts to slip.

# Chapter 35

## Renzo

I feel the moment Skylar connects with me, and it's only then I move down her body so I can have my way with her.

It's taking more strength than I knew I had not to throw her down and fuck her senseless.

*It's been five years since she's had sex. You can't just fuck her.*

As I feast on her breasts, I move my hand down between her thighs. When I brush a finger through her slit and feel the heat from her soaked pussy, I lose the grip I have on my self-control.

I move down and force her legs wider apart to accommodate my shoulders. With her pussy on full display for me, my tongue darts out to taste her, and just like at the restaurant, I lose my fucking mind.

I suck and bite at her clit while pushing a finger inside her tight warmth. I devour my woman until the friction makes her pussy feel scorching hot against my tongue.

"Oh God!" Skylar cries, her hips bucking from the assault. "Renzo! Shit. Renzo," she moans as she rubs herself against my hungry mouth.

I'll never be able to get my fill of her, and when her orgasm hits, I drink every drop of arousal from her.

"Jesus," she gasps when I finally lift my head. "Holy shit."

Grinning, I move back up her body and kiss the living hell out of her so she can taste herself on my tongue.

Her hands brush over my shoulders and back, and I let out a groan from how good it feels to have her touch me.

I position my cock at her entrance, and breaking the kiss, I lift my head so I can see her face.

The moment between us builds, and just to torture myself a little more, I wait as long as I possibly can before I thrust inside her.

I'm only able to enter her halfway before her narrow walls stop me, threatening to strangle the life out of my cock.

"Fuck, Skylar," I hiss, my body shaking from how good she already feels. "You need to relax. Your pussy is fucking strangling me."

"I am relaxed," she gasps. "You're too big."

"Fuck," I breathe as I press my forehead against hers.

I grab hold of the back of one of her thighs and lift her leg over my hip, and when I surge forward, I manage to push another inch into her.

"Christ, you're going to kill me," I groan.

"Not if you kill me first," she says through uneven breaths.

It's only then I think to ask, "You okay?"

She nods quickly, then lifts her ass, taking me deeper.

*Jesus. Fucking. Christ.*

I pull out, and with my fingers digging into her thigh, I fucking slam into her, forcing her to take all of me.

Her head tilts against the covers, and her back arches as a cry tears from her. She's so fucking beautiful as she takes every inch of my cock, I'm unable to give her a moment to adjust.

I begin to move, fucking her with hard, relentless thrusts while my eyes remain locked on her. Her nails claw at my back and sides, her breaths bursting over her parted lips every time I plunge into her.

Becoming one with Skylar is unlike anything I've ever experienced. From this moment onward, she owns me.

*I'm hers. Forever.*

"Renzo," she breathes, my name sounding like a prayer.

I press my forehead against hers again as I continue my relentless pace of conquering her.

"You're mine, *amo*," I groan. "You're fucking mine, and I'm never letting you go."

Her eyes shine like stars as she nods. Her body tenses, and knowing she's close, I fuck her as hard as possible.

"God," she whimpers, her features fucking angelic as she tenses right before her pleasure hits.

Her pussy grips my cock tighter, and it's all it takes for ecstasy to rip the air from my lungs. I drop down on her as my body jerks, and pushing my arms beneath her, I crush her to me as I ride out my orgasm.

The first thing I become aware of when my senses return is our rushing breaths. Then I feel her trembling body, every inch plastered against mine.

Lifting my head, I look at her face, and it's just in time to see love shining in her eyes.

She quickly turns her head away from me, but I grab hold of her jaw and force her to look at me.

"Stop fighting it," I say, which only makes her shake her head.

"Skylar." I give her a pleading look, which isn't something I do easily. "There's nothing wrong with you loving me, and I'll never use it against you. You're safe with me."

She lets out a sob, and pulling her jaw free from my hold, she buries her face against my neck.

It takes her a moment to regain control over her emotions before she whispers, "I just need time to process everything."

"Take all the time you need, *amo*," I say before I press a kiss to her hair.

*She loves me. I saw it in her eyes.*

I can wait until she's ready to say the words out loud.

The corner of my mouth lifts as relief fills my chest. I don't know how I fucking made her love me, but I'm thankful.

I kiss the side of her neck before I pull out of her, and getting up, I walk to the bathroom so I can dispose of the condom.

When I enter the bedroom again, it's to see Skylar gathering her clothes.

"You're not going anywhere," I mutter before I take the clothes from her hands and toss them back onto the floor.

Lifting her off her feet, I fall on the bed with her in my arms. She lets out a chuckle as I move over her, and with a smile on my face, I stare down at my woman.

"Christ, *amo*. You're so fucking beautiful," I whisper before pressing a tender kiss to her lips.

"What does *amo* mean?"

"Love."

Her smile widens, and lifting her hand, she brushes her fingers through my hair. "I like your hair when it's all ruffled. It makes you look hot."

"Glad to hear you think I'm hot," I tease her.

She scrunches her nose. "You know you're attractive." Her eyes lower to my jaw as she trails a finger over my stubble. "Even when you put the fear of God in me, I couldn't help but notice. It's actually very deceiving and unnerving." Her gaze meets mine again. "It makes you more terrifying."

I press another gentle kiss to her mouth, then ask, "How so?"

"You don't expect beautiful people to kill at the drop of a hat."

I stare at her for a moment before I say, "I'm sorry for all the hell I put you through." Wrapping my arms around her, I pull her against my chest as I turn onto my side. "I lost my mind after Giulio died, and I took it out on you and your father."

She presses a kiss to my chest, then whispers, "Thank you for apologizing."

Needing to change the subject, I say, "I don't really like long walks on the beach, and I don't suck at cooking. It's just easier to order in."

Skylar chuckles, and lifting her head, she looks at me. "What else?"

I brush her hair back as I drink in the stunning smile on her face.

"You're the first woman in my bed."

Her eyebrows lift. "Really?"

I nod. "I don't let people into my private space easily."

"Did you take all your one-night stands to hotels?" she teases me.

I shake my head. "I've never had a one-night stand."

Her eyebrows draw together as she gives me a skeptical look. "Fine. All your girlfriends."

"I've only had three. Excluding you."

She stares at me, trying to figure out whether I'm telling the truth.

Opening up to her about my past, I say, "They were all Sicilian, and my parents arranged the dates in the hope I'd pick one of them to marry. After my father died and I took over as the head of the family, I stopped that shit, and I've been single ever since." I take a deep breath and let it out slowly before I add, "I never planned to marry and have children of my own. That's why I made Giulio my heir."

Her expression grows serious, then she says, "I don't know whether I'll be able to have children. I had a shattered pelvis, and they had to reconstruct my bladder. You know all about the kidney failure." She lets out a sigh. "It's not something I've thought about until now."

"We'll adopt," I say. "You've been through enough, and I don't want the strain of a pregnancy putting your life in danger."

She looks up at me. "Really? You won't mind?"

I shake my head. "Not at all." While we're on the subject, I mention, "We need to get you a birth control implant. I don't want any accidents happening."

"Okay."

Pushing her onto her back, I cover her breast with my hand and press kisses to her jaw. "God, I love your body."

Skylar reaches for the drawer and grabs a condom. "On your back," she orders. "I want to be on top."

Grinning, I do as my woman says, and I lean back against the pillows. While she rolls the condom onto my cock, I'm struck, once again, with how much I love her.

It just happened, and I had zero say in the matter. One second I wanted to strangle her, and the next, I wanted to fuck her.

# Chapter 36

## Skylar

The past week has been pretty uneventful. Other than going to the clinic for the implant, I haven't left the penthouse.

I'm wiping down the counters when I realize I'm not a prisoner anymore.

Swinging around, I look at Renzo and say, "I can go out."

"What?" he mumbles before he lifts his head from where he was reading something on his phone.

"I can leave the penthouse."

A frown forms on his forehead. "Yeah?"

"I need to go to the mansion to get my wallet." I begin to walk to the elevator, then pause to ask, "Can Vincenzo or Fabrizio give me a ride?"

There's still a frown on Renzo's face as he asks, "You want to go out? Right now?"

"Yes." If he tells me I can't, I'll lose my shit.

"Okay."

Excitement bursts in my chest, and when we enter the elevator, I grin up at him.

The corner of his mouth lifts, and gripping hold of my jaw, he presses a hard kiss to my mouth. "Your smile will be the end of me."

"Why?"

"Because you're fucking stunning when you smile," he mutters.

The doors slide open, and as we walk to the Bentley, Renzo tells the guards, "We're heading to the Davies mansion."

During the drive, my excitement dies away, and my grief crawls back into my heart.

Renzo notices my change in mood, and linking our fingers together, he kisses the back of my hand.

It's something Dad used to do when I was in the hospital, and the memory has me taking a deep breath while I do my best to stop the grief from overwhelming me.

It's getting easier to fight back the tears, but the pain is still raw, and I don't expect it to lessen anytime soon.

When the Bentley pulls up to the mansion, I glance around the garden that needs tending. I'll have to decide what to do with the place. It's big and needs a lot of upkeep.

We climb out of the car, and as we walk to the front door, I say, "I think I should sell the property."

"Whatever you want, *amo*. I can handle the sale for you," Renzo offers while he unlocks the door.

For the past three years, Dad's handled all the finances, and Renzo took over when he kidnapped me. At some point, I'll have to take back control.

I probably need to get a cellphone if I'm going to look for work.

I'll have to update my resume.

I have no idea what my bank accounts look like.

"You okay?" Renzo asks as we walk through the foyer.

"I'm just thinking about everything I have to do. Dad took control of my life after the car accident, and then you happened."

He tugs me to a stop at the foot of the stairs and turns me so I'll look at him.

"What do you mean by *everything*?"

"I need to sort out the bank accounts. I don't have a cellphone. I want to start working again." I gesture around the foyer. "I have to pack up everything."

Lifting his hands to the sides of my neck, he leans down and holds my gaze captive. "I can do all of that for you."

I take hold of his wrist and ask, "You won't mind?"

"No, *amo*. Not at all. You're mine, and it's my job to take care of you."

"You don't think it's pathetic that I let my dad handle everything?"

He shakes his head and pulls me against his chest. "No. You were on the brink of death and had to deal with a kidney transplant. If anything, I think you're fucking strong."

Closing my eyes, I let Renzo's words sink in before I whisper, "I miss him."

"I know." Renzo brushes his palm over my hair. "But you have me, and I meant it when I said I'll take care of you."

I snuggle closer to the man who's quickly taking over my heart. "Thank you."

He holds me for a moment before he pulls away and says, "Let's get everything you need."

We spend the next couple of hours gathering the last of my belongings and going through Dad's office for all the financial documents and his laptop.

"I'll have to get Dario to break into the laptop," Renzo says when we're stopped by the device needing a password.

I try Mom's birthday, and when the screen unlocks, I grin at Renzo. "His passwords are always my or Mom's birthdays."

"That makes things a hell of a lot easier," he says as he shuts the laptop again. "Let's get out of here."

When we walk toward the foyer, I murmur, "Can I just have a minute alone before we leave?"

"Sure." He presses a kiss to my forehead, then heads to the front door.

As I walk to the kitchen, I glance around my family home. The sorrow grips my heart, and I don't fight the tears as they come.

In the kitchen, I trail my fingers over the counters where I've spent many hours practicing the art of cooking.

Dad ate every meal and never complained. He was my biggest cheerleader.

"God, I miss you so much, Daddy," I whisper.

I think about how Louisa would complain about all the dirty dishes, but whenever I offered to help clean them, she'd shoo me away.

Wiping the tears from my cheeks, I suck in a deep breath.

This place isn't home without them. It's become a graveyard for the moments I shared with them.

Turning around, I leave the mansion and lock the door behind me. Walking to the Bentley and the man who loves me, I decide to stop fighting to keep Renzo out of my heart.

It's not a fight I would've won anyway.

When I reach him, I wrap my arms around his neck and pull him down so I can kiss him. Breathing in the woodsy scent of his cologne, I relish in the feel of his embrace.

With my lips against his, I whisper, "I love you." I pull back and meet his eyes. "The good, the bad, the ugly, and the beautiful. I love all of you. I might regret it one day, but there's no way to keep you out of my heart."

A devastating smile curves his lips, and happiness fills his eyes. "Thank you, *amo*. I know I haven't made it easy for you, but thank you for loving me anyway."

"I didn't have much of a choice," I tease him. "You took my heart captive, and I just had to make peace with it."

He shakes his head, his expression filling with tenderness. "You won't regret loving me, Skylar. I promise."

I press another kiss to his mouth, then say, "Take me home."

# Chapter 37

## Renzo

After I finish checking a shipment of Uzis, I walk to the office and take a seat on the couch.

Business is good, but I'm not making any progress with The Harvest. Servando Montes is nowhere to be found, and my patience is wearing thin.

I think he got wind of Enrique being killed and went into hiding.

The streets of New York are quiet, but my men are still on high alert and searching for anyone related to The Harvest.

It's frustrating. I want to put this matter to bed and get on with my life.

My life which now includes Skylar.

Every day, she's doing a little better. I've sorted out all the paperwork concerning Harlan's estate and her finances and made it easy for her to handle them should something happen to me.

I've invested the bulk of her inheritance, and I'll add the money from the sale of the mansion once it comes through.

I got her a cell phone, which she hardly uses. Her routine hasn't changed much, and she spends most of her time in the kitchen.

I've been playing with the idea of firing Chef Alain and giving her the position of head chef at La Torrisi. It's either that or I buy her a restaurant.

Climbing to my feet, I leave the office again and gesture to Vincenzo that we're leaving. Whenever I have to go out, I leave Fabrizio with Skylar.

When she starts working again, I'll assign guards to her. Maybe Carlo and Antonio.

"Where are we going?" Vincenzo asks.

"Home."

As he drives us back to the penthouse, I dial Dario's number to check in with him.

"What's up?" he answers.

"Nothing. Just wanted to check in with you."

"No news yet. The moment the fucker pops up, you'll be the first to know," he says, sounding preoccupied.

"Am I interrupting something?"

"No. I'm watching one of the ballerinas."

My eyebrow raises, and the corner of my mouth lifts. "Watching or stalking?"

"Both."

Letting out a chuckle, I can't resist taunting him. "You gonna be her mystery man?"

It's what Samantha called Franco when their relationship started.

"Nope, that's Franco's title." He's quiet for a moment, then says, "She knows I'm watching, and I think she loves it."

"Hmm...sounds like you have the hots for her."

"Watching her dance calms me," he admits.

"You can do with some calmness in your life." Vincenzo parks the car in the basement, and it has me saying, "I'll talk to you later. Enjoy the show."

"I will," he chuckles.

Ending the call, I tuck the device back into my pocket before I climb out of the Bentley.

I give Fabrizio a chin lift as I press the button to call the elevator, and stepping inside, I press the keycard to the pad.

*I need to have one made for Skylar.*

When the doors slide open, and I walk into the penthouse, the aroma of Skylar's cooking fills the air.

"Something smells good," I say as I enter the kitchen.

"I'm trying something new. It's Asian with a little special touch."

Taking the chance, I ask, "Why don't you open your own restaurant?"

"I wouldn't know where to start. I'm not a businesswoman. I just want to be a chef and not worry about the ins and outs of running a restaurant."

"I'll employ people to run it for you," I offer.

Her eyes dart to me. "You already have a lot on your plate."

I shrug as I lean against the island and cross my arms over my chest. "I don't mind, *amo*. I think it's a great idea. You'll call the shots and won't have to report to anyone. It will give you the freedom to create the menu."

She switches off the stove and focuses all her attention on me. "That sounds like a dream."

"Let's do it." I push away from the island, and wrapping my arms around her, I press a kiss to her mouth. "Let's open another restaurant."

"I get to pick the name," she chuckles as she flattens her hands against my chest.

"Okay."

"I want an Asian restaurant."

The corner of my mouth lifts. "Okay."

"Can I choose how to decorate it?" she asks, giving me a seductive look that has my cock hardening at the speed of light.

"Yes," I agree. "Whatever you want, *amo*."

Lifting her eyebrow, she asks, "Whatever I want?"

I nod as I lean down to press a kiss to her mouth.

When I lift my head, she says, "I want you."

*Those three words. Christ, I love hearing them.*

I'm just about to pick her up so I can carry her sexy ass to the bedroom, where the condoms are, when I remember she has an implant.

Claiming her mouth with a hard kiss, I grab hold of her hips and lift her to sit on the island.

Knowing I can take my woman bare, I rip her panties off.

While I remove my Glock and set it down beside Skylar, she makes quick work of my belt and zipper. When her fingers wrap around my aching cock, I groan into her mouth.

Stepping closer, I take over and position myself at her entrance. Her hands grip my ass, and when I thrust into her, the pleasure is instant and fucking overwhelming.

Lifting my hand to the back of her neck, I devour her mouth as I begin to fuck her.

Each thrust has the pleasure between us building, making me lose my mind with a need for more.

I want everything she has to offer.

Breaking the kiss, I grab hold of her hips so I can keep her in place as I fuck her even harder.

"Renzo," she moans, her fingers digging into my ass.

I watch as ecstasy tightens her features, and once again, I fall in love with her.

When my orgasm hits, and I fill her, I feel so fucking close to her, nothing will ever be able to tear us apart.

As my cock jerks inside her and I ride out the last of my pleasure, I claim her mouth again. I kiss her with all the love I feel for her.

I don't stop thrusting into her, loving the feel of us joined together. It doesn't take long before her moans spill into my mouth, and this time, I take it slow as I make love to her.

I drag down the zipper of her dress, and breaking the kiss, I pull the fabric over her head. I get rid of her bra, and pushing her back until she's lying down on the granite top, I cover her breasts with my hands.

With my woman spread out before me, I touch every visible inch of her body before I drag the tip of my finger over the length of the surgery scar on her side.

The anger I used to feel whenever I thought about the kidney transplant is gone, and in its place is thankfulness.

Something good came from it all. Giulio gave me Skylar.

*Thank you, brother.*

Skylar notices the emotion on my face, and sitting up, she wraps her arms around me and holds me to her.

I bury my face in her hair, and crush her to me as I bring us closer to our orgasms. When our pleasure hits simultaneously, we're both overcome with emotions and clinging to each other.

"I love you," I whisper. "With everything I am."

She brings her hands to the sides of my jaw and presses a tender kiss to my mouth. "I love you, Renzo."

# Chapter 38

## Skylar

Since Renzo spoke to me about opening my own restaurant, my excitement has been growing.

We've secured a building a few miles away from La Torrisi, and Viviana has agreed to manage my restaurant as well.

Every day I play around with Asian dishes, and I'm slowly putting together a menu so I'm ready for when the doors open.

Today I'm choosing my signature dish, and I'm torn between two.

Setting both meals down in front of Renzo, my tone is professional as I point at the plate on the left. "This is *Banh xeo*, a savory Vietnamese pancake filled with pork, shrimp, onions, and bean sprouts." I gesture at the other plate. "And this is *yukhaejang*, a Korean spicy brisket soup." My eyes meet Renzo's. "Tell me which one you like most."

He nods as he turns his attention to the dishes, and taking a bite of the first one, he focuses on the taste.

I push his glass of Italian Prosecco closer so he can use it as a palette cleanser.

When he takes a bite of the Korean soup, my heart beats faster and nerves spin in my stomach.

Sitting back, his eyes meet mine, and I swear the man is trying to torture me when he doesn't immediately give me his feedback.

"The Korean spicy brisket is your signature dish," he says. "You got nervous when I took a bite, which means it's important to you." The corner of his mouth lifts. "It doesn't matter which one I like more."

*He's right.*

Tears fill my eyes, and before I can try to stop them, they spill down my cheeks.

*I've just chosen my signature dish.*

He stands up from the chair and wraps me in a tight hug.

This moment has been in the making since I started my career as a chef. I'm so overwhelmed because, after the accident, I never thought I'd get the chance to have my own signature dish.

"For the record," Renzo murmurs. "The beef brisket soup is my favorite."

I let out a chuckle, and pulling back, I look at him.

He wipes the tears from my cheeks with his thumbs before pressing a kiss to my mouth. "Congratulations, *amo*."

"Thank you." I smile as I glance at the two dishes.

The *banh xeo* is an excellent addition to the menu, but the *yukhaejang* is special because it was one of Dad's favorites.

"I've decided on a name for the restaurant," I say.

"What?"

"*Yukhaejang*."

A smile spreads over Renzo's face. "I should've guessed. I'll get the sign made. Just write it down for me, or I'll butcher it because I can't pronounce that word for the life of me."

Wrapping my arms around his waist, I stare up at him. "Thank you for being so amazing."

He kisses my lips, then says, "You make me want to be amazing."

His phone starts to ring, and I let go of him so he can take the call.

"Hey," he answers.

He listens for a moment, then his eyes flick to me, and I watch as his features change from loving to cold and ruthless.

My stomach clenches, and my heartbeat speeds up because it's a look I won't ever get used to seeing. Honestly, his brutal side still scares the living hell out of me.

Renzo lifts his hand and wraps his fingers around the side of my neck as he mutters to whoever's on the other end of the call, "I'll be at your place in thirty minutes."

He ends the call, and shaking his head, he steps closer to me and says, "Don't be afraid of me, *amo*. I'll never do anything to hurt you."

"Knee-jerk reaction," I murmur. I suck in a breath of air, then ask, "What was the call about?"

"Dario found Montes. We're flying to Mexico. The fucker's been laying low in some village in the middle of nowhere."

*That explains the reason for the ruthless expression on his face.*

Renzo is going to kill the leader of the group responsible for all the heartache we've suffered. The man who ordered Dad's death.

Realization shudders through me, and my voice is hoarse when I say, "Go and put an end to this nightmare for us."

"I should be back before you go to bed," he murmurs as he leans in to give me a kiss.

"Please be careful." I wrap my arms around him before he can walk away. "I won't survive losing you as well."

He lets out a chuckle. "You won't lose me. I've done this a hundred times, and I'll have Dario for backup. He's good with a sniper rifle."

"I love you," I say as I stand on my tiptoes to give him another kiss.

"Love you too, *amo*."

He pulls away from me, and I watch him walk to the elevator. While he waits for the doors to open, he makes another call.

"Get the men ready. We're going to Mexico to kill Montes."

He glances back at me, one last time, then steps into the elevator.

Standing in the kitchen, I let out a slow breath before I start to clean up.

I always thought I'd end up with some kind of businessman who works nine to five and plays golf on the weekends. Instead, my man works all kinds of hours and kills people left, right, and center.

I put the leftovers in plastic containers in case Renzo is hungry when he gets back, and once the kitchen is spotless, I take a seat at the island and pull my laptop closer.

Trying to stay busy so I won't just sit and worry about him, I look at different concepts for the menu.

I work for a while before my thoughts turn to Renzo.

*He's going to be okay. Don't start worrying. It will drive you crazy.*

Knowing I won't be able to focus on work, I let out a sigh and close the laptop. Getting up from the chair, I walk to the sliding doors in the dining room. I pull them open, and stepping out onto the balcony where Renzo kissed me the first time, I suck in a deep breath of the cool air.

*Winter will be here soon.*

Leaning over the railing, I stare down at the traffic and start counting yellow cabs.

*You've seen Renzo deal with the bastards. He's capable of keeping himself safe. Nothing bad will happen to him, because he's the monster everyone fears.*

I realize what I'm thinking and let out a burst of laughter.

I fell in love with the beast, and I don't want him to change. I really love all of him, even though his brutal side still scares the ever-loving hell out of me.

# Chapter 39

## Renzo

The motorcade leaves a cloud of dust as we drive out to the village where Montes was last seen.

Dario, Carlo, Emilio, and I are in the first SUV while my men fill the other four. We used a couple of my private jets to get everyone into Mexico, and I had to reach out to the local cartel and give them a heads-up so there are no misunderstandings.

With a little luck, Servando Montes dies today.

Dario's phone buzzes, and he checks it quickly, then says, "We have a face to put to the name."

He holds the device so I can see. There's a photo of a man having a cigarette outside a shitty house. He seems to be in his late fifties and loves heavy gold chains way too fucking much.

"Zero style," Dario says as if that's the biggest crime the man could commit.

I let out a chuckle, then mutter, "Doesn't look like he knows we're on the way."

"The soldier that sold him out made sure Servando doesn't catch wind of what's going on."

"At least one of his soldiers has enough common sense to rat him out to stop us from killing every last one of them," I mention.

It's a sad day when your own men turn on you.

"We're going to have to move fast once we're in the village so Montes doesn't get away," Dario says.

"Send the photo to my phone," I request.

A second later, the message comes through from Dario, and I send it to all of my men.

Lifting the two-way radio to my mouth, I press the button and say, "I've sent you all a photo. Kill anyone who looks like the fucker."

"One minute out, boss," Carlo informs us.

I check my submachine gun and Glock for the third time before I suck in deep breaths, readying myself mentally for the action we might encounter. I'm bracing for a war so I'm not caught off guard.

"The fucking bulletproof vest is digging into my side," Dario complains.

"Don't you dare take it off," I mutter.

The fucker bats his eyelashes at me. "When are you going to admit you love me?"

As we close in on the village, I lock eyes with the man who's been there for me every step over the years and helped me get through the past few months.

"I love you."

Dario's mischievous expression fades away, and he looks a little shocked. He quickly turns his head and glances out of the window.

"If you cry, I'm going to shoot you," I mutter.

He looks at me again and pretends to wipe a tear from beneath his eye, then the fucker aims to hug me. I slap his arms away, giving him a look of warning.

Letting out a burst of laughter, he says, "Love you too, brother."

"Jesus," Carlo mumbles from the driver's seat. "Get ready!"

I roll my shoulders, and the second the SUV comes to a stop, I shove the door open and get out.

I watch as Carlo and Emilio run to the front door. Emilio throws all his weight against the door, and it shudders open.

The other SUVs stop, and my men pile out.

"Move your asses!" I order.

Dario stays by the SUV with his rifle resting on the roof of the vehicle.

Walking to the house, my fingers flex around the handle of my Glock while I keep glancing around us. People peek through curtains, but there's no one out on the streets.

I hear gunshots, and picking up my pace, I walk into the house and glance around the living room.

"Carlo?" I call out.

"In the back," he shouts. "The fucker's in the basement."

I head in the direction of his voice and find my men standing on either side of a door.

When Carlo sees me, he says, "The lights are out, and it's fucking dark down there. He'll pick us off one by one."

"I'll be right back," I mutter before I head out of the house. Opening the backdoor of the SUV, I dig in the bag of weapons and find what I'm looking for.

I grab two smoke grenades, and when I straighten up, Dario yawns before asking, "What's happening?"

"The fucker's in the basement, so we need to flush him out."

When I head back to the house, he calls out, "Okay then, I'll just wait here."

The corner of my mouth lifts, but the smirk quickly fades away when I reach Carlo and Emilio. I pull the pin out and throw the grenade into the darkness before moving out of the line of fire.

*Three. Two. One.*

Coughing sounds up, and I hear movement.

Pulling the pin on the second one, I throw it down the stairs and move back again.

I hear a woman screaming in Spanish and a couple of people coughing.

A moment later a woman crawls into the hallway. Emilio grabs her and shoves her to the side. He keeps one of his guns trained on her.

"*Por favor,*" she begs.

I gesture with a flick of my head for her to go. She scrambles to her feet and runs away as fast as she can.

A couple of seconds later, a guy in his thirties comes out, suffering from a bad coughing fit.

Emilio yanks him out of the way and slams the butt of his gun into his head, rendering him unconscious.

Growing impatient, I let out a heavy breath.

I'm a heartbeat away from going down there, but knowing the effects of the smoke, I hold out a little longer.

Finally, the fucking rat appears, and as he crawls into the hallway, I kick him hard, making him gag as he falls to his side.

I let out an audible breath, then say, "Emilio, get rid of the other one."

"No!" Montes shouts through ragged coughs. "He's my son."

"Ooooh." Carlo grins at me. "Two for the price of one, boss."

Crouching by Montes, I press the barrel of my gun to his head and say, "You took my heir from me. I feel it's only fair I repay the favor."

"No. Please. It was a mistake." His eyes are bloodshot as he looks at me. "You already killed the men who fucked up. You got your revenge."

I shake my head slowly. "It wasn't a mistake when you came into my city and butchered my brother. It was a mistake that you got caught."

I glance at Emilio, and he doesn't hesitate to shoot the son in the head.

"Nooooo!" Montes cries.

I grab his jaw and force him to look at me. "Be thankful for the merciful deaths I'm giving you and your heir. I could've gutted you like I did the others."

When I let go of him and I rise to my feet, he crawls to his son. Lifting his son's head to his chest, he cries as the sorrow engulfs him.

For a moment, I play with the idea of letting him live so he can suffer the loss for the rest of his life.

*He was responsible for sending the men who killed Giulio and Harlan. Because of this man, Skylar and I suffered.*

*She would want him dead.*

Lifting my hand again, I train the barrel on him and pull the trigger three times. The smell of gunpowder hangs in the air, and my ears ring.

*It's over, amo.*

Turning around, I order, "Leave the mess for someone else to clean up. We're going home."

# Chapter 40

## Skylar

I look at the time again, and seeing it's past three in the morning, I stand up from the couch and struggle to hold the tears back.

*Where is he? It's taking too long.*

I drag my fingers through my hair, and unable to stop the sob, it bursts over my lips.

*Please let him be okay. I can't lose Renzo.*

*I swear I'll throw myself over the balcony because there's no way I'm living without him.*

Realizing just how much I love Renzo, I cover my face with my hands and pray to all that's holy he'll come home to me.

Suddenly I hear the elevator doors slide open, and my head snaps up. I run toward it as pure relief washes over me.

Just as Renzo steps into the penthouse, I throw myself at him and wrap my arms around his neck. Sobs wrack through me as I get to smell his cologne and natural scent.

*Thank God.*

"Hey, what's wrong?" he asks, his tone tight with worry and his arms crushing me to him.

I shake my head and cling to him with all my strength.

Renzo lifts me so I can wrap my legs around his waist before he carries me to the living room. He sits down on one of the couches, and I straddle his lap, refusing to let go of him.

"Skylar?" he asks. "Talk to me. What happened?"

"I t-thought something h-happened to you," I sob. "I c-can't lose y-you."

"You won't, *amo.*" He rubs his hand up and down my back. "I'm sorry it took me so long. I should've called you."

I pull away so I can see his face and drink in the handsome sight before my eyes. "I love you," I whisper.

He wipes my tears from my cheeks, looking at me as if I'm all that matters in his life.

"I *really* love you," I say. "Not knowing if you were safe or dead in a ditch somewhere, I realized how much I love you."

Framing my face with his hands, he presses a kiss to my mouth before saying, "Next time I have to go somewhere, I'll text you every hour so you won't worry. Okay?

Lost sobs drift over my lips as I whisper, "Okay."

A smile tugs at the corner of his mouth, then he says, "Montes is dead. It's over, *amo*."

*It's over.*

I stare at Renzo as the words sink in. All the hell we've been through flits through my mind, and it feels like a weight rolls off my shoulders.

After everything I've been through, I deserve my chance at happiness, and I'm going to grab it with both hands.

Leaning forward, I press my mouth to Renzo's, and I kiss him with every ounce of love I have for him.

He takes over control, and just like all the times before, the kiss quickly turns wild and passionate. Our tongues dance, and our lips knead as if we'll die if we stop.

Renzo's hands move down my sides, and while he pushes my dress up my thighs, I undo his belt and pull down his zipper.

We're completely in sync.

I pull his cock free, and shoving my panties to the side, I sink down on him. Having him fill me makes my body shudder from how good it feels.

Renzo grips hold of my hips, and the pace is slow as we make love. The intimacy filling the air around us has me focusing on the taste and feel of the man who stole my heart.

I never believed I'd have this once-in-a-lifetime love. It happened in the most unconventional way, and the price we had to pay almost broke us.

*Maybe it did, and our broken pieces fit perfectly together.*

---

My stomach spins with nerves as I check that everything is ready for tonight.

I've made finger foods because all the heads of the Cosa Nostra are coming over for a poker game.

Renzo said they used to have it every two weeks, but two of the men got married and started families, so now it's once every other month.

At least their wives are also coming, so I won't be the only woman.

"Stop fussing," Renzo says from the living room. "Come sit by me."

"I just want –"

"Skylar, come sit your ass down right now!"

With a scowl on my face, I walk to the living room and say, "Don't take that tone with me. It doesn't work anymore."

His eyebrow lifts as he rises to his feet. "Is that so?"

"Yes. You don't scare me."

I watch as his features tighten until the predatory look I used to fear settles over his face like a dark cloud.

I shake my head and cross my arms over my chest.

Slowly, he stalks closer until I have to tilt my head back to keep eye contact.

A smile threatens to form on my face as I say, "It's actually a turn-on."

He can't keep up the pretense, and the corner of his mouth lifts as he chuckles. Just as he takes hold of me and pulls me closer, the elevator doors open.

"Not in front of the triplets," I hear a man say.

"What? I was just going to show them how they were made," Renzo jokes as he turns around and walks away from me so he can greet his friend with a handshake.

My eyes dart between the beautiful blonde, the strollers, and the man. They look like a typical family.

"Hey, Samantha," Renzo greets the woman.

He walks with them as they come toward the living room.

"Skylar, this is Franco and Samantha."

"Nice to meet you," I say, a polite smile on my face.

"Franco is my closest friend," Renzo adds as he comes to wrap his arm around my shoulders.

"I see you're taking my advice," Franco says as his eyes flick between us.

"Yeah-yeah. I'll let you take the credit," Renzo chuckles.

I move from under his arm, and peeking into the strollers, I whisper, "They're so adorable."

"You don't have to whisper. We got them used to sleeping with noise," Samantha says.

"Clever," Renzo mutters.

The elevator doors open again, and I hear Dario say, "You better smile around the women. You look like a murder waiting to happen."

Instead of Dario, a man walks toward us and mutters, "Get him off my back before I kill him."

"Dario cut it out," Franco says.

My eyes are wide on the man who really looks like a murder waiting to happen. He helps himself to a tumbler of whiskey before his eyes flicks from one person to the next before stopping on me.

*Oh Jesus.*

I dart back to Renzo's side and feel some relief when he places his arm around me again.

"Don't worry, he always looks like that," Dario says as he comes to stand on my other side.

"Damiano, this is Skylar," Renzo introduces us.

*Damiano, as in the head of heads. That explains a lot.*

"Is she yours?" Damiano asks.

"Yes." Renzo tightens his arm possessively around me.

Damiano nods before taking a sip of his drink. "Dario told me you took care of the problem?"

Renzo nods. "Everything's dealt with."

"Good."

Samantha comes closer and says, "I see food in the kitchen, and it looks mouthwatering."

I glance over my shoulder, and pulling away from Renzo, I say, "Yes, I made finger foods. I thought we could hang out in the kitchen while the men play poker in the dining room."

"As long as I'm close to the food, I don't care where we sit."

I let out a chuckle, and when we reach the island, I say, "Please help yourself."

"Christ, come look at this spread," Dario says from behind us. "Fuck poker. I'm sitting with the women."

"The hell you are," Franco mutters.

I hear the elevator door slide open again, and glancing over my shoulder, I see another couple with a toddler coming in. The woman's heavily pregnant and has a sweet smile on her face.

"Finally," Renzo says. "We were about to start without you."

Everyone greets the couple, and it takes a minute or so before Renzo says, "Skylar, this is Angelo and Vittoria."

"Nice to meet you," I say before asking, "Can I get anyone something to drink?"

"Tori and I will have soda," Samantha answers.

"Tori, is that what I should call you?" I ask Vittoria as I walk to the fridge to get the sodas.

"Please. Only the men call me Vittoria."

I pour the cans of soda into glasses before handing them to Samantha and Tori.

We take a seat at the island, and the men come to help themselves to the food before they head to the dining table.

"Are you getting any sleep?" Tori asks Samantha.

I glance at Renzo and watch as he lets out a burst of laughter at something Franco said.

"Yes, they're finally getting into a routine," I hear Samantha answer.

Turning my attention back to the women, I ask, "How did you meet your husbands?"

Samantha lets out a chuckle. "I used to be Franco's PA."

"I didn't actually know much about Angelo when we got married," Tori says, making my eyebrows shoot into my hairline. "It was kind of a forced marriage situation. My stepbrother owed him money, and I was the payment."

My jaw practically drops to the floor. "You're kidding, right?"

She lets out a chuckle. "No, I'm not, but I learned to love him. He's an amazing man."

*I think I still hold the trophy for the weirdest way to meet the love of your life.*

"How did you and Renzo meet," Tori asks.

Samantha places her hand on Tori's arm and shakes her head while saying, "It's too soon for that question. I'm sure Skylar doesn't want to talk about it yet."

I give Samantha a thankful smile, then say, "Help yourselves to food."

"Oh yes!" Samantha exclaims before getting up to load a plate for herself.

I glance at Renzo again and catch him staring at me with a soft smile tugging at his lips.

"Yep, the fucker is in love," Franco mutters.

Renzo looks at his friend, then says, "You fell first, brother."

I watch the men banter and argue as they start a poker game, then turn my attention back to Samantha and Tori.

This get-together feels refreshing, and with a little luck, I can become friends with the women.

# Chapter 41

## Renzo

When Fabricio brings the Bentley to a stop at the cemetery, I open the door and climb out. Walking around the back of the car, I wait for Skylar before I take hold of her hand.

I had the headstones placed recently and wanted to make sure they did a good job.

Walking to Harlan's grave, Skylar's fingers tighten around mine.

It's the first time we've been back since the funerals, and I know it's going to be hard for her.

When we stop in front of the graves, I read the words engraved on the granite.

**Harlan Davies**

**The most selfless and loving father.**

**Devoted husband.**

**A guardian angel who walked among us for too short a while.**

"God," Skylar whispers, tears shining in her eyes before the spiral over her cheeks. "The headstone is perfect. Thank you, Renzo."

"You're welcome, *amo*."

I let go of her hand and wrap my arm around her shoulders. Pressing a kiss to her temple, I take a deep breath of her soft scent.

*She's doing well, Harlan. No problems with the kidney, and she's opening her own restaurant. You can rest in peace.*

Skylar moves from under my arm, and I watch as she places fresh flowers at her parents' graves.

"There's so much to tell you," she says to her parents. "I chose my signature dish. Obviously, I cried my eyes out. It's the Korean spicy brisket soup you loved, Daddy. I think it's going to be a winner." She sucks in a trembling breath before she continues, "I'm opening my own restaurant, and I'm calling it *Yukhaejang*. Renzo's done most of the work, though."

She's quiet for a while before she says, "Renzo's good to me, Daddy. If you're looking down on me, I don't want you to worry. I'm safe and happy."

She presses a kiss to her fingers, then presses them to each of the headstones. "I'll visit again soon."

She comes to take my hand before we walk to Louisa's grave, where she also places flowers.

She sucks in a deep breath before letting it slowly. "I actually miss your meatloaf." A chuckle escapes her. "I hope you're happy and getting a lot of rest wherever you are."

I give Skylar all the time she needs, and when she's ready, I wrap my arm around her shoulders and lead her to the final grave.

"I saw you here when we came to visit Mom right after I got out of the hospital," Skylar murmurs.

"I know." I hug her to me. "Sorry for being creepy as fuck."

She lets out a chuckle. "Hey, at least my stalker was hot."

When we reach Giulio's grave, my heart clenches with sorrow. It's manageable now and more like an empty wind blowing through me.

There will always be emptiness because nothing can fill the spot Giulio had in my life.

Thinking of his infectious smile, my mouth curves up.

*Christ, I miss his smile.*

Skylar moves away from me to place the last bouquet of flowers by his headstone.

"Hi, Giulio," she whispers. "My name is Skylar." Her shoulders shudder as she tries to keep the tears back, and her voice is strained when she says, "Thank you for saving my life. Having a piece of you inside me makes me feel close to you."

*Christ.*

I glance away as my eyes begin to burn.

"I'll live life to the fullest for the both of us." Her voice cracks over the words. "And I'll do everything in my power to make Renzo happy."

I exhale slowly as the emotional moment threatens to overwhelm me. I know it will get better with time, and eventually, the memories of Giulio will make me smile.

Turning my gaze back to Skylar, I see her pressing a kiss to her fingertips and brushing them over Giulio's headstone.

When she walks a few feet away to give me some privacy, I stand and stare at his grave.

"I killed them all, brother. I hope it gives you some peace." I clear my throat before whispering, "Love you, Giulio."

Turning around, I walk to where Skylar is waiting, and gripping her hand, I head to the Bentley.

When we climb into the back seat of the car, I say, "We're going to Skylar's restaurant."

"Yes, boss," Fabricio answers as he starts the engine.

When we leave the cemetery, I glance at Vincenzo and say, "Have Carlo and Antonio join you tomorrow. I want you to train them so they're ready to guard Skylar once she starts working." I glance out the window, then think to add, "Tell them to bring one of the armored SUVs so they can drive her around in it."

"Yes, boss," Vincenzo replies before he makes the calls to Carlo and Antonio.

Skylar doesn't say anything about the guards I'm assigning to her, and it has me asking, "You okay with the guards?"

She nods quickly. "It's for my safety."

Leaning into her, I press a kiss to the side of her head. "You ready to meet all the staff?"

She nods again, a smile spreading over her face. "Thank you for handling everything for me."

"Anything for you, *amo*." When we turn up the street where the restaurant is, I say, "Close your eyes."

She obeys with a chuckle. "I'm excited."

Fabrizio stops the car right in front of the restaurant, and I quickly get out and walk around the back of the Bentley to open Skylar's door.

Taking hold of her hand, I help her out of the back seat. I position her where I want her, then say, "You can open your eyes."

Her eyelashes lift, and when she sees the sign in cursive letters above the windows, her hands fly up to cover her mouth.

"Oh my God. I love it!"

I feel the happiness burst from her like a living force, and I imprint this moment to memory so I'll never forget it.

She makes an excited peeping sound that's fucking cute and rushes into the restaurant. I trail behind her, my eyes glued to her face as I watch her look at the bamboo on the walls and the lanterns hanging from the ceiling in the seating area.

"It's so beautiful," she murmurs in total awe.

We walk to the kitchen, where Skylar pauses to stare at the space where she'll create her masterpieces. She chose all the appliances and décor but hasn't had a chance to see the final result yet.

All the chefs and kitchen staff stop what they're doing, and turn to look at her. With a slight bow of their heads, they unanimously say, "Chef."

Skylar steps forward to greet the staff she chose for her kitchen.

She'll be the Chef de Cuisine.

The queen of her own empire.

*My queen.*

When she starts to talk about the menu with her staff and inspect the freezer and equipment, I turn around and walk to the office where Viviana is hard at work.

"Hey," she says when she notices me. "Everything is almost ready. I'm just waiting for the tablecloths to arrive. I've advertised the opening and every table's been reserved. It's going to be a busy night."

"That's good to hear," I say as I take a seat across from the desk. "Skylar's getting to know the kitchen staff."

"She's here?" Viviana asks while climbing to her feet. "Introduce me!"

Letting out a chuckle, I stand up again and follow Elio's wife to the kitchen. The woman's managerial skills are unmatched, and I know she'll be able to run the two restaurants.

Entering the kitchen, I say, "Skylar, give me a minute."

She excuses herself, and when she sees Viviana, her smile widens as she says, "God, I've wanted to meet you for the longest time."

The women shake hands, then Viviana admits, "I was heartbroken when I heard you were in a car accident. I wanted to steal you so you could help La Torrisi get a Michelin Star." Viviana sucks in a breath, looking a little awestruck. "Luckily for me, fate brought us together."

"Fuck fate. She's here because of me," I mutter, which makes the two women laugh.

Viviana continues as if I didn't interrupt her. "I want you to know you don't have to worry about the business side of things. Just focus on the kitchen."

"Thank you, Viviana. I'm looking forward to working side-by-side with you."

"I better get back to work. We'll talk soon," Viviana says before returning to the office.

I take Skylar's hand and pull her closer. When she looks up at me and I see her blue eyes sparkle with life, my heart overflows with love for her.

"Happy?" I ask.

She nods and stands on her tiptoes to press a kiss to my mouth. "Incredibly happy."

# Chapter 42

## Skylar

Renzo and I are peeking around the wall at the full restaurant.

"Oh my God. Half the critics in New York are out there," I whisper, my stomach a tight ball of nerves.

"They better not dare say anything bad," Renzo mutters. "Or there will be bodies floating in the Hudson."

I slap his chest and scowl at him. "You'll do no such thing!"

Turning around, I head back to the busy kitchen.

Renzo grabs my arm, and I'm yanked backward. He grips hold of my jaw and plants a hard kiss to my mouth.

"Good luck, *amo*. You've got this."

Shooting him a thankful smile, I pull free and rush to my station so I can continue cooking.

"I need spring onions," I call out.

"Yes, Chef!"

A few seconds later, a bowl of finely chopped spring onions is placed on my counter. I quickly add it to brew, and while it boils, I check on the spicy brisket soup.

The orders come fast and non-stop, and I get lost in my work.

Two hours into my opening night, Viviana walks toward me and says, "A customer would like to meet you, Chef Davies."

I glance at Chef Ji and say, "Keep an eye on everything."

"Yes, Chef."

I follow Viviana to the table where a woman is seated. A polite smile forms on her face when she sees me.

Standing up, she offers her hand, and as I shake it, she says, "I'm glad to see you've opened your own restaurant after the accident. I was worried we wouldn't get to taste your food again."

Not knowing who she is, I ask, "Again? I'm sorry, have we met?"

She shakes her head. "I'm Klara. I was the inspector who recommended *Dame* for their Michelin Star."

*Holy shit.*

The blood drains from my face, but she quickly adds, "Relax. I'm only here to enjoy your food. I'm no longer with the organization."

I let out a breath of relief and smile at Klara. "Thank you for coming to my opening night."

"I just wanted to compliment your signature dish. It's an explosive sensation I thoroughly enjoyed. I'm confident it will make the headlines soon." She begins to walk away, then pauses to add, "I'm glad you're back, Chef Davies. You were missed."

"Thank you so much. It's good to be back."

When she heads to the door, I turn around and walk to the kitchen in a daze of pure happiness.

The rest of the night goes by in a blur, and by the time the kitchen is clean and the staff leaves, I let out an exhausted breath.

I glance around the space, and feeling satisfied with the successful opening night, I begin to think about tomorrow and the week ahead.

"You were amazing tonight," Renzo suddenly says.

My eyes dart to where he's leaning against a counter, a proud smile on his face.

Walking to him, I plant my face against his chest and let out a sigh. "I'm so tired."

"Let's go home, *amo*."

The next moment, he picks me up bridal style, and chuckling, I wrap my arms around his neck.

I don't complain as he carries me out of the restaurant and sets me down on the back seat of the Bentley.

I watch as he locks the door of the restaurant, and when he comes to slide in beside me, I snuggle into his side.

During the drive home, I nod off several times, but when Fabrizio parks the car in the basement, I'm wide awake again.

When we walk into the penthouse, I kick off my shoes and let out a groan as I wiggle my toes. My eyes fall on a massive bouquet of red roses that takes up all the space on the coffee table in the living room.

"Holy crap, that's huge," I gasp as I walk closer.

"It was the biggest arrangement I could fit into the elevator," Renzo says. "I was aiming for a rose for every tear you cried because of me."

"Renzo," I breathe as I brush my fingertips over the petals. "You didn't have to."

"Yes, I did."

I turn around to thank him for the beautiful flowers but freeze when I see him down on one knee.

Shock shudders through me, and after the busy and emotional day I've had, I can't keep my eyes from misting up.

"Even though I kidnapped you, you were the one who took me captive. You've seen me at my worst and still chose to love me."

Tears stream down my cheeks as I stare at the man who's changed my life in so many ways it's still hard to believe it happened.

He clears his throat then says, "This is me officially asking you to be my girlfriend and partner in crime."

I let out a burst of laughter as I move forward. "Get up so I can kiss you."

Renzo climbs to his feet then takes a small box from the inside pocket of his jacket. Opening it, he holds it out to me so I can see the Sapphire ring.

"This is a you-belong-to-me ring. It has a tracker so I can find you if you're ever in trouble." He takes it from the box and slides it onto my ring finger. "I want every fucker out there to know you're taken."

"It's beautiful," I murmur before I lift onto my tiptoes to kiss my man.

Suddenly he lifts me from my feet and carries me bridal style up the stairs. "I want to see you naked with only my ring on your finger."

"Hmm...I like the sound of that," I chuckle as I press kisses to his neck. "A perfect ending to a perfect night."

Walking into the bedroom, he places me on the bed, and staring down at me, he says, "A perfect beginning to a perfect life, *amo*."

# Epilogue

## Renzo

**(Two years later…)**

The first year after our marriage, we focused on ourselves and work to make sure we were ready for the next step.

So here we are, standing in an orphanage with way too many cute faces looking for a home.

"We should buy the orphanage and adopt them all," I mutter.

"This is hard," Skylar says, looking a little panic-stricken.

A little boy runs into my legs and bounces back. Landing on his ass, he bursts out laughing.

Crouching down, I pick him up, and when we're face-to-face, I ask, "You okay, little guy? That must've hurt."

He shakes his head. "I'm tough."

The smile on his face is filled with mischief, and it does something to my heart.

"Renzo," Skylar whispers. My eyes flick to hers, then she nods quickly. "Him."

I look back at the little boy, then ask, "What's your name?"

"Georgi." He points to where a little girl is sucking her thumb while holding a blanket to the side of her face. "That's my sister, Raya."

I glance at Skylar. "We can't split them."

"Definitely not." She walks to the little girl and picks her up, then turns to smile at me.

I glance between the two kids, and when the little girl lays her head on Skylar's shoulder and I see the emotion on my wife's face, I know it's a done deal.

We came for one, and we're leaving with two.

I turn around and walk to where Sylvia is standing. She's helping us with the legal side of things.

"Can we arrange the adoption for both Georgi and Raya?"

"Are you sure?" she asks. "Taking on two children can be daunting."

"Dead sure." I look at Georgi again. "Get everything sorted out. We'd like to take them home."

"Take us home?" Georgi asks, his eyes wide on me.

It's only then I think to ask, "Would you like that, little guy?"

His eyes flick to his sister, then he puts on a brave face and nods. "But Raya's coming with me."

A smile tugs at my mouth. "Definitely. You're her big brother and have to take care of her."

He nods again, his eyes constantly going to Raya.

Christ, I love the protectiveness he has for his sister. This little guy will grow up to be a force to be reckoned with.

My eyes flick to Sylvia, and I order, "Get the paperwork done."

When Sylvia heads to the office, I glance at Skylar and say, "Come, *amo*. Let's go sign everything."

Heading to the office, I sit down and keep Georgi on my left knee while I sign everywhere that's needed.

It takes a while before we're allowed to leave with the kids, and as we carry our son and daughter out of the orphanage, Georgi asks, "What's your name?"

My eyes meet his. "Renzo."

"Do I have to call you dad?" he asks with a serious expression.

I shake my head. "You can call me Renzo or Dad or Papa. Whatever you're comfortable with."

He nods and once again looks for Raya.

"I'm Skylar." My wife says as we reach the car.

We huddle together for a moment, just taking in the special occasion and staring at our children.

"You have a nice car," Georgi mentions. "What's your house like? Is there space for us? I always share a room with Raya so she doesn't get scared."

"Our home is way up in the sky in an apartment building," Skylar answers while Raya snuggles closer to her, her little fingers playing with strands of Skylar's hair. "It's big, and there's lots of space. You can share a room with Raya, and one day, when she isn't scared anymore, you can have your own room."

A smile starts to tug at Georgi's mouth, and suddenly, his chin starts to tremble. He fights the emotions so fucking hard it has me wrapping him up in a hug.

"I'm here now, Georgi. I'll help you take care of Raya. Okay?"

He nods and hides his face until he has control over his emotions again.

Lifting his head, he stares at me for the longest moment, and I see how tired he is from having to be strong all the time.

"You're safe with me," I promise.

He nods again, whispering, "Thank you, Renzo."

"Let's go home," Skylar says, her voice hoarse from the emotional moment.

We strap the kids into the back seat before I signal to Vincenzo and the other guards that we're leaving.

When I slide behind the steering wheel, I glance in the rearview mirror and see Georgi's eyes locked on me.

Skylar pulls on her safety belt, then says, "We need to get clothes, and toys, and I need to decorate the rooms, and... shoot, what else –"

"Breathe." I chuckle as I steer the car away from the orphanage. "Don't forget to breathe, *amo*."

"Yeah, right. That too." She looks at me with a happy smile and places her hand on my thigh.

---

# Skylar

**(Another two years later...)**

"Look at my boy go," Renzo praises Georgi when he finally has the hang of skating.

I hold Raya's hand tightly as she carefully shuffles over the ice. "You've got this, baby," I encourage her. "Just hold onto Mommy."

"Okay," she murmurs, all her concentration on not falling. She slowly gets better and excitedly says, "Look, Mommy. I'm doing it."

"I see, baby. You're even better than Daddy."

"Daddy's about to see his –" Renzo loses his balance and falls on his ass.

Georgi quickly skates back to Renzo and tries to help him up. "Are you okay, Dad?"

Renzo chuckles while I do my best not to laugh out loud.

"I'm fine. Help your old man get to the side where it's safe."

Skating in small circles with Raya, I watch as Georgi helps Renzo to the bench on the side of the frozen pond.

"Mommy, I'm cold," Raya says. "I want to go to Daddy."

"Okay." I lead her carefully across the ice, and smiling at Renzo, I say, "She wants Daddy."

He lifts her to his lap and engulfs her against his chest, while I look at Georgi and ask, "Want to race?"

"Yes!"

We get ready, and before I can count down to one, Georgi shoots forward.

"Hey, that's cheating," I call out as I set off after him.

We spend another twenty minutes on the ice before we head back to Renzo and Raya.

After we've changed out of the skates and into our shoes, Renzo asks, "Who's hungry."

"Me," Georgi replies. "Can we have hotdogs?"

"Sure."

We walk to a hotdog stand, and I order four hotdogs which we eat on our way back to the car.

While the kids climb into the back seat, Renzo leans in and presses a kiss to my mouth.

"What's that for?" I ask.

"Just because I love you," he says with a grin tugging at his lips.

Looking at the man who's given me the world, my heart can't contain all the love I feel for him.

"I love you too."

"Happy?" he asks as he opens the passenger door.

"Very happy," I murmur and steal another kiss before I get into the car.

# The End.

# Published Books
## *In Reading Order:*

---

## MAFIA ROMANCE

### THE KINGS OF MAFIA SERIES
*Mafia / Organized Crime / Suspense Romance*
*(Can be read in this order or as standalones)*
This series is not connected to any other series I've written, and there will be no spin-offs.

Tempted By The Devil
Craving Danger
Hunted By A Shadow

*Coming May 2024...*
Drawn To Darkness
*Coming 2024...*
God Of Vengeance

**(The Saints, Sinners & Corrupted Royals all take place in the same world)**

### THE SAINTS SERIES
*Mafia / Organized Crime / Suspense Romance*
*(Can be read in this order or as standalones)*

Merciless Saints
Cruel Saints
Ruthless Saints
Tears of Betrayal
Tears of Salvation

## THE SINNERS SERIES
*Mafia / Organized Crime / Suspense Romance*
*(Can be read in this order or as standalones)*

Taken By A Sinner
Owned By A Sinner
Stolen By A Sinner
Chosen By A Sinner
Captured By A Sinner

## CORRUPTED ROYALS
*Mafia / Organized Crime / Suspense Romance*
*(Can be read in this order or as standalones)*

Destroy Me
Control Me
Brutalize Me
Restrain Me
Possess Me

# CONTEMPORARY ROMANCE

## BEAUTIFULLY BROKEN SERIES

*Organized Crime / Suspense Romance*
*(Can be read in this order or as standalones)*

Beautifully Broken
Beautifully Hurt
Beautifully Destroyed

## ENEMIES TO LOVERS

*College Romance / New Adult / Billionaire Romance*

Heartless
Reckless
Careless
Ruthless
Shameless

## TRINITY ACADEMY

*College Romance / New Adult / Billionaire Romance*

Falcon
Mason
Lake
Julian

The Epilogue

## THE HEIRS

*College Romance / New Adult / Billionaire Romance*

Coldhearted Heir
Arrogant Heir
Defiant Heir
Loyal Heir
Callous Heir
Sinful Heir
Tempted Heir
Forbidden Heir

**Stand Alone Spin-off**
Not My Hero
*Young Adult / High School Romance*

## THE SOUTHERN HEROES SERIES

*Suspense Romance / Contemporary Romance /*
*Police Officers & Detectives*

The Ocean Between Us
The Girl In The Closet
The Lies We Tell Ourselves
All The Wasted Time
We Were Lost

# STANDALONES

LIFELINE
*(FBI Suspense Romance)*

UNFORGETTABLE
**Co-written with Tayla Louise**
*(Contemporary/Billionaire Romance)*

# Connect with me

Newsletter

FaceBook

Amazon

GoodReads

BookBub

Instagram

# Acknowledgments

Renzo and Skylar's book hit differently. There was no plot, and I wrote their story straight from their hearts. This book is all them. I just typed what they wanted to say.

Thank you to Sheldon for all the help with graphics, formatting, and research. Without him, I'd be a mess, and there would be no books & To Tayla for being my sanity and biggest cheerleader.

My editor, Sheena, has nerves of steel with all the deadlines wooshing past us. Thank you for putting up with me and always being honest with your feedback. I appreciate you so much!

To my alpha and beta readers – Leeann, Brittney, Sherrie, and Sarah thank you for being the godparents of my paper-baby. Thank you for all your time and feedback.

Candi Kane PR - Thank you for being patient with me and my bad habit of missing deadlines.

Sarah, from *Okay Creations* – I love, love, love the Kings of Mafia covers! Thank you for doing such an amazing job with them.

My street team, thank you for promoting my books. It means the world to me!

A special thank you to every blogger and reader who took the time to participate in the cover reveal and release day.

Love,
Michelle.

Made in United States
Cleveland, OH
03 November 2024

10421800R20219